The Devoted HUSBAND

B. LOVE

Published by
BLACK ODYSSEY MEDIA

www.blackodyssey.net
Email: info@blackodyssey.net

This book is a work of fiction. Any references to events, real people, or real places are used fictitiously. Other names, characters, places, and events are products of the author's imagination, and any resemblance to actual events or places or persons, living or dead, is entirely coincidental.

THE DEVOTED HUSBAND. Copyright © 2025 by B. LOVE

Library of Congress Control Number: 2025902593

First Trade Paperback Printing: July 2025
ISBN: 978-1-957950-75-4
ISBN: 978-1-957950-76-1 (e-book)

Cover Design by Ashlee Nassar of Designs With Sass
To the extent that the image or images on the cover of this book depict a person or persons, such person or persons are merely models and are not intended to portray any character in the book.

All rights reserved. Black Odyssey Media, LLC | Dallas, TX.

This book or parts thereof may not be reproduced in any form, stored in a retrieval system, or transmitted in any form by any means—electronic, mechanical, photocopy, recording, or otherwise—without prior written permission of the publisher, excepting brief quotes or tags used in reviews, interviews, or complimentary promotion, and as permissible by United States of America copyright law.

10 9 8 7 6 5 4 3 2 1

Manufactured in the United States of America

Distributed by Kensington Publishing Corp.

The authorized representative in the EU for product safety and compliance
is eucomply OU, Parnu mnt 139b-14, Apt 123
Tallinn, Berlin 11317, hello@eucompliancepartner.com

Dear Reader,

I want to thank you immensely for supporting Black Odyssey Media and our ongoing efforts to spotlight the diverse narratives of blossoming and seasoned storytellers. With every manuscript we acquire, we believe that it took talent, discipline, and remarkable courage to construct that story, flesh out those characters, and prepare it for the world. Debut or seasoned, our authors are the real heroes and heroines in *OUR* story. For them, we are eternally grateful.

Whether you are new to B. Love or Black Odyssey Media, we hope that you are here to stay. Our goal is to make a lasting impact in the publishing landscape, one step at a time and one book at a time. As always, we welcome your feedback and kindly ask that you leave a review. For upcoming releases, announcements, submission guidelines, etc., please be sure to visit our website at www.blackodyssey.net or scan the QR code below. And remember, no matter where you are in your journey, the best of both worlds begins now!

Joyfully,

Shawanda Williams

Shawanda "N'Tyse" Williams
Founder/Publisher

DETECTIVE JONES
July

THE ONLY SOUND that could be heard in the car was the flicker of Jones's lighter as he lit his cigarette. His eyes were zeroed in on Dante Williams, watching his every move. It had been a while since Jones felt so invested in a case. The murders of Patrice Baker and Trina Roe haunted him. Willow Frank was still missing, and Jones couldn't rest until he found her. There was no doubt in his mind that Sade was responsible for all three—he just had to find a way to prove it.

So far, they had hair from the scene of Patrice's murder and a few drops of blood from Trina's. Neither the hair nor the blood had a DNA match in their system. Unfortunately, Patrice's murder was ruled a robbery gone bad, and the case was closed because they didn't have any more evidence. Jones's gut was telling him it was no robbery at all. That the murder was intentional and the reason the intruder, Sade, was there to begin with. His captain may have wanted him to drop the case, but Jones wouldn't—not until there was justice for all three women.

Jones had been keeping a close eye on Sade and Dante. The more he learned about them, the more convinced he was that Sade had committed these murders because she was trying to keep Dante's identity hidden. It wasn't a coincidence that multiple murders happened in the small town of Vanzette when Dante arrived. Even with Sade trying to keep him hidden, Dante had become a link attached to Patrice, Trina, and Willow just like she was. If Dante wasn't involved with their murders, he had to have knowledge of them. Jones refused to believe Sade had carried out two murders and a possible kidnapping by herself.

While he had no proof Willow was alive, Jones assumed she was since her body hadn't popped up. And until her body was found, he was convinced he still had time to save her.

A part of Jones was at peace to learn Sade and Dante were leaving town. That meant the murders would stop if Sade were actually behind them. He would have preferred they stopped because she was in prison, though. Even with her leaving, Jones would still work the cases until he got the answers he sought.

Dante looked around casually before tossing three black bags into the small body of water behind the house.

"Hmm." Sitting up in his seat, Jones set his cigarette in the ashtray. "What are you getting rid of?"

Jones watched as Dante jogged back toward the shed. Something important was in those bags. Something worth hiding. But what? Jones itched to fish them out, but anything he found would be inadmissible in court without a warrant.

Cursing under his breath, Jones waited until Dante left the house for what appeared to be the last time. He alternated between wanting to check the house and the shed or letting it go. Technically, he would be trespassing. The law made it hard to break the rules at times.

"Fuck it," he grumbled, unlocking his car. "I'm going in."

Casually, Jones made his way down and across the street. He wasted no time picking the lock and entering the home. It was empty and immaculately clean. As he headed into the backyard toward the shed, a medium-sized moving truck pulled into the front of the house. Cursing under his breath, he looked around for a place to hide. As spaced out as the homes were, the open space between the homes was blocked by a few trees.

Deciding not to hide, Jones walked toward the two men who had hopped out of the truck.

"Hey, do either of you know where I can find the owners of this house?" Jones asked, looking from one to the other. "I want to look inside. Thinkin' about moving into this neighborhood."

The movers looked at each other.

The taller, leaner one of the two shook his head and was the first to speak up. "No, we haven't seen them since yesterday. We just have to clear out the shed, and then we'll be done."

"I think the realtor's number is on the sign in the yard," the other mover spoke. "You might need to just speak directly to them."

With one bob of his head and a forced smile, Jones thanked them both before heading down the street toward the car. Instead of driving off, he watched as they cleared the shed of typical things one would find there—tools, a lawn mower, chairs.

Suddenly, his phone rang, pulling his attention away from the men doing their job.

"Jones," he answered, not bothering to look and see who it was.

"Uh, hi. This is Amanda Baker . . . Patrice's mom. You called and left me a voicemail."

"Oh yes. Yes, Mrs. Baker. Thanks for returning my call. I was wondering if I could stop by and talk to you for a moment."

"You're the detective who was over her case, you said?"

"Yes, ma'am."

"I'm sorry. I'm not exactly sure what's going on. The case was closed, right? Has it been reopened?"

"It hasn't, not officially."

"Detective Jones, we're still grieving the loss of our daughter. It's traumatizing going over the details repeatedly without it leading to anything. We've told you and other detectives everything we know about what was going on with our daughter around the time of the robbery. We have nothing else to offer."

"I'm not looking for answers from you; I actually have information to give."

"Do you have a suspect in the robbery?"

"That's the thing. I don't think it was a robbery. That information was classified and won't be shared now that the case is closed, but you deserve to know. Is your husband home? If I could just speak to you in person, this would all make sense."

"I-I guess you can come over."

After Amanda rattled off their address, Jones put it into his GPS and headed that way. It was wearing on him to work his cases with the Vanzette Police Department along with the trio of women on his off days, but bringing Sade to justice would make the sacrifice worth it. She may have left town, but she'd forever be on his radar. There was nowhere she could run and not be within his reach.

JONES

Pictures of Patrice as a child made Jones's heart ache. In almost every photo of her on the fireplace and walls, she was smiling—happy. The light in her eyes began to dim as she aged. There were three pictures of her while she was in high school that Jones took pictures of with his phone. He knew about her connection to Imani, but seeing Patrice in a cheerleader outfit beside her made things all too real.

Turning, he looked at Amanda, whose smile was sad as she watched him. Her husband, Elliot, seemed more hardened to the situation than his wife. Still, Jones appreciated them opening their home to him. He made his way over to the brown leather recliner beside the sofa they were seated on. Amanda took Elliot's hand into hers as he sat down and pulled out his small notebook.

"My wife said you don't believe this was a robbery-homicide," Elliot said, sitting up in his seat.

"No, I don't. Originally, we believed the robber or robbers were hiding in Patrice's car, and because she came out quicker than they expected, they killed her and left before they could take anything."

"What makes you think that is no longer the case?" Elliot continued.

"Well, for starters, it was daylight. Vanzette is a fairly safe and crimefree town. We hadn't had many murders before this year, and we haven't had multiple murders in the same year in a while. I don't think it's plausible that someone was trying to rob your daughter during the day and then killed her when they were caught. If that's the case, I believe it was a drifter passing through town looking for money or jewels to pawn before their next stop. Even so, they wouldn't have left without taking *something*."

"So, you have no proof that this wasn't a robbery gone bad. Just an assumption?"

"Not quite. Patrice had connections to another woman who was murdered shortly after her. I don't believe that was a coincidence."

"Who was the other woman?" Amanda asked.

"Trina Roe. Is that name familiar to either of you?" Amanda's head shook as Elliot gave a firm no. "What about Willow Frank?"

"Neither one," Amanda answered. "But it's not a surprise. We didn't know too many of Patrice's friends as she aged. She worked a lot and didn't go out too much, but there were a few women she would hang with occasionally."

"Imani Williams." He paused. "She would have been Imani Griffin while in school with your daughter. Do either of you remember her?" Jones asked, getting comfortable in the recliner.

"She was one of Patrice's closest friends while they were in high school and college," Amanda replied. "Has something happened to her too?"

Chuckling, Jones crossed his ankles. "I guess you could say that. She was recently sent to federal prison for several crimes, including credit fraud."

Gasping, Amanda clutched her chest. "Not little Imani. She seemed to have such a bright future ahead of herself."

Elliot sucked his teeth and crossed his arms over his chest. "I'm not surprised. I always felt like she was a bad influence. That's why I was glad Patrice moved here and didn't continue their friendship after college."

Amanda's eyes rolled as Jones requested, "Tell me more about why you believed Imani was a bad influence."

"She brought out the ugly in my daughter. Patrice's attitude completely changed when they started hanging out. She was no longer my bubbly, innocent child. Patrice became catty, bitter, and downright mean."

"They were accused of being bullies," Amanda added. "The fights Patrice got in, Imani was often the center of them. I thought Patrice was trying to be a good friend, but Elliot believed Imani was getting Patrice into trouble and that she needed to stay away from her."

"Did you know Imani's sister . . . Sade?" Jones asked.

"I don't think so, no," Elliot replied, looking at his wife. "Do you recall Patrice ever mentioning Sade?"

"I . . . I don't know. Maybe vaguely." Amanda laughed softly. "It's been so long."

"I understand," Jones said. "I'm asking because I have reason to believe Imani and Sade were involved with Patrice's murder." He paused, giving them time to register what he'd said. "Patrice and Sade were not friends in high school. I believe that Sade was one of the girls Patrice and Imani bullied."

"Wait," Elliot chortled before licking his lips. "Why would Imani bully her own sister?"

"That's a conversation for another day. What I *can* say is that Imani admitted to the toxic relationship she had with her sister and that Patrice was a part of that. Now, Patrice and Sade came back into contact with each other earlier this year. I don't have proof, but I believe Patrice was murdered because she knew about a secret Sade was keeping from her sister."

"What secret could have been worth taking my child's life?" Amanda asked.

"I'm not sure if you kept up with the news a couple of months ago, but a man was killed after breaking into a Vanzette resident's home and trying to rape her . . ."

"Yeah, I heard about that," Elliot replied.

"That was Sade. The man who broke in was her sister's boyfriend, Adam. Adam was on his way here to kill Dante, Imani's husband." The couple's confused and surprised expressions made him smile. "You heard that right. She had a husband and boyfriend. Now, the husband was missing. Turns out he had amnesia and had been in Vanzette the whole time with Sade.

"I don't know if he really had amnesia or if that was a lie, but that's his story to justify leaving Memphis while the police were looking for him. Anyway, Sade was helping Dante after his accident and while he had amnesia. I believe that's why she killed your daughter. I believe Sade didn't want anyone to know Dante was here with her, and Patrice found out. Because they all went to school together, Patrice knew Dante was considered missing in Memphis. So Sade killed her to keep her quiet."

"Do you have any proof of this? If there's a suspect, why is the case still closed?" Elliot asked.

"I don't have any actual proof yet. There was hair in the car that didn't belong to Patrice, but we didn't get a DNA match. Even if we did, any good defense lawyer could argue the hair belonged to someone who had been in the car with Patrice and not to the murderer."

Amanda shook her head. "That doesn't make any sense. I don't understand why Sade would keep her brother-in-law hidden from her sister and go as far as killing someone to do it, even if she didn't have the best relationship with our daughter."

"It's my understanding that Dante was facing the charges Imani was recently convicted of. If so, that's motive for murder—protecting him. Also, I did a little research and learned Imani's boyfriend tried to have Dante killed, which is how he ended up with amnesia. If Sade believed Dante was in danger in Memphis, she wouldn't want anyone to know where he was."

"So if Patrice found out, there is a chance Sade would try to silence her," Elliot said.

"Exactly," Jones replied.

Again, Amanda shook her head as she stood and began to pace. Wringing her fingers, she clicked her tongue.

"I can't accept that without proof. I want to know who did this to my daughter and why, but this seems like something in a movie. If Sade really killed Patrice, I need you to be able to prove it. Until then, I can't accept this."

"That's exactly what I intend to do," Jones said. "I know Sade killed your daughter. I feel it in my gut. I might not have all the proof and details now, but I know this is the truth." Standing, he added, "Keep this under wraps for now. Sade has left town and if she knows I'm still looking into this, she won't return. But I promise I will get the answers you need."

They both thanked him before Jones made his way out and headed to the house of Trina Roe's parents ... determined to connect the dots and paint a picture that showed him exactly what happened to both women and why.

DANTE

Three Weeks Later

"ARE YOU SURE you don't want to come home?" Olivia asked.

Dante's head shook as he stared at the beautiful view of New York that his penthouse apartment offered. He was sure he'd enjoy this view with Sade, but she abandoned him. As hurt as Dante was behind her choice, he meant it when he said he would take the time to prepare things for her before going after her.

For the last three weeks, he'd been going from New York to Decatur, then San Diego, making sure each abode was furnished comfortably in a way that complemented his style and Sade's. His ego wanted him to let it go, but his heart told him she needed this, that she needed him to plan for their future. That she needed proof that he was serious about her ... about them ... and Dante was more than willing to give her that.

"Nah, not right now, at least. I still have a lot to do to prepare."

Olivia scoffed. "And what if she never comes to you?"

"She will, Ma. That girl loves me, and I love her too."

"I don't deny that, but love isn't everything."

"You're right, but it's a foundation and a start. What I'm doing might not make sense to you, but it does to me. Sade is mine, and I have to be prepared for when I get her back."

"All right, baby. If that's what you want, I support you. I just hope you don't end up disappointing yourself by waiting for her for too long."

Dante laughed softly with a shake of his head. "She watched me marry her sister, Ma. I'm going to wait for as long as it takes."

JONES

Receiving the box of Willow's belongings made Jones feel like a kid at Christmas. Because she had been missing for months and was behind on her mortgage payments, her parents didn't know what they should do. They struggled with trying to keep her house from going into foreclosure and letting fate take its course. Her mom expressed not wanting to get rid of Willow's home, and she returned to nothing. Her father wanted to accept that she was gone forever so they could start to grieve and heal.

Jones offered a solution—renting the home for a year or until she returned, whichever came first. The Franks agreed and asked what he wanted in exchange for his great idea. His request? Access to her phone logs again and any diaries or to-do lists she may have had in her home. They granted Jones access to both.

There hadn't been any outgoing calls or text messages from her phone, further causing him to believe she was dead. She didn't have a diary, but they gave him her planners and the legal pad she scribbled random notes on while seated at her desk.

Jones made himself comfortable, going through each item one by one. The legal pad was mostly random thoughts and grocery lists or recipes. She had three planners—one for work, one for the night classes she took to get her master's degree, and one for traveling.

While the planners didn't tie Willow to Patrice, Trina, or Sade in any way, it further humanized her in Jones's eyes. She seemed proud to be back in school and happy to almost be done with it. She loved to travel and had several trips lined up. It didn't make sense for her to drop her life and move somewhere else without contacting her family. Jones was sure Sade had ended her life unexpectedly and prematurely, and he wanted her to pay for it now even more than ever.

SADE

August

"*This is our last night here. How do you feel?*" *A soft smile tugged at the corners of Dante's lips as he looked down at Sade.*

Sade relaxed more against his frame, enjoying the warmth of his body against hers. Dancing with him was probably her favorite thing to do . . . outside of making love to him.

"*I feel hopeful. Tomorrow is the start of our new lives. How do you feel?*"

"*Relieved.*"

"*Yeah? Why?*"

"*I'm finally with the girl of my dreams.*"

Sade's eyes playfully rolled as she tried to pull herself out of Dante's grasp, but he held her closer—tighter.

"*Spare me, Dante.*"

He chuckled. "*Why don't you believe I've been in love with you since we were kids, Smiley?*"

"*Because you friend zoned me and got with my sister.*"

"*I didn't friend zone you. We just didn't date back in the day. And Imani . . . that just happened. I never should have let it. That's probably my biggest regret in life.*" *Dante placed a kiss on the center of Sade's forehead.* "*Even if I had never worked up the courage to go after you and risk our friendship, I never should've gotten with your sister.*"

Sade's hands slid down his chest. It didn't seem to matter now. Imani was in prison, and after decades, Sade finally had her man . . . even if it was temporary.

They continued their sway before pigging out on Chinese food. The relaxed, intimate moment seemed like the perfect way to end their time in Vanzette and, unbeknownst to Dante, their time with each other.

Sade's thoughts were so clouded by memories of her time with Dante that she forgot where she was and who she was with. The feel of fingers grazing her cheek pulled her out of her thoughts. But they weren't Atlas's fingers. Her eyes shifted to the left, where a man stared at her with a grin on the opposite side of the escalator.

"Damn, you fine."

Before Sade could calculate a response, Atlas grabbed the man by the collar of his shirt and lifted him onto their escalator.

"Atlas, no!" she whisper-yelled, watching as he dragged the man down the escalator.

If this indicated how things would go between them during their time in Memphis, Sade already wanted to return to her island.

"Stop!" she yelled, tugging at Atlas's neck. The action didn't seem to faze him as he repeatedly punched the man in his face. "Are you trying to get put on the no-fly list? Get up!"

"Hey!"

At the sound of security, Sade tried one last time before deciding she'd leave him there.

"Atlas! Get your butt up! We have to go!"

Tugging with all her might, she was able to remove him from the unconscious man's body. They rushed out of the airport. Sade wasn't sure if the run or her anger had her heart racing as they jumped into Atlas's car. Before she could stop herself, she slapped him.

"What is *wrong* with you? Are you out of your mind?"

Sucking his teeth, Atlas swerved out of the parking space. "He disrespected me and touched you, so he had to pay for that."

Rolling her eyes, Sade stared out of the window. She hoped they could pay for parking and leave without further issues. This was yet another example of the stark difference between Atlas and Dante.

Sade trusted Dante and knew he could defend himself and protect others. He also had a clearer head and wasn't easily swayed by his emotions. On the other hand, Atlas was quick-tempered and could become volatile quickly. There was no doubt in her mind that the only reason he was okay with her being with Dante for months was because they weren't in Memphis. Things would have gone differently if he had witnessed the affection between the two.

There was a time Sade thought Atlas's possessiveness and anger were cute ... passion, even. But those days and that perspective faded the moment a man's perusal of her body or harmless compliments led to arguments and fights. One time, she called him insecure, and the darkness that filled his eyes before he punched a hole in the wall beside her was something Sade would never forget.

With Sade, he'd always been romantic and sweet. It hadn't mattered that he was volatile and violent. Now, with a baby in her womb, Sade wondered if she'd made the wrong choice to return to him.

Hours later ...

Atlas placed kisses along Sade's neck that softened her toward him. Her body arched, making more room for his as she smiled.

"Does this mean you're calm now?" she confirmed.

"Yeah. I'm sorry about that. He touched you, and I saw red."

With a sigh, Sade turned in his arms. She was in the bathroom doing her makeup. They were supposed to go to his parents' home for dinner... which was the last thing she wanted to do. Still, she put her desires aside to please Atlas because she knew how important family was to him. There was a time when family was important to her as well—until her parents died and her sister became a terror.

"I won't deny that he was wrong for touching me, but that wasn't the way to handle it, baby. If you had gotten stopped and put on the no-fly list, who would I travel with to see the world? Not to mention, you could have gotten arrested. Then that would have been yet another reason for your family to hate me."

Atlas licked his lips, hiding his smile. "They don't hate you, Day."

"They do, and you know it."

His lips went from her forehead to her lips and neck. "They don't hate you. They just... hate how things played out." Sade pouted, her head lowering slightly. Atlas lifted it by her chin, gently forcing her to look into his eyes. "Hey, I love you, okay? I don't care what they think. I'm happy with you, and that's all that matters."

Except, that wasn't all that mattered. If it were, Atlas wouldn't shut down every time his family expressed their disdain for Sade being the reason Adam had been killed. It didn't matter how many times he told them Adam was killed while trying to rape her and shoot the police. In their minds, it was Sade's fault.

"Okay," Sade agreed softly, still unable to tell him she loved him too. The truth was, her heart was too busy reserving love for the father of her child.

"How much longer will you need in here?"

"Maybe like fifteen minutes."

"A'ight, I'm gonna go ahead and get dressed then."

"Okay, baby."

After giving him another quick kiss, Sade turned and looked at her reflection in the mirror. She couldn't remember the last time her smile reached her eyes. Even though the plan had always been to protect Dante and bring her sister and Adam to justice, blurring the lines and getting physical with Dante made things . . . sticky. She didn't think it was possible, but Sade loved Dante even more after their brief tryst as a married couple.

There were still times when she felt his hands between her thighs, around her neck. Times where flashbacks would bring tears to her eyes and a smile to her face. Times where she wished she wouldn't have taken the money and abandoned him at the airport to be with Atlas. But that was an action she couldn't take back now. Even if Dante planned to get her back, she had no idea if he still felt that way after learning about the money she'd taken. So far, he hadn't tried to contact her.

However, he updated his friends on Facebook about how life had been going for him, and Sade kept up with him through a spam page. Instead of starting his own financial firm in New York, he'd been traveling the world before planting roots back in Memphis. Apparently, he would become a partner with his old college friend, Ian Sanders—the same Ian Sanders who peeled the blindfold off his brain and unlocked a few memories.

Sade's hand ran across her flat belly. At only ten weeks pregnant, she had a long journey ahead, and with each day that passed . . . she was less and less sure it was Atlas she wanted by her side.

Shaking off the sadness that was trying to consume her, Sade finished her makeup and snapped a few pictures of herself to post on Facebook. Her mind was so caught up in thoughts of Dante that she sent them to him via text instead of posting them to her social media.

"Oh, crap!"

Before she could delete them or pray he'd changed his number, Dante read the message as if he were holding the phone when they were sent. Her heart palpitated as she waited for his response. How would she explain sending the pictures after a month had passed? Would he even care what she had to say? His dots began to bounce against the screen, and her breathing hitched in anticipation of his response. When it came, a quiet gasp escaped her.

Do *Not* Answer: Hello, Smiley.

SADE

The Thanksgiving Adam Came Back

THE DEFINITION OF *rage was violent, uncontrollable anger. That was exactly how Sade felt at the sight of Imani being a little too flirty with Adam. Imani failed to mention he and his cousin, Atlas, would be coming around—otherwise, she wouldn't have joined them for the evening. Sade found it suspicious that Imani opted out of the family trip with Dante and his family to Denver for the holiday, and now, she knew why. Imani's original excuse was that she didn't want to make anyone miserable because she was miserable and suffering from a stomachache. She was perfectly fine now.*

Sade's eyes squeezed shut at the sound of Imani's giddy laughter. Hot tears slipped down her cheeks as she fought to pull in short, ragged breaths. It was one thing for Imani to cheat on her husband; it was altogether different for Imani to cheat on Sade's best friend. Though she and Dante didn't hang out as much as they used to, he was still and would always be her best friend. They spent time together twice a month alone and went on quarterly trips. Her heart felt as if it were breaking into pieces at the thought of Imani cheating on the man Sade had wanted since they were kids. When she couldn't take it anymore, Sade stormed through the living room and lifted Imani off Adam's lap.

"H-hey!" Imani slurred, trying unsuccessfully to claw herself out of Sade's grip. "W-what are you . . ." She hiccupped, then giggled. "What're you doing?"

"No, what are you doing?" Sade asked, shoving Imani into a seat at the kitchen table. "Why are you sitting on that man's lap, giggling in his face and letting him touch on you like you're not a married woman?"

Scoffing, Imani gave her big sister a dismissive wave of her hand. "Who are you to question me?"

"Your sister and your husband's best friend."

Sucking her teeth, Imani crossed her arms over her chest and tried to look at Sade with a serious expression, but it turned into another fit of giggles. "B-baby, that man in there has touched me with my clothes on a-and off. This ain't nothin' new."

Sade remained silent, giving herself time to process what her sister had said.

"You've had sex with him?"

Imani's eyes rolled. "Duh. He's the twins' father." Standing, she wobbled and gripped the table for support. "Now leave," she slurred, pointing her finger in Sade's face. "I want him to fuck me and make up for all the lost time he's been in prison. You can stay if you want to hear."

"Are you crazy?" Sade almost whispered, turning as Imani headed out of the kitchen. "I'm not leaving you here with him. We haven't seen this man since college. How do I know you're safe with him?"

"God, you're s-slow." Imani gripped Sade's forearms. She blinked rapidly and pulled in a deep breath before adding, "I've been seeing Adam the whole time he was locked up. Trust me, there's nowhere safer for me to be than with h-him. Now, get out unless you want to hear your little sister get her back blown out."

For a while, Sade just stood there. The sound of Imani's cackling grew quieter and quieter as she retreated. Her first thought was to call Dante and tell him about his wife. Her second thought was to hold on to that information. Because of their past, people always swore the sisters were lying just to one-up the other. She would have to literally record Imani and Adam if she wanted Dante to believe her. After tucking the truth about Nila and Mila not being Dante's children into the back of her mind, Sade decided she'd force her sister tell him the truth. Finally, she had a way for Dante to be free of the woman who had never truly appreciated him.

As she went outside, Sade's heart began to feel like a brick. Yes, Dante was her best friend, but he was also the best friend who chose Imani over her. Was Imani cheating his Karma? Did he deserve to have Sade come to his aid? Sade was so conflicted internally that she didn't pay attention to where she was walking.

Her knee went into Atlas's back as he sat on the porch, and she almost toppled over. Had he not caught her and effortlessly sat her on his lap, Sade didn't want to think about the damage that would have been done. As Atlas's arms wrapped around her, he surveyed her face.

"Why you runnin' outta there like that?" he asked with a teasing smile.

"Sorry. . . . . Apparently, they're about to have sex, and I did not want to hear that."

Atlas's head bobbed. "I'm surprised they waited as long as they did."

"So you knew about them?"

"Of course. Me and Adam are like brothers. We tell each other everything."

Sighing, Sade confessed, "I wish me and my sister were that close. I also wish she wasn't a cheater."

"What that got to do with you?"

"Cheating is wrong. Plus, Dante is my best friend. I can't know something like this and not tell him."

Atlas shook his head. "Nah, I don't think you should tell him."

"Why not?"

"*From what my cousin has told me, you and Imani have always had beef, right? And Dante was at the center of it most times.*"

"*Yes, that's true.*"

"*Who's to say he will believe you? I think he'll believe her, and that will make things worse between y'all.*"

"*I thought about that, but if the twins aren't his, all it would take is a DNA test to prove it. Then he'll know I'm telling the truth.*"

"*Yeah, but at what cost? Ruining his happy family? Taking away the kids he married her to be there for?*"

Sade nibbled her cheek and thought over what Atlas said. "*I hadn't thought about it like that.*"

Sighing, Atlas ran a hand over his face. "*I can promise you that their marriage is over now that Adam is out. Let him find out the truth on his own. You stay out of it and just be ready to help him pick up the pieces.*"

Sade stood. "*I, um . . . I have to go. Sorry about falling on you.*"

Atlas chuckled as she scurried away quickly to her car. "*It's cool, Sade. You can fall on me or for me . . . I'm cool with either one.*"

Her feet stopped moving momentarily.

Is he . . . flirting with me?

Looking back, she took in his playful eyes and smile as he winked. Giving him a smile of her own, Sade waved before walking away.

ATLAS

THE INCESSANT VIBRATING of Sade's phone was driving Atlas crazy. Usually, she kept it on Do Not Disturb. Because they were temporarily back in Memphis, Sade wanted to see her family, which was why she said she had her notifications on. That ringing, those text messages, they weren't from her grandparents.

Who the hell is blowing up her phone?

Atlas put his car in park, releasing a long breath as he gritted his teeth.

"Who keeps texting you?" he asked, calmer than he actually felt.

"Hmm?"

Chuckling, he looked over at Sade as he cut off the car. "I said, who keeps texting you?"

"I-I'm not sure."

"Then let me see." As he reached for her phone, which was in the cup holder, Sade did the same.

"Atlas, no—"

"Get the fuck back." His hand wrapped around her neck, and he pressed her body into the window. Holding her in place, he unlocked her phone. "Why do you make stuff so difficult, Sade?"

"Let me go." The more she wiggled underneath his grasp, the tighter he pinned her to the window.

"Nah. You must want me to handle you like this because you don't know how to tell the truth."

His brows wrinkled, and his heart stopped beating when he saw several text messages from someone named "Do *Not* Answer." Atlas looked over at her, not swayed by the sight of her watery eyes.

"Who is Do *Not* Answer? Dante?" When she didn't respond, Atlas released a low laugh and began to read the messages he'd sent.

Do *Not* Answer: Hello, Smiley.

Do *Not* Answer: You changed your mind about talking to me?

Do *Not* Answer: That's okay. I'll still wait for you. I miss you.

Do *Not* Answer: Tell me when you're ready for me to come get you. I'll always come.

"What does he mean 'tell him when you're ready for him to come get you'? You been talking to this man?"

Sade clawed his hand from around her neck. "No. I accidentally sent him some pictures earlier. As you can see, I didn't text him back."

"But you sent him pictures of you. Pictures that you took before going to spend time with *my* family."

"It wasn't on purpose," she muttered, causing Atlas to laugh. The mechanism of laughter usually calmed him down. That day, it wasn't working.

"How do you *accidentally* send someone pictures of you?"

"I was trying to put them on Facebook, but I was thinking about Dante and . . . wasn't paying attention."

While Atlas appreciated her honesty, he didn't like how the honesty made him feel. Why was she thinking about him? They agreed that she wouldn't talk to him anymore. He knew he couldn't control her thoughts and feelings, but based on what Sade said, she was detached from Dante and didn't want to be with him. Something wasn't adding up.

Deciding that wasn't the time to address it, Atlas tossed her phone onto her lap. "We'll talk about this later."

Her head bobbed softly, and her hand wrapped around her neck as she looked away. Regret immediately filled Atlas. His shoulders slouched as he gently grabbed her thigh.

"I'm sorry, Day."

"If you *ever* put your hands on me again . . . I'll kill you."

Sade got out of the car, not bothering to wait for him. If it were any other woman from his past, Atlas would have assumed she was playing. But this was Sade—the woman who had proven she had no problem taking a life for the right reason. And Atlas didn't want to find out if the next reason would be his abuse.

Nibbling his bottom lip, he stared her down as he headed toward his parents' front door. Maybe she only killed for Dante. Was he even special enough? Chuckling, he tried to reel his emotions in because he was losing his fucking mind. To think . . . He wanted to question her about his worthiness through something as toxic and evil as a kill.

"I can't touch you at all?" he asked softly, stepping directly in front of her on the porch. Atlas allowed his fingers to glide gently down her arm. She shivered, and her nostrils flared. "You're driving me crazy, Sade." Entangling his fingers with hers, Atlas lifted her hand to his lips and kissed it. "Just the thought of you cheating and being with another man takes me to the edge." When she tried to lower her head, he lifted it. "I gave you to him for months. I'm never sharing you again." He wrapped his arms around her and pulled her close. "Tell me you understand that, baby."

Atlas hadn't told Sade because he didn't want to appear weak, but the whole time she was with Dante, his insecurities and paranoia began to brew. Though she kept telling him the ploy was in play to keep him safe, Atlas was aware of their bond and how tight it had been. Imani had often made jokes about how she took Dante from Sade. Every night, the thought of another man touching his woman plagued him, causing him to lose sleep from those images. Sade returning to him pregnant was his biggest fear. The only thing that made it easy for him to accept was her agreeing to never see or talk to him again. Now . . . It didn't appear that it had been the truth.

"Sade," he pleaded.

"I understand," she replied quickly—crisply.

"Tell me no one else can have you."

Releasing a shaky breath as her eyes fluttered, Sade put her hand on his heart. "You accepted me and saw me when my past forced me to hide myself. No one else can have me, Atlas."

He stared into her low, underturned eyes, needing the truth to be there. He became so hypnotized by her beauty he no longer cared. As he stroked her cheek, he confessed, "God, you're so beautiful. These eyes . . . your smile. I can never get enough of you."

He hadn't given the compliment to soften her toward him, but it worked. She cupped the back of his neck and gave him a sweet kiss.

"I want to validate you, but I also need you to know I'm not cheating on you. Please, don't do this again. If I feel like me and my baby won't be safe with you—"

"You both are. It'll never happen again. I swear."

Satisfied with his answer, Sade nodded and put some space between them. Atlas knocked, then opened the already unlocked door. Immediately, the smell of soul food assaulted his nostrils in the best way. He hadn't had his mother's cooking in a month, and though he enjoyed being on the island, he missed the morsels and his people. Initially, the plan was to lie low on the island until they were sure Dante wouldn't try to come after them for taking his money. Sade being pregnant changed their plans. She would have to travel regularly for doctor's appointments, so they agreed to leave the island indefinitely.

Memphis was the last place she wanted to return to, but because her family was there, she agreed. Sade feared people would think she was a horrible person because Dante was with her in Vanzette. Memphis was a small, big city. It felt like everyone knew everyone. In this instance, people were more grateful that Dante was alive and well than anything else. Unless they were a part of the sisters' or Dante's family, they didn't know the personal details about his time away. So far, no one had an idea of Sade's temporary kidnapping of her best friend . . . even if it was with the good intention to keep him safe.

"Wassup, y'all?" Atlas greeted his mother, Vanessa, and his father, Clay, as they moved from one side of the kitchen to the other.

Vanessa's eyes lit up at the sight of him. She dropped the spoon in her hand and rushed over to him. Atlas released hearty laughter as he spun her around.

"I'm so glad you're home!" she cheered.

"That island food don' made you lose a li'l weight," Clay noticed, shaking Atlas's hand and using it to pull him in for a hug.

"Nah, it wasn't the food. It was all the working out I was doing in the sun. That was probably the most beautiful place I've ever seen. I never wanted to be inside."

Vanessa's eyes slowly scanned Sade's frame. Her smile dimmed as she crossed her arms over her chest. "Sade."

"Vanessa," Sade replied curtly, stepping closer to Atlas's side.

Since Atlas had always been a mama's boy, the women had never been close. His father and the rest of his family were more accepting of Sade. That changed a little when Adam was killed. They didn't just blame Sade; they blamed Imani too. The difference was that Imani had twins with their DNA, and because of that, she got a pass.

They also held Sade more responsible because of Atlas's loyalty to her. To his mother and her sister, Adam's mother, it was Atlas telling Sade about Adam's plan that made everything worse. If he'd been more loyal to his family and kept her out of it, Dante wouldn't have sought asylum with Sade, and Adam wouldn't have had to go after him.

"Hey, Sade," Clay spoke. "You look well. My son must be taking good care of you."

"He is, thank you," Sade replied as they briefly hugged.

"I didn't know you were bringing a guest, Atlas," Vanessa said, returning her attention to her marinara sauce.

"She's not a guest. She's my woman."

"Still . . . The family is in the backyard, and I don't know how comfortable she'll be. She can sit in the dining room, I guess."

Chuckling, Sade lifted her hands in surrender. "I'm just gonna go, baby."

"Nah, stay."

"If she wants to leave, let her leave," Vanessa said.

"Vanessa, be nice," Clay ordered.

"No, really, I'll go. I'll take the car. If you want, I'll just come and get you later."

"His family is here. Someone will bring him to you later," Vanessa replied before Atlas could.

"Fine," Sade agreed.

As she tried to walk away, Atlas grabbed her hand and pulled her close. "You want me to bring you and the baby back something to eat?"

"The baby!" Vanessa yelled. "Don't tell me you got her pregnant!"

Sucking his teeth, Atlas led Sade out of the kitchen.

"That woman would probably poison or spit in my food. Don't bring me anything out of her kitchen."

Atlas couldn't tell by Sade's expression if she was playing. "I'm sorry about that. I thought with more time passing, she'd ease up."

Sighing, Sade stroked his hand with her thumb. "I just don't get why she hates me so much. Her nephew tried to rape me. It's not my fault he died. His death was declared suicide by cop because he didn't want to go back to prison and reached for his gun. How am *I* being blamed for that?"

When her chin trembled and her eyes watered, it broke Atlas's heart. He remained silent until they were outside by the car, where he pulled her into his arms.

"Look, my cousin was wrong. Imani was like gasoline to his greed and bad habits. When he got out and started up with her again, he became a version of himself even I didn't recognize. I don't blame you for that, and that's all that should matter."

"But it's not," Sade chuckled as she wiped away a tear. "I know how much your family means to you. Eventually, them not liking me is going to become an issue. And on the off chance it doesn't, I'm not dealing with this every time I come around."

With a frown, Atlas crossed his arms over his chest as she leaned against the driver's side of his car. "What you saying?"

"I'm saying unless she starts treating me better, I'm not coming around."

"Come on, Day. You know I'll never let things get out of hand..."

"Out of hand? You shouldn't want me to be in a position where I'm uncomfortable or being disrespected. I don't care who it is."

Atlas rubbed his hands down his face, releasing a defeated sigh. "Just... Go back to the hotel and rest. I'll Zelle you some money for food." Not bothering to respond, Sade turned and allowed him to open the door for her. "Text me when you get there. I love you."

Atlas had grown used to Sade not returning the sentiment. He tried to convince himself his love for her wasn't dependent upon her love for him. While a part of him admired how cautious she was with his feelings and not wanting to lie to him or move too fast, the other part of him questioned how she could fake love for Dante for months. What about him made Atlas unworthy of the lie of love? At least it would have made him happy.

He watched until she drove away, then made his way back into his parents' home. Before going outside to see the rest of his family, Atlas stopped to tell his mother, "You gotta ease up on Sade."

"Did you get that woman pregnant?"

"No, it's not my baby, but I'm raising it."

Vanessa chuckled as she leaned against the counter. Her eyes stared outside toward his father.

"Seeing as she's not showing yet, I assume she's still in her first trimester." Vanessa pushed herself off the counter and walked over to him. "So that means whatever she had with that other man is still fresh." Her head tilted as she thought about it. "It's Dante . . . isn't it?"

"As far as the world knows, that baby will be mine. I don't need you telling anyone otherwise."

"I don't trust this, Atlas. I think you should let her be with Dante. Whatever the two of you had before that plan was made, that's over. She can tell you she wants to be with you, but seeing as she was having sex with him and is pregnant with his child . . . That's a lie."

"Ma, please. Of course, they had sex. She had to make him believe they were married."

Vanessa's tongue rolled over her cheek. "And that's *all* you think it was? Her *pretending*?"

"That's what I know it was. She doesn't love or want to be with him. She wants to be with me."

Their eyes remained locked for a while before Vanessa lifted her hands in surrender. "Whatever you say."

Atlas hugged his mother and kissed the top of her head before going outside. As normal as he tried to act with his family, Vanessa's words had him paranoid. It didn't help that Sade had been thinking about Dante and texted him. Was he a fool to believe they could have a healthy relationship? Would the day come when Dante and Sade decide to be together? Seeing as Atlas had gone against his cousin to be with her and tolerated his family's disappointment, there was no way in hell he'd let her leave him to be with another man—*especially* Dante.

SADE

The Christmas Atlas Made Sade Smile

SOFT SNIFFLES ESCAPED Sade as she stared into her mug filled with coffee and whiskey. Imani had played her—yet again. Her sister asked her to go on a girls' trip a few days before Christmas. While Sade was hopeful it would allow them to strengthen their unraveled bond, Imani had other things in mind. As always, Imani said what she needed to get what she wanted, and that was an excuse to leave Memphis without her husband asking her any questions.

Regardless of how toxic Sade and Imani's relationship was, everyone knew the sisters would protect and look out for each other when needed.

But their girls' trip wasn't a girls' trip at all. It was a ploy to get them in a cabin in Gatlinburg, where Atlas and Adam were waiting for them. Not only did it frustrate Sade to be played, but it also hurt her feelings. Every time she got her hopes up that things could turn around between her and her sister, Imani reminded her why that would never be possible.

Chuckling, Sade shook her head and wiped her face. "Why do I even bother?" she grumbled as she returned to the cabin. Thankfully, Imani and Adam had gone into town, so it was just her and Atlas.

Atlas was cool, a bit intense, but cool, nonetheless. And he was abnormally handsome. The kind of handsome that made Sade believe he'd never been single or faithful a day in his adult life. So far, she'd been avoiding him. Her vulnerable state caused her to head in his direction. He was on the couch watching one of the old westerns her grandfather loved to watch.

He looked over at her briefly but did a double take. Had he noticed she was crying? His brows wrinkled, and his mouth parted slightly as he peered at her face. Atlas always had a deep way of looking at her—as if he could see through her with his syrup-brown eyes.

"You were crying."

Her eyes watered again, but she wouldn't shed another tear over her sister. "I'm fine."

"Is it about your sister? I didn't think you'd be cool with coming here with us, so I was surprised when Adam told me you agreed."

Chuckling, Sade sat back in her seat. "Imani told me we were having a 'girls' trip,' and it would be just the two of us. Had I known y'all would be here, I would have said no."

"Damn," Atlas mumbled after a quick bark of laughter.

"Oh no. I'm sorry." Sade sat up, gripping his arm. "I didn't mean it like that. I just . . . You know how I feel about what she's doing with your cousin. Being here makes me feel like I'm a part of it, and I don't want to be."

"So, it's them that has you not wanting to be here . . . not me?"

"Yeah. You're cool. I don't really know you well enough to decide I don't like you."

His lips spread into a smile. "I want to make you like me, Sade."

She mirrored his smile. "Why?"

"Have you seen you? You're beautiful. Plus, you have character and morals. You seem sweet and softhearted. Caring. I think you might be a good person, so I want to get to know you."

"Thank you. You seem like you might be pretty okay too. I guess we can be friends."

"I'll settle for that for now, but I'm trying to be more."

Blushing, Sade looked away from his gaze. It had been a while since a man's charm or flirting unnerved her. With all the men she dated, none of them made her feel the way Dante used to. Even without them becoming a couple, he was a hard act to follow. With Dante, Sade had always felt seen, heard, safe, and cherished. If he made her feel that way as friends, she couldn't imagine how he would have made her feel as her man.

"Look at you," Atlas mumbled, turning her face back to his with her chin. His stare was intense. He wanted to watch the effects of his words. Sade wasn't sure how she felt about that. Open, exposed, yes . . . turned on? Maybe a little.

"Why do you look at me like that?"

Swallowing, he shook his head slightly as he stared at her. "Like what?"

"Like . . . You've never seen a more beautiful thing."

With a low chuckle, Atlas lifted her hand to his lips and kissed it. "I haven't."

His confession caused their lips to gravitate toward each other. There, they made love on the couch. He made her come more than she thought was physically possible before they moved to her room. The entire time he was inside of her, Sade tried to convince herself this was a one-time thing. But unfortunately, her heart was open, and her pussy was leaking, and that was a horrible, horrible combination.

SADE

Do *Not* Answer: You didn't have to steal from me.

Do *Not* Answer: I would've given you whatever you wanted, Smiley.

Do *Not* Answer: I think you know that, and you stole it because you thought that would make me hate you. I don't. I still love you.

After sending Dante pictures accidentally yesterday, it was like a dam had broken. He texted her sporadically over the past twenty-four hours, and it was getting harder and harder for Sade not to reply. She found herself constantly comparing him to Atlas and struggling with Atlas's love not feeling like enough. As much as she told herself she'd be a fool to be with Dante, her love for him made it harder to stay away. They may not have had the fairy-tale love she thought she'd have with a man, but he'd finally opened his heart to her, and Sade wanted desperately to walk in.

At the sound of the toilet flushing, Sade exited the one-way text thread. The last thing she wanted to do was deal with Atlas's attitude and insecurities. He'd convinced her to join his family for dinner that day. After hearing she was pregnant, his mother agreed to apologize for the way she'd been talking to and about Sade. Even though Sade didn't want anyone to know she was pregnant so early into her first trimester, if that was why she could make peace with Vanessa, Sade was okay with it.

Because she was only ten weeks pregnant, Sade hadn't fully even wrapped her mind around the fact that a baby was growing inside her. A baby that was half of Dante's, no less. After years of longing for her best friend and sister's husband, it seemed surreal that she was pregnant with his child, and the twins he thought were his had come from another man.

"You ready to go?" Atlas asked, drying his hands.

"Yeah, I guess."

Atlas gave her a warm smile. "Thank you for doing this. I know you and Mama haven't really gotten along lately, but she promised to be on her best behavior today."

With a nod, Sade stood. "Does she . . . know the baby isn't yours?"

"Yes, but I told her the baby *is* mine. She promised not to tell anyone otherwise."

Sade didn't trust that, but she didn't care enough to question him about it. They left their hotel suite as Atlas asked, "We need to start looking into our own home, Day. I know you're still early in your pregnancy, but the baby will be here before we know it. We can't bring him or her back to this hotel."

Sade sighed and nodded her agreement. "You're right."

"What's the holdup? Money isn't an issue. Is it because you don't want to settle down in Memphis?"

"That's part of it," she admitted as he took her hand into his. "I wouldn't mind staying here because of my grandparents and the twins, but this city has always held unhappy memories for me."

"Well . . . We can create some happy ones with our baby. But if you really want us to leave, we can. I'm cool with anything except the island. I know that's your place of peace, but it's a bit too far."

"Yeah, I agree. I wouldn't want to take the baby there prematurely. Not to say I think the baby will have medical issues, but I wouldn't want to have to rely on the ferry if we ever had an emergency."

They continued to talk on the way to Stoney River in Germantown, and Sade found peace in his commitment to her and her child. She hoped being in the steak house instead of Vanessa's home would allow them to have a peaceful encounter. When she saw Adam's mother, Samantha, sitting next to Vanessa ... Sade was sure that would no longer be the case.

"Hey, Ma," Atlas spoke. "Hey, Auntie."

"You knew she was going to be here?" Sade whispered, referring to his aunt.

"Yeah, I mean ... I think it's best y'all tal—"

Before he could finish his statement, Samantha was leaping up from the table and charging toward Sade. In his attempt to separate the women, Atlas pushed Sade backward, causing her to topple over a table.

"Ma!" he yelled, pushing his aunt back as Vanessa cackled. "Are you serious right now? You promised me you'd apologize."

"Yeah, but I didn't say my sister would. That ho is the reason her son is dead. Did you *really* think she'd behave?"

Releasing a growl, Sade grabbed a knife and tossed it at Samantha. She shrieked and ducked, her eyes wide in disbelief.

"That bitch just tried to kill me!"

"Oh, hell no!" Vanessa yelled, frantically trying to close the space between her and Sade.

With haste, Atlas picked up Sade and carried her out of the restaurant. Sade fought against him, swinging until he put her on her feet.

"Baby, I'm sorry. I didn't know they would do that."

"I'm done! That was the final straw. Anything could have happened to me and my baby, and it would have been *your* fucking fault!"

"Sade, I—"

"I don't want to hear it, Atlas. I can't believe you thought it would be a good idea to have me in the same room as the two of them, regardless of *what* your mom said."

"Look, I really thought I could trust what she said."

"It doesn't matter anymore. I told you this wouldn't work because they hate me. I'll never ask you to choose between me and them, so we have to be over."

Atlas stared at her for a while before laughing. "Choose?" His jaws clenched, and he closed the space between them. "I already chose. I chose when I came to you with Adam's plan. I chose when I told the Feds the truth, so ya boy wouldn't have to serve time. I chose when I agreed to be the father of another man's baby. What other choice could you possibly want me to make?"

"Maybe the one where you don't put me in a room with your crazy-ass aunt." Sade pulled in a deep breath as he looked toward the sky. "Baby, you won't be happy with just me and the baby. Your family means too much to you. But I'm telling you right now, if I ever see either one of them again, I'm going to try my very hardest to beat their ass. So . . ." She shrugged and looked away, squeezing the back of her neck. "I think it's best if we end this now. We tried, but it just won't work."

Atlas massaged his chin as he released a hard breath. "We can pause while I figure out how to fix this, but it's me and you for life now, Day. I'm not sure what part of that you don't understand."

"There's no way to fix this," she muttered. "Either you never deal with them again or let me go."

"How are those the only options?" he asked with a bitter laugh.

"You set me up. You put me in a position to be attacked. I don't feel safe with you."

"Stop with the dramatics, Sade. You act like I knew they planned this."

"How did you *not*? You know your family far better than I do, and even *I* knew what time it was when I saw your aunt. They will disrespect me when they see me and talk about me when they don't. I'm not dealing with that. So unless you can stand here and tell me you won't have anything to do with them ever again, we're over." Atlas stared at her, his eyes growing weary.

Chuckling, Sade shook her head. She grabbed his wrists and stood on the tips of her toes to give him a tender kiss. "Goodbye, Atlas."

When she tried to walk away, he grabbed her hand. "It ain't gotta be like this, Day."

She pulled her hand away. "It does. I will not subject myself to this drama while I'm pregnant."

"And what about after? Can we try again then?"

Her eyes rolled as she pulled her phone out to call an Uber. Gripping her arm, Atlas pulled her side into his chest.

"Atlas—"

"After you have the baby, I'll have them together. We can try again then."

Shaking her head, she looked toward security as they escorted his family out. "Go with your people, Atlas. Please. You can get your things from the hotel today. I will go to my grandparents' house to give you time."

"Day, please. Don't do this."

Ignoring his request, Sade put distance between them as she busied herself to get a ride. A part of her was scared shitless to go through her pregnancy alone. The other part of her felt a little peace, no longer being attached to Atlas. As happy as she was to be with him after she left Dante, that feeling subsided quickly with each passing day. Atlas had some great qualities, but being with him felt like settling compared to Dante. Maybe she'd be better off alone.

ATLAS

The Reveal of Imani and Adam's Plan

*I*T DIDN'T MATTER how many times Sade said what they shared was only about sex. Every time Atlas made love to her body, he tried to touch her heart and mind too. The closer they got, the more honest she was with him. After hearing about her childhood and the things that happened between her, Imani, and Dante, Atlas hated them both. Still, he decided to be honest with Sade about Imani's plan with Adam.

As he pulled himself out of her leaking center, he rolled over onto his back and stared at her bedroom ceiling. Visiting her in Vanzette had become his escape over the last six months. The small town was quiet and perfect. If he didn't have family and worked in Memphis, he'd move there to be closer to her. Atlas wasn't sure what about him made Sade have her guard up with her heart, but he was confident he could break it down.

Sade got out of bed and returned with two towels to clean them off. When she finished, Atlas wrapped her in his arms. He held her close, sporadically placing kisses along her face and neck.

"I like it when you visit," she announced.

"I bet."

Her giggle made him smile.

"I like you too, Atlas."

"You know how I feel about you. I've liked you since we met." His exhale was hard as he sat up to look down at her. "And I hate that I have to tell you this now that you're finally starting to open up to me."

"Oh, God. Please don't tell me you have a wife or something."

"What? No." Atlas waited until his laughter died down to give her a sweet kiss. "The only woman I want is you."

"Then what do you have to tell me?"

"First, I need you to promise it won't mess up what we have going on."

Sade sat up and leaned against her headboard. "Okay. Now, you're scaring me."

The sight of her tugging the sheet against her body angered Atlas even more. He hated the position Imani and Adam had put him in . . . put them both in.

"It's about your sister." Her shoulders relaxed. "I told you she'd want to end her marriage now that Adam was out, and I was right."

"She actually said that?"

It didn't surprise Atlas that Sade didn't know what was happening back in Memphis. After Imani's last stunt around Christmas, Sade stopped contacting her sister and hadn't bothered to check in.

"Yeah, but it's not that simple. She's been doing some illegal shit, and the Feds have been watching. To avoid jail time, she plans to blame it on Dante."

"What!" Sade roared, causing the sheet to lower.

"That's not the worst part. On the off chance that Dante figures out what she did, tries to run, or ends up getting away with it . . . They have a backup plan to get him out of the way."

"Which is?"

Squeezing the back of his neck, Atlas momentarily avoided her eyes. "They want him dead, Sade. In fact, that's what Adam wants most. He agrees to let him take the fall for the charges that Imani will soon face, but he wants him dead anyway. And he . . . He wants me to kill him."

Sade stared at him before laughing in disbelief. "No, that's... You're joking, right?"

He shook his head. "I wish I was. Imani thinks Dante will have time to be arrested and face his charges. Adam wants him dead before that could even happen. I've been trying to talk them both out of this, but they aren't hearing me. So I agreed to kill him if he ran or found out Imani was the one who set him up. I have a feeling, though, that Adam will have me go after him before he can face a judge."

"Why would he ask something like this of you... unless you've done it before?" she asked, scooting away from him. "Have you... do you... Are you a murderer, Atlas?"

"Look... that's... neither here nor there. I'm telling you that your sister wants to set her husband up for fraud and that my cousin wants him dead. Now, I agreed, but I won't kill him because I know how much he means to you. But you need to find a way to get Dante here with you or at least out of Memphis."

"How could you agree to this, Atlas?" she yelled, hopping out of bed.

"Because I'm falling in love with you." Atlas rolled out of bed and took her naked frame into his arms. "If I didn't say yes, Adam would bring someone else into his plan who would kill Dante. He won't lose his life with me. Could you focus on that? I'm trying to help him—for you. I know this is a lot to take in, so I'll leave now so you can process this. But we need to come up with a plan to keep him safe. They are going through with this regardless of whether I'm involved. Help me save your best friend's life."

ATLAS

For Atlas, falling in love with Sade was the sweetest *and* most dangerous thing for him to do. He'd never felt so exposed and vulnerable in his life. Teetering on the edge of obsession and delusion, he read the text message that Dante sent her. He'd downloaded software that allowed every call and text message that she received to come to his phone . . . and he was also able to see her responses.

For the last week, Atlas was pleased. Sade hadn't been responding to the text messages. He believed he still had a chance. That changed that afternoon. It appeared she finally lost her ability to ignore him.

> **Do *Not* Answer:** I'm in Cali . . . Think I'm gonna go to that Mexican spot you love. The one in Old Town that makes the tortillas in front of you.

> **Do *Not* Answer:** Remember when we did the tequila tour and got fucked up? I think we hit every Mexican spot and tequila bar on that block.

> **Do *Not* Answer:** I wish you were here with me . . . smiling wide . . . toasting tequila . . . eating good . . . making love on the beach. I love you, Smiley. I've always loved you. I hope one day you will let me show you that.

Do *Not* Answer: I'll always be your devoted husband. You'll always be my loyal wife. And my best friend.

Sade: God, I miss you so much it hurts.

Do *Not* Answer: You don't have to. Tell me where you are, and I'll come to you.

Sade: I can't, babe.

Do *Not* Answer: Why not?

Sade: You didn't choose me. You always chose her. Regardless of how toxic our relationship was, that was my sister.

Do *Not* Answer: Quite frankly . . . I don't care about any of that. I want you, and I'm going to have you. We got years of making up to do . . . but I'll wait until you're ready.

Do *Not* Answer: Meet me where you are.

Sade: Dante . . .

Do *Not* Answer: Go to a Mexican restaurant and eat at the same time as me. I'd love to see you or hear your voice, but just knowing you're doing the same thing as me at the same time will be enough.

It took a while, but eventually, Sade agreed. Now, Atlas was seated in the booth behind her. She was so frazzled over what she was doing she barely took in her surroundings. Even if she had, the hat and shades Atlas wore would have made it difficult for her to recognize him. He'd purposely hung his head and casually made his way into the booth as she ordered what she always did—chicken fajitas.

When the waitress came to take his order, he pointed silently at the first thing on the menu to get her to walk away. He didn't have an appetite, but Atlas didn't want to risk being asked to leave if he didn't order something.

Sade released a shaky breath before sending Dante a Facetime request. As soon as it connected, she began to sob.

"Sade . . ." Dante said. "Baby, what's wrong?"

"I can't say," she whined. "I messed up badly, Tay. I-I never should've ended things the way I did."

"It's okay, Smiley. We can fix this."

She shook her head adamantly. "Not after what I did."

"Is this about the money? I told you I don't care about that."

Sniffling, Sade wiped her face. "No, it's not the money."

"Then what is it?"

Atlas waited, hoping she wouldn't mention the baby. If she didn't, there was still hope. There was still hope that she would choose him over Dante.

"Can we just . . . eat and act like what happened didn't happen? I really just need a moment with my best friend."

Dante didn't respond immediately, but when he did, it was with, "Whatever you need."

Atlas sat there for an hour and forty-five minutes, listening to them laugh and reminisce. Though they didn't talk about their love for each other or a future, Atlas realized at that moment their bond was deeper than Sade had been alluding to lately.

Did she not love him because she loved Dante?

Had she been playing him all along?

What was her motive?

Her intentions?

Atlas didn't know, but as he tossed two twenties on the table to cover his untouched food, he decided to find out just that.

Sade's body tensed at the sight of Atlas leaning against the wall next to the door of the suite they once shared. Her eyes shifted as she took small steps in his direction.

"Did you leave something here?" she asked.

"Yeah, you."

She shook her head as she released a tired sigh. "Atlas, please. I've had a draining day."

"You wanna talk about it?"

"No, I don't."

She unlocked the door, and before he could follow her inside, Sade planted herself in the door frame and held the door to her body.

"Can we please talk, Sade?"

Atlas's foot tapped the floor. If she gave in to Dante and didn't give him the same grace . . . he'd flip.

"Fine," she agreed, immediately dousing the fire that had started to build within him.

He followed her into the suite, eyes fluttering as he inhaled the scent of her perfume. It was fruity and floral. Her hair was in its signature '70s-style curls. That beautiful brown skin was covered in a kaftan with different shades of red. Red always looked good on Sade.

Kicking off her sandals, Sade sat in the chair closest to the window. Atlas sat in the one on the opposite side of the light-colored round table.

"I miss you" were the first words out of his mouth.

"I miss you too, but I still think it's best if we stay apart."

"Can you explain why?"

"I did at the restaurant."

"You act like I can't have a healthy relationship with you and protect you from my family."

Scoffing, Sade sat up in her seat. "You shouldn't *have* to protect me from your family, Atlas. There's no coming down from what happened a week ago. It will only get worse. They're going to come for me every time they see me, and I swear to God, I will kill them before I let them hurt my baby."

"Pipe down with the threats, a'ight? That's my mama and aunt you're talking about."

"Exactly. That's *exactly* why this won't work. You'll never choose me. Not over them."

"I don't know why you keep saying that when I did choose you, Day. My cousin is dead because I chose you."

"Your cousin is dead because he tried to rape me!" she yelled, slamming her fist down on the table.

"Nah." Atlas sat up in his seat. "If I would have just stuck to his plan and not included you, he'd still be alive. Ya boy would be dead or in prison, and you wouldn't be pregnant with his baby. But that's what you wanted, isn't it?"

"I think you should go," she blurted.

"You never wanted me. You lied to me. All this time, you've been stringing me along. *That's* why you never told me you loved me."

"That's not true." Her eyes blinked back tears. "I did want to be with you, Atlas. I saw myself falling in love with you eventually. But . . . I was . . . hesitant."

"Why?"

"I knew we wouldn't be able to remain in our own little bubble on the island forever. I felt like your family would be an issue, and they were. On top of that, you're way too possessive. The fighting over me and putting your hands on me . . . red flags. I think ending it before you fall harder is best, and I get more attached."

Tugging his ear, Atlas pulled in a deep breath. "I want to be here for you and my baby."

"It's . . ." She chuckled and licked the corner of her mouth. "It's *not* your baby, Atlas. It's Dante's."

"No, it's not. You said you never wanted him to know."

"That's true, but that doesn't mean I'm going to stay with you." Standing, she headed toward the door and opened it. "Can you please leave?"

Standing, Atlas looked around the room before heading in her direction. "I went against my family to be with you. You're out your damn mind if you think I'm going to let you end things so easily." When she didn't respond, Atlas wrapped his hand around her neck and used it to pull her closer. "I don't think you really want me to."

"Atlas," she whimpered against his lips before he kissed her. "I can't do another toxic relationship again."

Light laughter escaped Atlas as she clung to the hem of his shirt.

"Nah, that's exactly what you want." He lifted her into the air and wrapped her legs around him. "You want me crazy about you." He kissed her. "You want me to not let up off you." He kissed her again. That time, she wrapped her arms around his neck. "You want me to work for you because that nigga never did." He kissed her a third time. And that time, she kissed him back.

Kicking the door closed, Atlas carried her over to the bed.

"This doesn't change anything," she assured him.

"Yeah, okay," he agreed, though he didn't believe her. And by the time Atlas finished reclaiming her body, he was sure Sade would change her mind.

SADE

THE CONSTANT VIBRATION of Sade's phone pulled her out of her sleep, but she was too lazy to roll over and pick it up. As much as she hated to admit it, having sex with Atlas was the stress reliever she needed. Her mind had been jaded after having dinner with Dante over Facetime. She felt horrible for not telling him that she was pregnant and was battling whether she should continue with the secret or tell him the truth.

Though Dante suggested there wasn't too much she could do to make him hate her, *everyone* had a breaking point. Would keeping his baby a secret be his?

The phone rang again, and Sade groaned as she rolled over. It wasn't her cell phone that time; it was the phone in her suite.

"Hello?" she answered groggily.

"Sade, I hate to call you so early, but it's an emergency."

At the sound of her grandmother's words, Sade's eyes shot open as she sat upright. "What is it, Grandma?"

"Imani was attacked. It's bad."

"Oh God." Clutching her chest, Sade pulled in a deep breath as her heart skipped a beat—and not in a good way. Heat filled her body as she sat on the edge of the bed. "Where is she?"

"She's at The Med. She can't have visitors, but we can go up there to get updates on her and at least be in the same space as her."

"Yeah, yeah, of course. Um . . . Let me hop in the shower real quick, and I'll meet y'all there. Do the twins know?"

"Not yet. I didn't think we should tell them."

"I agree. Give me about an hour, and I'll be there."

"Okay, baby."

Sade stood and frantically pulled pieces of clothing out of the closet. Regardless of how things were between her and her sister, Sade took pride in being her protector. Knowing someone had attacked her sister made Sade want to get arrested just to avenge her.

"Atlas!" she yelled, rushing into the bathroom to cut on the shower. "Atlas, you have to wake up!"

"Hmm?" He sat up, rubbing his eyes. "What's wrong?"

"Imani was attacked. I'm going to the hospital. Grandma said they won't let them see her, but everyone has a price. I'm going to go up there and see if I can."

"Damn, okay. You want me to go with you?"

"No, I'll be fine. Plus, I meant what I said yesterday. Us having sex didn't change anything."

Atlas stood and made his way into the bathroom. She tossed him the extra toothbrush set she had and quickly brushed her teeth and washed her face before getting in the shower. Her eyes scanned his frame as he took off his boxers. Her mind was telling her to tell him to wait until she finished. However, her pussy was telling her to let him come inside.

Turning her back to him, Sade began to wash her body. He did the same . . . keeping his hands to himself until she grabbed her yoni wash. Atlas plucked it from her hand and squirted some into his palm. He spread her legs slightly before washing her center, using slow movements and paying extra attention to her swelling clit.

"Atlas, ... I really have to go."

"Then hurry up and come."

Even if she wanted to hold it off, she couldn't. Sade erupted into his hand before washing the suds from her body. He lowered to his knees, feasting on her pussy until she came a second and third time.

"I'm going back tomorrow," Sade said softly to her grandparents. "Someone is going to let me see her. I'll stop by the bank and get some cash. Maybe that will help."

"Hopefully, by then, she'll be awake," her grandfather, Barron, said.

"I just don't understand how this happened," Ava, her grandmother, said. "She's supposed to be safe there."

"How safe can you really be in federal prison?" Sade asked.

"Still, someone is going to have to answer for this." Barron massaged his temples. "The moment she wakes up and can tell us what happened, someone is going to have to pay."

Silence found them for a while as they watched the twins bounce on the trampoline at Urban Air. They hadn't shared with them what happened to their mother, but the guilt over the ordeal had all three adults wanting to love on Nila and Mila a little bit more.

"Hey, baby." Atlas kissed her cheek, and Sade practically leaped out of her skin.

"Atlas! What the hell are you doing here?"

He gave her a smile she used to find sexy as he shook Barron's hand and hugged Ava.

"I wanted to see my little cousins. You know they are more like my nieces because Adam was like my brother."

"Yeah, but how did you know where we were? I didn't tell you where we'd be."

His smile fell. "Yes, you did."

"No, I didn't. I didn't even know where we were going until we left the hospital and were on our way here." Pausing, she pushed him away from her grandparents' earshot as she asked, "Are you . . . Are you following me?"

"What?" He released a nervous chuckle and rubbed his palms together. "No. I think you'd know if I was following you, Day."

"Then how did you find us?"

"You share your location with me."

"I cut it off after what happened at the restaurant."

His mouth twisted to the side as he processed her words. "I didn't come here to go back and forth with you. I came to check on you and Imani and see the twins."

Nodding, Sade eyed him skeptically before pointing to where the twins were. She had no idea how he tracked her down, but she planned to take her phone to the nearest store to have it looked at before doing the same to her car. If Atlas was keeping up with her in any way, he wouldn't tell her, and she would have to figure out how herself.

JONES

DETECTIVE JONES HAD been watching Sade all day.
Her trip to the phone store.
Her trip to the mechanic.
Memphis may have been out of Jones's jurisdiction, but he was taking photos and documenting Sade's every move. On the off chance she did something to incriminate herself, Jones wanted to be the one to catch her.
Jones was tired of people getting away with crimes because the police didn't want to put in the work. That would end with Sade. He was sure of it.

DANTE

For the entire ten miles that Dante jogged, Sade was heavy on his mind and heart. He had the means and resources to find her but decided to give her space—for a while. It was silly of him to think it would be easy to get to their happily ever after. Since their teenage years, Sade had to watch him build a family and life with her sister. Their fate would have been different if she had expressed her desire for him before he got Imani pregnant. But Dante couldn't blame Sade for her hesitance because he'd also been tightlipped about his feelings for her.

After plopping down on the bench, Dante fought to catch his breath. He drank some water, removed his headphones, and poured the rest atop his head. Looking out into the bustling branches and bright sun, Dante laughed under his breath.

I really miss my girl.

Dante pulled his phone out to text Sade, and at the sight of two missed calls from her grandfather, he quickly called Barron back. Sitting lower on the bench, he draped his arm across it and settled in for the unexpected call.

"Hello?" Barron answered.

"Hey, Grandpa. You called?"

"Yeah. Couple things I wanna talk to you about." Dante nodded silently. "But first, how's New York treating you?"

"I'm actually in Baltimore now. I can't really stay in one place for too long without going crazy thinking about your granddaughter."

Barron chuckled. "Which one?"

Returning his laughter, Dante used his free hand to wipe his face and head. "Sade, of course."

"Hmm. Well, I wanna talk to you about her too, but first, Imani. Did Sade call and let you know someone attacked her in prison?"

With a frown, Dante stood and began to pace as his heart dropped. Regardless of how things played out between him and his ex-wife, Dante would never want any harm to come to her physically.

"No, she didn't. Is she all right?"

"She's . . . hanging in there, but it's bad, son. She's in a medically induced coma because of the swelling on her brain."

"*What?* What the hell happened?"

"We don't know. Conveniently, the warden had no video footage of the attack, and no one was in the room when Imani was found. All we can do is wait until she wakes up to tell us what happened."

"Damn. I hate to hear that. How are the twins taking it? Were they able to see her?"

"No, no one has. Sade is working on it, which may be why she didn't reach out to you."

"Honestly, Grandpa, she probably won't tell me even when she has the time. Unless I blow her up until she can't take it anymore, she's not talking to me."

"I need you to change that."

Dante's feet stopped moving. "Is she okay?"

"She is . . . but . . . I'm concerned."

"About what?"

"She's been acting distant or hesitant, even when in the same room as us. Like she's holding something back. And Atlas has been hanging around her a little too much for my liking."

"Wait." Chuckling, Dante ran his fingers down the corners of his mouth. "Atlas? Adam's cousin? The one who ran me off the road and didn't have to do a day in prison for it because he snitched?"

"That one. Now, I don't know what's going on between them, but when we were out with the twins earlier, Sade seemed extremely uncomfortable around him. She didn't know how he found out where she was. She left us and said she would have her phone and car checked out to see if he's put some kind of tracker on it."

"I think I'm missing something. For what reason would Atlas be stalking Sade? She's been apart from me for what . . . a little over a month? Has she moved on with him?"

Barron released a huff. "I don't want to get into her personal business. That's something you'll have to ask her yourself. I just wondered if you knew anything about Atlas from your time with Imani. Was he around at all with Adam? Or was it just while you were in school?"

Dante thought back over his marriage again. Now that the truth about Imani's affair with Adam and it leading to Dante not being the father of her twins had come out, he'd found himself looking for signs of the truth he'd missed. Any changes in priority or behavior . . . lowered libido . . . lies he'd gotten her caught up in. He looked at countless pictures of the twins, noticing less of himself and more of Imani and Adam every time.

"He was around while we were in college. I didn't notice any flirting or anything between Day and Atlas at the time. What happened between them after Adam got out is beyond me. Imani kept that from me, so if they were seeing each other, Sade did as well."

"From what you remember about him, is he someone I need to worry about? Can I write off what he did to you as loyalty to his blood, or was that a sign of how violent this man is?"

"I wish I could be more helpful, but I honestly don't know. Anyone willing to do what he did to me—regardless of whether for family—should be avoided. I can say Adam was willing to do whatever to get Imani and the girls, but that wasn't Atlas's excuse. If he was willing to do that simply because his cousin asked, I can't imagine what he's capable of if he's truly upset with someone. I'd say you have cause for concern. If the relationship was romantic and ended, or if he wanted more than she was willing to give, he might go after her."

Barron sighed heavily into the receiver. "That's what I was afraid of." He chuckled. "I disapproved of what she did with you while you were married to her sister, but at this point, I wish she would have stayed with you. At least then, I wouldn't have to worry about this."

Dante smiled with one side of his mouth. He hadn't considered if her grandparents' feelings toward their relationship were another reason Sade left him. They were all she had, and it wouldn't have surprised him if they influenced her more than he realized. While they hadn't straight up told her they didn't want Sade and Dante together, she did express her grandmother's warning that she'd be punished for what she did with him.

"I'll . . . uh . . . look into Atlas and see if Sade will open up to me about it. If things look like they are getting to be more than she can handle, call me, and I'll be there—whether or not she wants me to be."

"Sounds like a plan. Talk soon."

After disconnecting the call, Dante returned to the bench to gather his thoughts. His mind wouldn't allow him to believe Sade had moved on already . . . especially with the man that tried to kill him. There had to be another explanation for this—one where Atlas wanted something from Sade that she wasn't willing to give, and it didn't include her body or heart.

Refusing to believe his best friend could sleep with the enemy, Dante decided there was only one way to get to the bottom of this: to go to Memphis and confront her himself.

SADE

"I THINK YOU SHOULD journal," Ava said.

Sade's head tilted as she processed her grandmother's words. She hadn't been honest with them about a lot of things lately—being pregnant, her relationship with Atlas, missing Dante like crazy. It didn't take Ava long to realize things were sitting on her granddaughter's heart. Sade didn't want to go into detail, but she did admit to having a lot on her mind. Journaling, apparently, was Ava's solution.

"Huh?"

Ava smiled and covered Sade's hand with hers. They just had a late breakfast after getting the twins off to school. It had been difficult for Sade to watch her grandparents care for the twins since she'd been back in Memphis. Even though that's where Nila and Mila wanted to be, a part of Sade wished they'd wanted to come with her. She blamed herself for the distance between her and her nieces.

They might have been closer if she hadn't moved to Vanzette.

All that mattered was that they were loved and happy in a stable environment, and her grandparents provided that. But if they ever expressed their desire for Sade to take over, she'd do so willingly.

"If you have a lot on your mind and are not ready to talk about it, journaling is a great way to get it out. I've journaled since I was eighteen."

"Really? Do you keep them all and reread it or something?"

"Not all of them. Sometimes, I might read them to reminisce, but most of the time, once I write it out, I never open it again. There are many different kinds of journaling so that matters too. I have a prayer journal that I'll reread. The ones that are darker and about painful things, I don't open those. And there's a gratitude and daily one that I'll use for anything. I sometimes read over those."

"Hmm . . . Okay, maybe I'll do that. Thanks, Grandma."

"Anytime, baby. And you know you can always come to me, right?"

Before January, Sade believed that. After the slight judgment over what happened while Dante was with her in Vanzette, she wasn't so sure. Her grandmother's honesty was always out of love and respect, even if it wasn't something Sade wanted to hear. But Dante had always been a soft spot and sacred topic for her. Because she hadn't been able to have him the way she wanted until earlier in the year, Sade held what they had near and dear to her heart. Outsiders may not have understood it, and she didn't want their perceptions to taint the whirlwind love.

So, as much as she wanted to talk to someone about how she was feeling, she kept her thoughts to herself. The last thing she wanted was for her pregnancy to be something else that made her grandparents disappointed in her.

"Thanks, Grandma. I'll try the journaling, and if that doesn't help, I'll take your ear."

Pleased with her answer, Ava changed the subject, and they talked for a little longer before Sade headed out. She'd finally gotten an officer guarding Imani to agree to let her see her sister. He also agreed to send her daily updates. Unfortunately, the warden didn't think Imani's condition was serious enough to update her family regularly. But . . . the six figures Sade offered to pay Reggie, the guard, made Imani's condition *very* serious in his eyes.

Sade ended up leaving earlier than planned to try the journaling thing. Even though she stopped by the store to grab a notebook and pens, she decided to send herself a voice memo on her phone instead. That seemed more authentic to her.

As she stared out of her window at passing cars, she spoke. *"I'm pregnant with my best friend's baby, and he has no idea."* She chortled. *"All I've ever wanted was Dante. This year, I finally got him . . . and I let him go. Thinking back on it, I had a lot of reasons. But lately, those reasons don't seem like enough to stay away.*

"I wanted him to suffer for not choosing me, but I'm suffering too. I thought about how taboo it would be for us to be together, but I don't care about that anymore. At the end of the day, I have to live with the choices I make—not anyone else. Who cares if people approve of what I do or who I'm with if I'm unhappy?"

With a sigh, Sade nibbled her bottom lip. *"And then there's Atlas. When we first started messing off, I didn't tell Dante because I didn't want it to make him think about Adam. Then Atlas told me about Imani and Adam's plot against Dante, and I had to keep it a secret to protect him. I really liked Atlas, but something about him made me hesitate to commit. Now that I've been with him more, I know exactly where that hesitancy came from. It was my intuition telling me he had a few loose screws."*

She snickered. *"And I'm sure people can say the same about me, but that's all the more reason for us not to be together. But I wanted to be with Atlas because he was loyal to me . . . and Dante. He chose me. He made me feel like a genuine prize, and even if it was unintentional, Dante made me feel like I wasn't worthy of him and his love because of what he did with Imani. So, I guess a part of me felt like I owed Atlas.*

"Both men are on different ends of the spectrum. Atlas loves me more than I love him, and I love Dante more than he loves me. That's

why I need to stay away from Dante, and that's why I need Atlas to stay the hell away from me. But Dante deserves to know about his baby, right? God, this shouldn't be so hard. Could we actually coparent and not be together? I don't think I can watch him marry someone else, and he'd kill me if he knew I was with Atlas, even if it was brief.

"In his eyes, Atlas is the man who tried to kill him for his cousin. How will I explain being with him? That will probably make me look just as bad as my sister. No. I should just . . . keep my distance from Atlas and keep things platonic with Dante. I'll tell him about the baby and, no matter what, agree to coparent only."

Feeling lighter, Sade ended the recording and headed to the hospital. Reggie would soon be clocking out, and she needed to see her sister before he left for the day. It didn't take Sade long to get to the hospital, and when she did, she thought she saw a man who looked like Detective Jones from behind. Convincing herself she was only seeing things, she headed to the second floor and smiled at the sight of Reggie.

"Hi," she greeted, casually setting the black bag with his cash inside beside where he was seated.

"Hey. Please be quick."

"Of course."

As she went into Imani's room, Reggie stood and guarded the door. Her eyes immediately watered at the sight of her sister chained to the bed, unconscious. Her head was wrapped with a white bandage. There were no marks on her face—or her body. This couldn't have been a fight; this was an attack.

What had Imani done to warrant this?

Sade took Imani's hand into hers and gave it a gentle squeeze.

"I'm sorry I wasn't there to protect you. I need you to wake up and tell me who did this to you so I can make them pay. I love you, sissy. Rest well." After kissing Imani on the cheek, Sade left the room. "Were you able to get an update from her doctor?"

Reggie nodded. "Yeah, the swelling is going down. They think they will be able to take her out of the coma soon."

Relief flooded Sade as she smiled and placed her hand on her chest. "Good, good." Her fear was this might be another Dante "situation," where her sister would wake up and have amnesia. "Thanks again, and if she wakes up before I come back . . ."

"I'll give you a call ASAP," he assured, squeezing her hand gently.

Sade gave him a warm smile before leaving. Once she got to the car, she decided to go and tell her grandparents the great news.

ATLAS

THE SOUND OF knocking turned into a dull bell. Atlas was so drained of his energy he didn't want to get up to answer. It felt like Sade was his life source, and not being around her made him feel depleted. Atlas's eyes closed as the doorbell sounded again. He pulled in a deep breath before rolling out of bed. His eyes scanned his dirty room—the stacked pizza boxes and to-go food containers . . . clothes that he had tossed around haphazardly.

He caught a glimpse of himself in his dresser mirror, but he didn't look for more than a second . . . afraid he wouldn't be able to face himself. He looked out of the peephole and released a sigh at the sight of his father. Atlas opened the door and stepped to the side to let Clay in.

His father's frown didn't sway Atlas as he stepped inside. With a scowl, Clay told him, "When was the last time you bathed?"

"What day is it?"

With a scoff, Clay shook his head. "It looks like I got here just in time."

"I'm not really in the mood for company, Dad."

"It looks like you're not in the mood for a lot of things," Clay said, heading for the kitchen. He grabbed a garbage bag, returned to the living room, and began to clean. "What's this about?"

"Sade," he admitted. "I think she's going to leave me."

Clay eyed him skeptically, shoving a plastic cup into the bag. "What makes you think that?"

"She's been different since we came home. Things are perfect between us when it's just us with no one else around."

"That doesn't sound like the kind of relationship you should be in, son. If she changes when other people are around, maybe she's hiding something."

"I don't think that's it. I think it's because she's too loyal to Dante. Even when he's not around, he's ruining things. I won't let him stop me from raising my baby."

Clay's movements stopped. He leaned against the couch. "You said it wasn't your baby."

Atlas sucked his teeth. "Not biologically, but it *is* my baby. I promised to raise them, and I just . . . I don't want Sade to lose focus on what we're trying to build. She's been questioning me about things that don't matter . . . things she should trust me on . . . and I can't shake the feeling she's going to leave me."

"Well, if she does leave, it'll be her loss. However, if you want to try to prevent that, try reminding her of how good you two are together. How good you are for each other. If that doesn't work, nothing will."

Atlas nodded in agreement and tried to take the bag from his father, but Clay kept it. He told him to get freshened up and that he'd take him for a drive when they were done, hoping a little sunshine and vitamin D would further pull his son out of his depression.

A Week Later

Atlas stared at Vanessa's lips, trying to focus on what she was saying. His mind was racing, making it difficult for him to keep up. He put his hands over his ears, squeezed his eyes shut, and shook his legs as he rocked back and forth. Vanessa stood, then sat beside him, wrapping her arm around him. The tight restriction of her embrace grounded him. Atlas wasn't sure how much time had passed, but his mind was settled when he lowered his hands and looked at her.

"Atlas," she called softly—carefully. "Have you been taking your medicine, baby?"

Standing, Atlas began to pace. How *dare* she question him? He was a grown man. If he'd stopped taking his medicine, that was *his* prerogative.

"Is that what you came over here for?" he questioned, staring down at her. "To keep tabs on me?"

"Of course not. I'm just . . . a little concerned. I haven't seen you all week. And now it looks like you're having difficulty focusing on me. Last time this happened, you had an episode, and if that's what's happening now, I want to make sure we're prepared."

Gritting his teeth as his nostrils flared, Atlas looked away. He pulled in a shaky breath, trying to maintain control of his emotions. Had he been taking his medicine? No. Would he tell his mother that? Absolutely not. Did Atlas feel he was on the verge of an episode? Perhaps. Would that make him take the medicine or speak with a psychiatrist? Not at all.

"I'm fine, Ma. I just needed some time to figure things out with Sade. I thought I had a way to get her back, but I think she really wants me to stay away."

"That's her right, Atlas. Besides, I don't like her anyway."

His head whipped in her direction. "Well, you'd better find a way to get along with her because I'm going to make sure she doesn't go anywhere."

Chuckling, Vanessa ran her hands up and down her thighs. "I get that you may be a little enamored by her because she is beautiful, but let's not forget she's why your cousin is dead, son."

"Can we stop with that? Adam is dead because he was about to pull his gun out on the police. Sade was his victim. If they would not have shown up, he would have raped her. I won't let you demonize her to put him in a positive light—cousin or not."

Their eyes remained locked before Vanessa scoffed and stood. "Wow. Well, I guess I'd better go. I was coming to check on you, not argue with you. Remember, though, family comes before anything and anyone."

"Yeah, and that includes my family with Sade. She's carrying *my* baby, and she's going to be *my* wife. Get behind that, Ma, because it's going to happen."

Her head tilted in confusion as she squeezed his arm gently. "That's not your baby, Atlas. You promise me that you're taking your medicine?"

With a chuckle, Atlas licked the corner of his mouth. "Yeah, Ma. I promise."

SADE

After hugging the toilet and releasing all the contents in her stomach, Sade stood to shower, brush her teeth, and wash her face. She was completely drained of her energy and wanted nothing more than to climb back into bed. At the sound of someone knocking on the door, she thought back to the night before, wondering if she'd ordered breakfast, but she hadn't.

"Yes?" she called at the door.

"It's me, baby."

At the sound of Atlas's voice, her eyes rolled. She should have known he wouldn't stay away forever, but a part of her hoped he did. That would have made getting him out of her system easier. But with him popping up and trying to get her back, not to mention the sex, Sade could admit that had been easier said than done.

She opened the door and leaned against it slightly. "What do you want, Atlas?"

"Are you okay? You don't look too good."

"I don't feel good either, so I'd like to lie down. What do you want?"

"Is it the baby? Can I get you anything?"

She shook her head. "I'll be fine."

Atlas squeezed the back of his neck. "I haven't been fine. Not without you."

"Atlas—"

"Nothing matters to me without you. What my mom and aunt did... That was wrong. I promise I'll never put you in a situation like that again. We can leave the city, and you never have to be around them again. Just... please... Let me fix this between us."

"There's nothing to fix, Atlas. We've never been in a relationship. We agreed we'd try once the dust cleared, but what is even clearer is that we don't need to be together. I appreciate everything that you've done for me and were willing to do for my baby, but what we had is over. Please... Make this easier for both of us and just stay away."

His expression hardened, causing Sade to push herself off the door and prepare to close it. As she did, he said, "I'll be seeing you," and unfortunately, Sade knew that was the truth.

Just Under One Week Later...

Since it appeared Sade would be staying in Memphis indefinitely, she decided to make arrangements. The first thing on her list was finding a gynecologist, then an apartment. Going from owning her own home to renting an apartment felt odd, but because she didn't have to worry about maintenance, her lawn, or anything else, Sade was looking forward to having less stress renting instead of owning. Plus, the apartment she'd chosen was close to her grandparents. She'd be able to move in at the start of the next month and planned to stay in her suite until then.

A part of Sade wanted to tell Ava that she was pregnant so she could accompany her to her appointment. Before things with Atlas's family caused a rift between them, Sade expected to do this with him. Now, she felt even more alone. Since she'd changed her number, she hadn't seen or heard from him outside of that one pop-up a week ago. He watched her stories on social media but didn't engage, for which Sade was grateful.

Imani had been taken out of the medically induced coma, but currently, she was still unconscious. Her doctor assured Reggie that it was common for people to remain in a vegetative state and that she'd wake up when her mind and body were ready. Though the swelling had gone down almost completely, her doctor stressed it was imperative she rest. That gave Sade hope.

When her alarm sounded, Sade ended the voice memo she was recording and headed inside for her twelve-week checkup. The fact that she'd be able to hear her baby's heartbeat was bittersweet. Dante should've been there. Would he forgive her for keeping him away?

Before she could get lost in her guilt, the sight of Atlas waiting for her by the front doors caught her by surprise.

"What in the *hell* are you doing here?"

ATLAS

"What in the *hell* are you doing here?"

Sade was beautiful—even when she was mad.

Atlas's eyes scanned her frame. She didn't look like she was pregnant. Bloated, maybe, but not pregnant. She looked tired, though, as if she hadn't been getting as much rest. That angered Atlas. He was supposed to be there, helping her, making this pregnancy as easy as possible. Instead, she'd shut him out, but that wouldn't be the case for long.

"Why did you change your number?" he replied.

"How did you find me?"

"I followed you," he admitted. "Had you not changed your number, I could simply call you to make sure you're okay."

Sade released a low hum of laughter and licked her lips. "You know you're crazy, right?"

"About you? Absolutely." He took a step in her direction. She lifted her hands, and he saw the moment she held her breath. Her reaction to him made his heart ache. "Are you scared of me? You know I'd never do anything to hurt you, Day. I love you."

"You're stalking me. You don't think that's hurting me?"

"I just wanted to make sure you were okay. I promised you I'd be there for you and the baby and—"

"I told you that was no longer needed. Stop following me, or I will get a restraining order."

"Damn, it's like that?" When she didn't respond, he laughed. "Is this about Dante?"

She released a low breath. "No, Atlas. We can't be together. There's no reason for you to try to keep tabs on me. Now, please, leave me alone."

"Fine," he agreed. "But if you change your mind, I'm here."

Not bothering to respond, Sade headed into the doctor's office. He watched through the door as she talked to the receptionist, then went to take a seat. Atlas made his way to her car, casually putting an AirTag on it. He'd grown tired of waiting outside of the hotel all day for her to make a move. When he was done, he headed back to the hotel.

He was in luck—the front desk receptionist was the young girl who liked how he looked. Every time he came, her eyes would widen, and she'd smile and stumble over her words. It was cute to him in the past. Now, he'd use her crush to his advantage.

"H-hi. I haven't seen you here in a while."

"Yeah, I've been away at work," he replied, leaning against the counter. "I think I left my card to the suite at my hotel in Atlanta. Can you give me another one?"

"Y-yeah, sure." After a few taps and the swipe of a new card, Mandy handed it to him. "Is there . . . anything else I can get you?"

"I'm good for now, beautiful, but thank you."

He shot her a wink that made her bite down on her bottom lip and smile before he headed toward the elevators.

In Sade's suite, Atlas hid several cameras and microphones. He also logged into her computer and iCloud account to secure her new number. With it, he was able to hack her phone and email again. Pleased with his efforts, he headed out, confident he'd be able to win his lady back once and for all.

Hours Later...

"Am I crazy? I feel like I might be. I feel like what Atlas is doing is wrong. There's no good reason to stalk someone . . . right? God, I'm so screwed up in the head I'm actually wondering if this man could truly love me, I guess, because the man I love most never put energy behind having me. Now, here Atlas is, doing literally whatever to have me. I can't lie and say the obsession isn't creepy, but it's also a little cute. Still, those red flags can't be ignored."

She sighed. "I wished he would have just . . . been present from a distance and gave me space to make my way back to him. Now, I feel like I can never trust him. And don't get me started on his family. It's just too messy of a situation, but I can't lie and say I don't miss him."

She paused. Atlas sat up in his seat, locked in. He watched her record a voice memo on her phone as she lay in bed. "I cried after my appointment earlier. I wished he could have been there with me. Since he's unable to be my partner, that's all the more reason for me to tell Dante he has a baby on the way."

"No." Standing, Atlas tried to conjure up a plan.

"I can't believe I got myself into this mess."

Dialing her number, Atlas lowered the volume on his computer. He stared at the screen as she watched her phone ring with his Facebook messenger call request. Her eyes rolled slightly before she said, "This can't be a sign."

Sade answered with, "Yes, Atlas? How did you get my number?"

"Ava," he lied quickly. "I know you want me to stay away, but I just wanted to know how the appointment went. Is everything okay with you and the baby?"

Her body relaxed in bed as she smiled softly. "Everything's fine. I heard his or her heartbeat, so that was cool."

"Wow. Wish I could have been there."

"Me too."

"Baby, I know I didn't go about things the right way, but I just . . . I want you to know that I love you more than anything in this world. I'll continue to give you space, but if you ever need me . . . Please, remember I'm here."

With a nod, she almost whispered, "Okay."

"Get some rest, a'ight?"

Her mouth opened and closed, and Atlas held his breath . . . waiting for the invitation.

"We can't be together, Atlas," she said as if it was more for herself than him.

"I know, baby."

"And . . . . I don't want to play with your emotions."

"I understand."

Sitting up, she looked around her empty room. "Can you . . . Can you come to the hotel? I just feel really emotional and alone right now."

"I'll be there in less than an hour."

"Okay, thanks."

Atlas could barely contain himself as he ended the call and showered. Regardless of how often Sade said they couldn't be together, she was his, and he wouldn't stop until she realized that.

SADE

SADE STARED DOWN at Atlas as he slept. He'd come to her suite last night and hadn't left since. She didn't want him to. Things felt normal between them, and she knew it was because they were closed off from the rest of the world. When they were alone, things were perfect. It was when they were out in public or when they were with his family that they started to have issues.

In Atlas's arms, she found rest. As carefully as she could, Sade slipped from his embrace. She wanted to call Dante before she lost her courage. Instead of going out onto the patio, she stepped outside. Sade walked down the hall and waited for Dante to answer. When he did, she smiled.

"Hello, Smiley."

"Hi. Are you busy?"

His low chuckle made her heart skip a beat. "I'm never too busy for you."

"Can you come to Memphis? There's something I need to talk to you about in person."

"Of course. I've been waiting for you to call." He laughed softly. "It's been hard as hell waiting."

"Well, you don't have to wait anymore."

"I'll look up flights and tell you when I'll be there. But you're good, right?"

"Oh yes, I'm great. I just think this is something I should tell you face-to-face."

"All right, Sade. Let me look into some flights, and I'll text you."

"Okay, thank you."

"I love you."

Gritting her teeth, Sade blinked back her tears. "I-I love you too, Dante."

After disconnecting the call, she went back into the suite. Atlas was up, brushing his teeth. "Good morning."

"Good morning, beautiful. You good?"

"Yeah. I'm actually glad you're up."

"You about to kick me out?"

Sade laughed softly with a shake of her head. "No. I just wanted to talk."

"Cool. Let me take a shower, and then I'm all yours." He paused. "You wanna join me?"

"No. I don't trust you to keep your hands to yourself."

"Smart woman."

The sexy smile he gave her caused her to blush. His locs were longer now and a dark brown color at the ends. The scruff that usually lined his jaw had grown out into a beard. Those syrup-brown eyes were as beautiful as they always were against his milk chocolate-brown skin. Sade turned, not wanting to get so aroused by the sight of him that she joined him for that shower anyway. They didn't have sex last night, and she wanted to keep it that way. Sex was always easy between them, but it would complicate things even more.

After Atlas finished dressing, they went to the hotel restaurant for an early lunch. They'd placed their orders, and Sade felt it was a good time to tell him what was on her heart.

"I'm going to tell Dante about the baby." Atlas only stared at her, so she swallowed hard and continued. "He deserves to know, Atlas. He was a great father to the twins, and he's my best friend. I can't deny him of the opportunity to be a father to our baby just because I decided I don't want to be with him."

Atlas's head tilted. He licked his lips and rolled his tongue over his teeth. "You still don't want to be with him?"

She considered her response carefully. Things had been good between them since last night, but Atlas was still the possessive man he'd always been. The possessive man she'd need to be careful with.

Did she want to be with Dante? Absolutely. Would she tell Atlas that? Not a chance in hell.

"I want him to know about his baby and be here," she said carefully. "I want my best friend back. My priority right now is having a healthy and stress-free pregnancy, so I'm not trying to be in a relationship with him or you."

His head bobbed once . . . His jaw set. "Okay, so what do you want from me? To stay away while you work things out with him?"

"Not quite." Sade shifted in her seat and took a sip of her water. "I would like to keep you in my life but as a friend. I don't want to go around your family, and I also don't want us to have a romantic relationship because that's what makes you get crazy. Dante can be here for the baby . . . but I want you here with and for me."

"How will that work if you want to hide me and what we have?"

"I'm not hiding it; I'm just not making it public. I know Dante, and he will need some time to process the fact that I knew what Adam and Imani had planned and that you and I were . . . intimate. It wouldn't be good if I tried to bring you around him any time soon. I'm already springing a baby on him, Atlas. I don't want to tell him that I was fucking the man that tried to kill him too."

Atlas scoffed with a shake of his head. "So, that's all it was for you? Sex?"

Her eyes rolled as she released a tired breath. "No, but we weren't in a relationship. The specifics don't matter. What matters is you and I are perfect when we're alone, and no one else is in our business."

"I can't argue with that."

"So, I want it to stay like that while I'm pregnant. If by the time I have this baby, you aren't as violent when it comes down to other men looking at me and flirting with me, and we can trust Dante not to go crazy over you being around me and the baby, we can talk about taking things to the next level. But I can't make any promises, Atlas. If that's not good enough—"

"I'm cool with that, baby," Atlas said, and Sade hoped to God that was the truth.

ATLAS

Though he agreed to them keeping a low profile, that didn't mean Atlas wouldn't put forth the effort to make Sade just as crazy about him as he was about her. She was a laid-back woman who was easy to please, and that made Atlas want to give her the world. He looked over everything he'd done in his home again before heading to the door to let her in.

The TV was up and a medical drama was queued for them to watch. He had several crossword puzzles and the extra-large mahjong tiles for them to play. The coffee table had all her favorite snacks, and candles were lit all over the room.

As much as he wanted to take her somewhere to show her off, this would have to do.

When he opened the door and waved in her direction, Sade exited the car. She looked as beautiful as always, dressed down in leggings and a crop top. Her hair was pulled up into a bun for a change, and her smile was as radiant as ever.

"Hi," she greeted him, puckering her lips for a kiss.

"Hey. Thank you for coming over."

"Of course." It wasn't a long walk from the entryway to the living room, so by the time Atlas was done locking up, he heard her gasp. "Aww, Atlas, this is so sweet."

"I know you want to stay low-key, so I've been looking up home date ideas. I figured something chill like this would be a good start."

She wrapped her arms around his neck and gave him another kiss. "This is a great start, Atlas, seriously."

Pride filled his heart as he released her. "Good. I ordered Chinese, and it's on the way. These snacks should last us for the rest of the night. Did you bring a bag like I asked?"

"Yes, it's in the car."

"Good. I don't want you to worry about driving back if you get sleepy. I'll go get it if I need to."

"Okay," Sade agreed as she sat down on his couch. "This is really cute, baby. Thank you."

"Anything for you."

Atlas sat next to her, and they talked about their days. It wasn't long before the food was delivered. After dinner, they started the show and began to play games. Three rounds of mahjong later, Atlas was upset over how good she was at it, but he didn't mind losing to her. They ended up falling asleep on the couch, and he didn't wake up for hours. When he did, he put Sade in his bed and went to get her bag out of the car, putting a new tracker on it in the process.

It took a second for Sade to stir, but Atlas didn't mind. He continued to feast on her center. When she hummed, it was like music to his ears. Sade gripped the back of his head, rocking her hips against his face.

"I swear you're using sex to keep me addicted to you," she slurred, sleep thick in her voice.

"Is it working?" he asked, slipping a finger inside her opening.

"God, yes," Sade purred as her back arched.

He stayed between her legs until she came on his tongue. Then he flipped her onto her stomach and slipped into her from behind. Each moan and whimper she released mixed with his groans and heavy breathing. Atlas wished she wasn't pregnant and that *his* seeds could plant life inside of her. Since that wasn't the case, he'd have to behave and be patient . . . and come up with a plan to get rid of Dante—*permanently.*

DANTE

Two Days Later

Originally, Dante was supposed to meet Sade the following day. When she texted him an hour ago and asked him to meet her at this restaurant, Dante was confused but wouldn't miss the chance to see his favorite girl. He didn't have to be escorted to the table by the hostess. He recognized her from behind as soon as he saw that thick hair and loose curls.

Dante approached the table, his feet slowing when he noticed someone sitting beside her. He wasn't sure, but it looked like Atlas. Instead of making his presence known, Dante hung back to listen to their conversation, unsure why Sade had asked to meet her while Atlas was there.

"I'm not sure what you want me to say to that, Atlas," Sade said.

"Say you agree."

She shook her head. "But I don't. I told you what my priorities were right now. Even being out with you right now is going against my desires. And now you want me to tell Dante about us?"

"I love you, and you don't have to say it, but I know you love me too."

"Look . . . I won't deny that I have a lot of respect and appreciation for you because of what you did to Dante for me, but—"

Dante couldn't believe what he was hearing. It was one thing to consider Sade dating Atlas. Had she just admitted to being in on the plan to have him framed and killed? How could she say she had Atlas do what he did? Unable to hear anymore, Dante grabbed Atlas by the back of his shirt and slung him to the carpeted floor.

Their eyes remained locked on each other's. It didn't matter how much Sade screamed for him to stop and pulled at his arms, Dante wouldn't let go. He wanted to watch as the life faded out of Atlas's eyes. Even when Atlas blacked out, Dante kept his hands around his neck. It wasn't until several arms wrapped around him that he got up.

"I can't believe you, Sade! *This* is what you wanted me here to say? That you were in on it with them? How could you betray me like this!"

"It's not what you're thinking!" she yelled with tears streaming down her cheeks, but they meant nothing to Dante.

He'd heard it with his own ears—Sade appreciated Atlas for what he did to Dante for her—*for her*. Atlas had only done one thing to Dante, and that was run into him and almost kill him.

What was the reason?

Was she so upset about him being with Imani that she wanted him dead?

Was *that* why she left him in Vanzette?

None of it mattered now because Dante vowed to make them both pay as he was pulled out of the restaurant.

SADE

SADE DIDN'T THINK anything would make her feel better after what happened at the restaurant yesterday, but getting the call that her sister had finally woken up did. All day, she'd been trying to process what happened. Of all the restaurants Dante went to, he chose the one she was at with Atlas. She didn't even want to be in public with Atlas, but he'd convinced her to go out for dinner so they could talk. If she had known that he wanted to discuss letting Dante know about them, she would have told him no. Sade knew her best friend and that he'd react violently to that truth, and that was why she didn't want him to know until after she had the baby.

"Thanks for calling," Sade said to Reggie.

"You're welcome. Your sister is being transported back to prison after her doctor clears her. I don't know when that will be, so make your visit quick."

Nodding, Sade went into her sister's room. Her eyes watered immediately at the sight of Imani sitting up in bed. Slowly, her head turned toward the door. Sade covered her mouth, fighting back her tears, causing Imani to groan and roll her eyes.

"You are *so* dramatic."

Laughing, Sade dropped her hand. She sniffled but didn't think her tears would fall.

"Shut up. You should be glad I'm happy to see you're awake."

"Mhmm. What are you doing here?"

"I wanted to set eyes on you and find out what the hell happened."

Imani sighed as Sade pulled up a seat next to her bed. "Honestly, I don't know what happened. One minute, I'm doing laundry. The next, I'm getting hit in the back of my head."

"And you don't know who did it?"

She shook her head. "No. I don't have any beef with anyone currently. It's been a while since I've gotten into a fight. I don't know."

"Damn. Well, hopefully, when you get back inside, someone will have some answers."

"Why do you care?" Imani scoffed. "You don't give a fuck about me."

Massaging her temples, Sade pulled in what she needed to be a calming breath. "I am sick of having this conversation with you, Imani. I *do* give a fuck about you. You're my sister, and I love you. I've told you this a million times—no one can beat you up but me." That made Imani smile like Sade hoped it would. "I wish there was a way to get you out of there. I wanted you to go to prison and pay for what you did, but I don't know. This makes you being there real. I don't like not being able to get to you when you need help."

"Well . . . if you want me out, maybe I could give that detective a DNA sample since he promised he'd help get me out."

That got a good laugh out of Sade. "I know you better not! If you helped Jones send me to prison, I'd commit another murder before my trial was over and do something to get you in there with me."

Imani laughed. "You know I wouldn't do you like that. The money has already cleared in my account."

They shared another laugh before Sade confessed, "I needed this. Can't believe the laughter is coming from you."

"What's wrong, sissy?"

Sade considered if she wanted to share what was happening with her sister. Technically, she was the reason they were in this situation anyway.

"Dante came back to Memphis, and he overheard a conversation between me and Atlas. I don't know how much he heard, but he now thinks I was in on the plan, and he tried to kill Atlas." Imani's eyes widened, and her mouth hung open. "And I'm not exaggerating, Imani. He literally choked Atlas in a room full of people until the man blacked out. If a few people hadn't grabbed Dante and carried him outside, Atlas would be dead."

"Damn. I wish I could say I'm surprised, but I'm not. It's best for all parties involved if those two are *never* in the same room. Dante's going after him every chance he gets."

"I tried to explain that to Atlas, but he didn't want to hear it. He's insisting I tell Dante about us like we're together now."

"Why does he care that Dante knows you two were fucking?"

Sade opened her mouth but quickly snapped it shut. She wouldn't tell Imani she was pregnant with her ex-husband's baby. Not yet, at least.

"It doesn't matter. Everything's all messed up, and I don't know what to do. I wanted me and Dante to get back to our friendship, but I fear that will never be possible now."

"Well, I'm sure everything will work itself out. Dante will forgive you for almost anything. You're perfect in his eyes. Once he calms down, I'm sure he'll hear you out."

"I hope so," Sade mumbled. She'd been calling him, but her calls were going straight to voicemail. This was the first time Dante's anger had ever been directed toward her. He'd been frustrated or disappointed in the past but never angry with her, and Sade didn't know what to do.

"How are my babies?" Imani asked, changing the subject.

"They're good. Thriving. I'm enjoying being able to spend time with them. They can't wait for me to get my apartment so we can have a sleepover there."

"Wait, so you're staying in Memphis?" Imani snickered. "Why?"

There she was . . . asking a question Sade didn't want to provide the truth for again.

"I just . . . think it's best if I be close to family right now," Sade decided on. "Grandma and Grandpa aren't getting any younger, the twins are getting older, and your ass is getting knocked out in prison. If I'm on the island, it'll take days for me to get here if anyone needs me."

Imani's eyes rolled as she chuckled. "Don't add me to that equation. You know if I needed you, you wouldn't be there. Not after everything I've done to you."

"You've done a lot of horrible things, but you're still my sister. Besides, I'm no angel. I've done some horrible things to you too."

Imani huffed, her head hanging. "Yeah, and sleeping with my husband is at the top of that list." Her head hung, and it was the first time she showed sadness over Sade being with Dante. It caught her off guard.

"I didn't think you'd care. I mean, you *were* cheating on him with Adam and wanted a divorce."

"That's *not* the point!" she yelled, jerking her cuffed arms against the bed. "That was my *husband*, and you were my *sister*. And I knew . . ." Her chin trembled, and her eyes watered. "I knew he'd finally choose you." Chuckling, Imani looked toward the ceiling as her tears rolled down her cheeks. "It didn't matter how hard I tried to make him want me. I knew he would always choose you."

Sade wiped her sister's tears. "He didn't choose me, Imani. He married you. He stayed with you."

"Yeah, because he thought the twins were his. If he knew I'd cheated on him with Adam, he would have been gone instantly."

"Would that have been such a bad thing? God, what did I do beyond exist to make you want the one thing, the one person who meant the most to me?"

Sighing, Imani looked toward the window with a shake of her head. "It doesn't matter anymore. You finally won, got the man, and got me out of your life."

This wasn't how Sade saw their visit ending, but she figured it was a good time to leave. "I'll, um . . . check on you through Reggie later. If you need anything, tell him, and he'll let me know."

As Sade walked away, Imani gritted, "Stop doing that."

"Doing what, Imani?"

"Being nice to me. I don't deserve it. The worse I treat you, the better you are to me. Just stop."

Chuckling, Sade turned to face her sister. "I'll never stop. The quicker you realize that and let me be a good big sister to you, the better off we'll both be."

She took a few steps more before Imani asked, "Can you . . . bring me a seafood bag?"

Sade's smile widened as she nodded. "Yeah, I got you."

Sade's head was killing her. Outside of feeling nauseated and tired, the headaches were the worst symptom of her pregnancy. She was curled up in a ball with the lights and TV off, waiting for the headache to pass. About two hours had passed since she left the hospital after visiting Imani. Reggie refused to uncuff her, so Sade had to feed her, and to her surprise, the gesture made Imani cry.

"I'm sorry, Sade, for everything," Imani sobbed. "I know that might not mean much, but—"

"It means everything, seeing as though you never apologize," Sade replied, shedding a few tears of her own.

"I love you. I'm really sorry."

Gasping, Sade wobbled in her seat. She couldn't remember the last time her sister told her she loved her . . . if ever. "I-I love you too."

A smile lifted the corners of Sade's mouth at the memory. Someone knocked on the door before it opened. Sitting up, she asked who it was. Relief filled her when Atlas announced himself . . . then she grew confused.

"How'd you get in? You left your key here when we called things off."

"I told them at the front desk that you weren't feeling good and asked for a new key so you wouldn't have to get up to let me in."

"Thanks, but I don't like how easy it was for you to get a key."

"They know I was staying here with you. I'm sure they wouldn't have given it to me if that wasn't the case." Satisfied with his answer, Sade lay back down. "How you feeling? Head still hurting?"

"Yes."

"And you sure you don't want to take anything?"

"I'm sure. My doctor told me I could take a low dose of Tylenol, but I don't want to. I'd rather let it go away on its own."

After Atlas undressed, he climbed behind her in bed. The moment his arms wrapped around her, Sade relaxed farther in bed. His presence and embrace may not have made her headache disappear, but it made her feel better.

"I'm sorry about Dante yesterday. I can't believe he showed up where we were. We were supposed to meet today, but he hasn't answered my calls. I actually think he has me blocked."

"You don't have to apologize for his actions."

"I still feel bad about it. He could have killed you."

"Him sneaking me from behind was some bitch-ass shit. If he wants to square up or shoot it out, we can always do that."

"Whoa." Turning in his embrace, Sade tossed her leg over his frame. "Now, that's what we're *not* going to do or even discuss. I told you how important it was to keep the peace. That's why I didn't want him to know about us. If I can't trust you to behave—"

"He choked me out. Ain't that much behaving in the world, Sade."

"Can you please just let it go . . . for me? You did run him off the road and give him a concussion. He temporarily had amnesia."

Sucking his teeth, Atlas didn't respond right away. This was what Sade was worried about. There was no way these two men could coexist in the same space. What Atlas had to understand was that if she had to choose between the two of them, he'd lose. She prayed he'd calm down and it wouldn't come to that.

Sade's Audio Journal

"My life is a mess like an unmade bed. I hope Imani's being sincere, but she's in my head. She's being all nice, and she apologized . . . and cried. What am I supposed to do with that? Do I trust it? Is it a part of a plot or scheme? And then there's Dante and Atlas. God knows I've always loved Dante. The months we spent together were the best months of my life. I can't describe how it felt to finally be his . . . even if it was temporary.

"Even if it was fake. It doesn't matter how much I tell myself I deserve better than a man who didn't choose me. I can't deny how much I love him. How much I've missed him. And then there's Atlas. He's been a little off his rocker lately, but he chose me. He's been so considerate and thoughtful about me. Or at least he was. I don't think I trust him entirely either, and I certainly can't trust him and Dante to be around each other.

"Is it even possible for me to have something with Atlas one day since I will be having Dante's child? Should I just cut Atlas off now before it gets too hard? Am I only attached to him because of how much he likes me? Because of the toxicity? I don't know, but I need to figure this out soon."

DANTE

RUBBING HIS HANDS together as his leg shook, Dante tried to direct his energy to one place. Ever since he found Sade and Atlas together, his emotions had been all over the place. The most frequent emotion had been anger... then confusion and hurt. He'd been replaying the situation, the conversation, over and over again. A part of him hoped he'd missed something, but that wasn't the case.

He got a call from Sade.

He agreed to fly out two days later.

They were supposed to meet the next day.

But instead, she sent a text with a time and place to meet after his flight.

He showed up and heard her telling the man confessing his love for her that she appreciated what he did to Dante for her.

So, truth—Sade had some kind of sexual or romantic relationship with Atlas. Truth, Atlas was the man who tried to kill him. Truth, Sade, his best friend, asked him to do that.

Whenever he thought about it, Dante wanted to go after Atlas again. He'd have the chance. That, Dante was sure of. His phone began to ring, and that was the third time he'd received a call from an unknown number.

He finally answered with, "What?" before taking a swig of his beer. That was all he'd been doing since he'd been back in Memphis—drinking... and thinking.

"Dante Williams?"

The voice was familiar, yet Dante couldn't place who it was. "Who is this?"

"This is Detective Jones from the Vanzette Police Department. Is now a good time to talk?"

Dante chuckled. "It's never a good time to talk to you, but what do you want?"

"This is something I'd prefer to talk to you about in person."

The last time he heard that, it was from Sade. And what she had to say, Dante didn't want to hear at all.

"I'm no longer in Vanzette, Jones."

"I know. You're in Memphis."

Dante's leg stopped shaking. He stood. "You're following me?"

"No, I'm following Sade and saw you approach her."

"Does she know you're following her?"

"No, and it's best if it remains that way."

Shaking his head, Dante massaged his temples. "I don't know what you're up to, but I want no parts of it."

"I just want to have a conversation. I'm not going to lie; I'm still going after Sade, and because I'm convinced you're the reason she committed several murders, this concerns you too."

With a sigh, Dante nodded his agreement. "Fine. Where do you want to meet?"

Even meeting with Jones felt like some kind of betrayal against Sade. But seeing as she was why he'd almost lost his life, Dante stuffed those feelings of loyalty inside to meet with Jones. As he stepped inside the coffee shop, his eyes scanned the room. He found Jones seated at a high-top round table in the back of the room. There was already a mug of something in front of the seat

Dante would occupy, so he didn't bother heading toward the front counter.

Sitting down, he eyed Jones before lifting the mug to his nose and sniffing it.

"It's just a cup of coffee," Jones said. "I didn't add anything else to it."

With a nod, Dante pushed the mug forward and waited for Jones to continue.

"I know you and Sade are together, but I was hoping that if I shared some evidence and my theory with you, you'd help me bring her to justice."

"We're not together anymore. If you saw us yesterday, I'm sure you know that."

Jones gave him a barely-there smirk before continuing. "As you know, I am investigating the murders of Patrice Baker and Trina Roe, along with the missing case of Willow Frank. All these women have a connection to each other and your wife. Or ex-wife. I'm not exactly sure how that works. Because you two weren't actually married, right? That was fake." Dante remained silent. With a chuckle, Jones nodded his head and licked his lips.

"We found a strand of hair at Patrice's nape that didn't belong to her. There was blood at Trina Roe's home that didn't belong to her. We still have no evidence of where Willow is, but we were able to tap into Patrice's phone, and she was talking to Willow before she came up missing. Would you like to know what they were talking about?"

"I don't care, but I'm sure you will tell me."

"They were talking about a missing man from Memphis they believed Sade was hiding. When we tapped Willow's phone and tried to track her location, those messages were deleted. They weren't, however, deleted from Patrice's phone."

"And?"

"You were the missing man. My theory is that Patrice tried to use Willow for information, and Sade killed her. Then she killed Patrice. And finally, she killed Trina. Because Sade's DNA is not in our database, I can't prove any of this, and that's the only reason she hasn't been arrested yet."

"What does any of this have to do with me?"

"Your testimony can help me put her away. If you can admit to having amnesia at the start of the year, that will line up the murders with the timing that Sade had you, and it will give her motive. I would also go as far as to suggest you file a police report and have her arrested for abduction. If we can get her convicted on the lesser charge, she'll be put in the system, and it'll be easier for me to get her DNA to prove she was at each scene."

Dante shook his head as he stood, but Jones continued. "Those women lost their lives because Sade wanted to keep you for herself. Doesn't that make you feel even the slightest bit guilty? I'm giving you the chance to do the right thing and help me get closure for their families. Help me put Sade where she belongs . . . in prison for the rest of her life."

Their eyes remained locked for a few seconds before Dante walked away. It was his hurt and anger that even allowed him to briefly consider helping Jones. But he couldn't do that . . . right? Despite what Sade had done, she still helped prove Imani was committing fraud and kept him out of prison, which didn't make any sense. If she wanted to destroy Dante, why not let him stay in Memphis to face those charges?

His head began to pound as he tried to put together the pieces. Maybe he needed to hear her out himself, but at the moment, Dante didn't trust himself to be around her. And he didn't know when, or if, that would change.

SADE

ONE THING SADE wasn't expecting was to be woken up from her nap by a Facetime request from Dante. Groggily, she sat up and cleared her throat as she looked around the suite. For a moment, she was so caught off guard by the call that she even forgot where she was. Answering the request, Sade rubbed her eyes. She had little energy these days and was always sleepy.

When she stopped rubbing her eyes and allowed them to settle on Dante, his frown made it difficult for her to smile because she was so happy to see him.

"Jones is here, and he's following you."

Swallowing hard, Sade nodded. "I thought I saw him at the hospital when I went to see Imani. Why? And how do you know?"

"None of that matters. Just . . . Don't kill anyone or do anything illegal while he's here."

With a chuckle, Sade avoided his eyes. "Wow. Everything I did, I did for you, Dante."

"Nah, don't put that on me. How am I supposed to believe that? Now, it's looking like you did what you did to keep your secrets. You sent Atlas after me. Maybe you killed them because you never wanted me to know."

"First of all, if I *did* kill them, I certainly wouldn't admit to it on this phone. And second, I didn't send Atlas after you. I can't believe you'd think I could do something like that to you."

"I didn't think it, but you admitted it yourself. And I'm still trying to figure out why you asked me to come here just so I could hear it."

"That's *not* why I asked you to come!" she yelled louder than she intended. "I didn't even know you were at the restaurant."

"You told me to meet you there!"

"No, I didn't, Dante. I asked you to meet me the next day. We were supposed to meet yesterday, not the day before."

"Sade . . . You texted me and asked me to meet you there an hour after my flight landed. You're going to lie about that too?"

"I'm not lying. Why on earth would I ask you to meet me while I was with Atlas? I didn't want you to find out about us until . . ." Her mouth snapped shut. This wasn't how she wanted him to find out she was pregnant with his child. "Months later. I promise I didn't text you to meet me there, and I promise I had nothing to do with what they did to you. That's not what I was implying." Pausing, Sade nibbled her bottom lip. "If I tell you the complete truth, do you promise to hear me out?"

Dante considered her request for a while as she made herself comfortable against the headboard.

"Go ahead."

"The Thanksgiving Adam came back, Atlas and I reconnected. I did not approve of her cheating on you. I wanted to tell you, but Atlas convinced me not to. He said there was a chance you wouldn't believe me, and I didn't want to risk messing up our friendship. I agreed to wait a little while and see what Imani would do. I thought she would just divorce you. I didn't think she would try to frame you for fraud, and I most certainly didn't think Adam would try to kill you."

"Were you in a relationship with Atlas?"

"No, but we did spend time together and have sex. Imani tricked me. You know that Christmas we were supposed to go on a girls' trip?" He nodded. "She lied. Adam and Atlas were there. I was angry and hurt that she lied to me and used me to cheat on you. Atlas . . . kept me occupied. We did have sex. I told him I didn't want a relationship, and he was cool with trying to change my mind.

"About six months later, that's when the FBI first approached Imani, and she decided to frame you. It was Adam's idea to kill you, and he asked Atlas to do it." She paused. "Atlas came to me because he knew how close you and I are, and he asked me to help him save your life. He knew how much it would hurt me if something happened to you. He agreed to Adam's plan but never planned to kill you. The accident was supposed to buy you time in the hospital while I helped you prove Imani was the one stealing and committing fraud."

"But I woke up with amnesia and didn't remember a damn thing for quite some time."

Sade smiled as her eyes watered. "Exactly. So, I brought you to Vanzette to make sure you wouldn't be arrested and charged with crimes you not only didn't commit but also didn't even remember your wife committing because you didn't remember her or anyone else."

"And that's what you want me to believe you were referring to?"

"Yes, Dante," she stressed. "I have thanked him a million times for warning me about what Imani and Adam were planning so I could help you. Adam wanted him to shoot you at your office that night. He chose not to. Trust me when I say I was working *for* you . . . not *against* you. I would never do anything to hurt you. I didn't even want you to know that I'd been sexually involved with Atlas—"

"Then why did you tell me to meet you there?"

"Babe, I swear I didn't."

With a huff, Dante lowered his phone. A few seconds passed before he sent her a screenshot of their text thread. Her brows wrinkled and her mouth parted as she looked at the text from her asking Dante to meet her a day early. Except it wasn't from her.

"So you didn't send that, Sade?"

"No, I didn't. That's not what I asked you to meet me here to discuss with you. I did *not* send that text, Dante."

"Then who did?"

Gritting her teeth, Sade hopped out of bed. "That motherfucker! Atlas knew exactly what he was doing! He wanted you to show up and hear that conversation so you'd be upset with me. I have to go."

"Wait, we need to tal—"

Sade disconnected the call and quickly dressed. Atlas sending Dante that text was the final straw.

Sade beat against the door, refusing to be ignored. Atlas's car was in his parents' driveway, which meant he was there too. The longer it took someone to answer, the more frustrated she became. Atlas trying to finesse the strings of her life and heart to make more space for himself could not be ignored or forgiven any longer. She felt like a fool inviting him back into her life—just for him to turn around and do this. But this would be the last time she ignored her intuition about Atlas . . . or anyone else for that matter.

Finally, the door burst open, and Vanessa was behind it.

"Why are you beating on my door like you ain't got no damn sense?"

Ignoring her question, Sade pressed her way inside. "Where is he?" she asked, charging through the living room.

"Who?"

"Atlas! Who else?"

"In his room, but I didn't invite you into my home. Get your ass out!"

Sade increased her pace down the hall until she made it to Atlas's room. She found him stretched out across the bed with his noise-canceling headphones on. Before she could shake him awake, the setup in the corner of his room caught her attention. She made her way over, her heart palpitating at the sight before her. Each monitor had a different angle of her hotel room on it. He had her text thread and email account pulled up as well. There was also a black screen with a map that looked to be tracking her car.

Covering her mouth, she gagged. Sade had never felt so violated before. He was watching her everywhere, through everything. Shaky hands pulled her phone out, and she took pictures of everything before sending them to her grandmother. There was no way in hell she'd be using that phone anymore. She barely wanted to drive her car. And she certainly wouldn't sleep another night in that suite.

Her eyes scanned the room, settling on his closet. She remembered he kept a bat there from previous visits. Vanessa and Clay had kept this room just as it was when Atlas left for college. Sade used to find it cute that he'd spend so much time there instead of at his own home. Now, she was disgusted by it and wondered how many other women he'd stalked and watched there.

Grabbing the bat, she began to hit each monitor one by one. Vanessa rushed in, shaking Atlas awake since the headphones kept him from hearing a thing. He immediately sprang into action, trying to grab Sade, but she lifted the bat and was fully prepared to swing.

"Don't come near me!" she yelled, taking backward steps toward the closet, then heading for the door.

"Do you know how much this shit costs?" Atlas questioned, syrup-brown eyes almost bulging out of their sockets.

"You think I care about that? You've been stalking me! My phone, my car, my suite . . . you've been watching it all! You're fucking *sick*!"

"Sade . . . Baby, it's not what it looks like," he said softly, getting a laugh out of Sade.

"No, it's *exactly* what it looks like." She looked behind herself to see how close she was to his door. "You're going to leave me the hell alone, Atlas. If you don't, I'm going to take my evidence of your stalking to the police and press charges against you. Do you understand me?"

Atlas chuckled. "You can try, but they won't do anything about it."

"Stay the hell away from me," Sade gritted before turning to leave.

She left the home as quickly as she could, running over her phone in the process. Sade went to her hotel and found every camera and microphone he had planted. After that, she searched her car for the AirTag. Sade boxed everything up and took it to her bank to put in her safety deposit box for safekeeping. Once she checked out of the hotel, Sade went to her grandparents' home. She was exhausted. As she neared the front door, she noticed a note pinned to it. She snatched it, and her heart sank when she recognized Atlas's handwriting.

Not even jail will separate me from you. You can get rid of the phone and cameras, and I'll still have eyes on you. You're mine, Sade— mine.

Her eyes blurred with tears, and her heart pounded in her chest. Fumbling with the keys, it took Sade what felt like forever to open the door and finally let herself inside. She didn't realize how disconnected she was until her grandmother grabbed her hands. Sade saw Ava's lips moving, but none of the words registered in her brain.

Short, choppy breaths escaped her as her tears began to fall.

"H-he's never . . . n-never going to let me go. I'm never going to g-get away from him."

Tears turned into sobs, and choppy breaths turned into not being able to breathe at all. And before Sade knew it, she passed out.

ATLAS

*T*HE LIGHT TAPS *against his door caused Atlas to stir from his sleep. With his feet on his carpeted floor, he gripped the side of his bed. After sitting there for a few seconds to fully wake up, he stood and went down the hall to answer the door. At the sight of Sade, he smiled.*

"Can I come in?" *she asked sweetly.*

"Y-yeah, sure."

Sade stepped inside and headed straight for his room.

"What are you doing here?" *Atlas asked, not that he minded.*

"I've been thinking and . . . maybe I reacted too harshly. You were watching me because you love me. That's not something I should run away from. That's something I should run toward. I think I made a mistake calling things off." *She turned and sat on the edge of his bed.* "I want to be with you, Atlas."

His heart palpitated as he made his way over to her. "Don't play with my emotions, Day. Are you sure about this?"

With a nod and a giggle, Sade wrapped her arms around his neck. "I'm positive. I want to be with you and only you."

"What about Dante?" *he asked, pushing her toward the center of the bed.* "I won't share you or our baby with him."

"You won't have to. We can run away together and raise this baby ourselves. He doesn't have to be involved."

Finally. That's all Atlas wanted to hear. But it was only in his head. The sound of his phone ringing proved that. Instead of answering right away, he sat up in bed and looked around the room—momentarily confused about where he was. When he realized he was alone and had only hallucinated Sade's presence, he picked up his phone and threw it across the room for ruining the dream that would probably never happen in his reality.

SADE

Sade was no longer able to hide her pregnancy. After she passed out, she wanted to go to the doctor to make sure her baby was okay. Her grandparents were so concerned they demanded to be able to go with her too. There, she told them the truth.

"Why didn't you tell us sooner?" Barron asked as they slowly walked out of the hospital.

Sade was okay, and the baby was too. The doctor said her blood pressure was a bit high, so they kept her until it returned to normal.

"I didn't want to disappoint you both yet again. I know you didn't like me being with Dante, to begin with. Now, I'm having his baby."

Ava wrapped her arm around Sade's. "You're a grown woman, and you're allowed to make your own decisions. I don't like how things played out, but I also don't like how Imani treated you and Dante. She wasn't being faithful to him, and it's a good thing they are divorced."

"How did Dante take the news?" Barron asked.

"He doesn't know yet, and please, don't tell him."

"What are you waiting for?" her grandfather continued.

"I planned to tell him when he first returned, but Atlas ruined that. Now, I have to wait until he's over that before I can tell him about the baby. I don't want anything to taint or ruin the news."

"Well, we won't tell him, but I think you should tell him about Atlas."

"I agree," Ava said.

"I'd already mentioned Atlas to Dante after what happened at Urban Air, and he said he would look into it and handle it if need be." Barron paused and stepped directly in front of his granddaughter. "Either call the police or let Dante handle it."

With a nod, Sade surrendered to the fact that Atlas had her beat in the crazy department. He was beyond her control, and she couldn't handle him herself.

Though Sade assured her grandparents she was okay, Ava insisted she rest for the evening. By the time she made it to the second movie with Nila and Mila, someone knocked softly on the door.

"Come in," Sade said, pushing herself up in the bed.

Excited squeals escaped the twins when Dante walked in. The white lilies in his hand softened Sade's heart. They were her favorite. Nila and Mila rushed over to him, each giving him lingering hugs. He caught up with them both before Ava called for them. Dante took slow steps in her direction, giving her time to take in his handsome features.

His wide frame. The tattoos that covered his chest and arms . . . She'd forced herself to forget how handsome his caramel brown-hued face was. How captivating those shiny eyes were. Clearing her throat, Sade forced herself to look away.

"Grandpa called and said you needed me," Dante said, handing her the flowers. "What's going on?"

"Thank you." Sade lifted them to her nose and smiled. His simple gesture of bringing her favorite flowers had already lightened her mood. "I figured he'd call you, but he said he'd give me time to do it on my own."

Dante chuckled as he slipped out of his shoes. She watched as he undressed down to his boxers before slipping into bed behind her. The moment his arms wrapped around her, all the noise in her head was silenced. In his arms, she always felt secure enough to shut down her heart and mind. In his arms, she always felt safe.

Turning in his embrace, Sade tossed her leg over him, and he immediately molded his arms around her. Dante placed a kiss on her temple before slowly rubbing her back up and down.

Sniffling, Sade lost herself in the peace and comfort that she never felt with any other man . . . including Atlas. On Dante's chest, in his arms, that was where she truly belonged.

Sade hadn't planned to fall asleep, but she did. When she woke up, the sun had gone down completely, and she was still in Dante's arms. Sitting up, she looked around the room, then down at him as he watched a low-volume video on his phone.

"Hey, sleepyhead."

Smiling, Sade yawned. "How long was I out?"

"Two hours."

"Jesus. I'm sorry, Dante. I'm sure you have more important things to do than lie here with me."

"Nothing is more important to me than you, Smiley. Now, tell me what's going on."

Dante exited the TikTok app and set his phone on the nightstand beside the bed. He sat up next to her and took her hand into his.

"It's Atlas. He's been stalking me."

"Seriously?" His grip tightened on her hand. "Like . . . for real, for real?"

Sade sniggled and bobbed her head. "For real, for real. He's used my phone, email, and car to track me. There were also cameras and microphones in my hotel suite. That's why I'm here. I'm staying here until my apartment is ready because I don't feel safe there anymore. I feel . . . way too exposed." Her eyes watered, and she tried to blink back her tears, but they fell anyway. "I've been intimate with that man, but this . . . This is a vulnerability I never wanted to feel with him or anyone else.

"He's watched me do things no one should be privy to without my permission, which shattered me. I ended up having a panic attack and passed out." Wiping away her tears, Sade confessed, "I don't know what to do, Dante. I don't know how to stop him. I feel like I'll only be able to get rid of him if I leave Memphis, but I don't want to."

Dante lifted her head and wiped the tears from her face. As hard as his facial expression was, his voice was full of emotion when he said, "I'm not going to let anyone run you out of this city. If you want to stay here, I'll take care of him."

Sade tilted her head and kissed his palm. "Did you kill Willow? Are you going to kill him too?"

Dante smiled with the left side of his mouth. "Like I said in my text, you proved your loyalty to me, and I proved mine to you. Willow was taken care of, and he will be too. The less you know . . . the better."

"Okay," she almost whispered, nodding her agreement. "Thank you, Tay."

"You know I'd do anything for you."

"Still?"

"Always."

Slowly, their mouths moved like magnets until they connected. Sweet pecks turned into a deep, passionate kiss that had Sade leaking between her thighs. Dante's hand slid down her frame, squeezing her ass. She moaned into his mouth.

"We don't have to do this," he said against her lips breathlessly, "especially here."

"Don't stop," she requested before reconnecting her lips with his.

Dante gently lowered her to the bed before covering her body with his. His hand slipped under her oversized T-shirt, and the moment his fingers grazed her leaking opening, she moaned. Much too much time had passed since the last time she'd felt his fingers on her or in her, and Sade feared it would overwhelm her.

"Mm . . . You're already so wet. Did this pussy miss me?"

Tugging her bottom lip between her teeth, Sade nodded. "Yes, babe."

"I'm going to put my fingers inside of you, but you have to be quiet, okay?" The warning intensified her arousal. She nodded, gripping his shoulders, attempting to prepare, but nothing prepared her for the pleasure he provided. His hand covered her mouth as moans erupted, silencing her until she came.

Dante pulled the shirt over her frame as she pushed his boxers down. Their lips reconnected as she wrapped her legs around him. She whimpered as he stretched her, prompting him to say, "Shh . . . Be quiet, or I'll have to stop."

"Mhm," she agreed, clawing at his back.

His strokes were slow, deep, long, and gentle—then hard. Her toes curled as he licked and sucked her nipples. It didn't matter how hard she fought to remain quiet. The slow knock of the bed against the wall, combined with the sound of her wetness covering his shaft, filled the room. If anyone walked by, they'd surely hear, which only turned Sade on more . . .

ATLAS

T HERE WASN'T MUCH Atlas regretted, but he did regret sending Dante that text from Sade's phone. If he hadn't, he would still be in her good graces. But because he wanted to speed up the process of their happily ever after, he decided to take matters into his own hands. His logic led him to believe that if Dante were upset over their relationship, he'd leave the city, and Sade would decide to keep the baby from him as she had initially planned. What he *wasn't* expecting was for the two to reconcile.

As he watched them make love, tears filled his eyes. Exiting the app that was connected to the camera he'd planted in the guest room at her grandparents' house, Atlas chuckled to release some frustration. He knew there was only one way to get rid of Dante, and that was through death.

DANTE

DANTE SHOOK HIS head in amusement at the sight of Jones in a parked car across the street. He made his way over to speak with him. Though he didn't like the idea of Jones following Sade, at least he wasn't following him. That meant Dante could take care of Atlas and not have to worry about anyone being on his trail.

Jones got out of his car and leaned against the driver's-side door. He lit a cigarette, placed it between his lips, and then crossed his ankles. Dante's eyes focused on the lighter. It was the most unique one he'd ever seen. It was shaped like a dragon.

"I've been calling you," Jones said. "Are you going to help me with Sade or not?"

"Not. Is it legal to follow someone in another city after a case has been closed against them?" Dante sucked his teeth, straightening his frame. "That has to be harassment, stalking, or something."

"Do you think I give a damn about that? Sade killed two, maybe three, women. I'm not stopping until she's behind bars. And since you won't help me . . . Maybe I'll make sure you end up there too."

Closing the space between them, Dante lowered himself to Jones's ear and told him, "Stay the fuck away from my wife. She's no longer a suspect, and this isn't Vanzette. If you keep on, I'm going to take matters into my own hands and forcibly remove you from wherever she is."

"Did you just threaten me? I should end your life right now!"

"You could, but then you'd have to explain to your superiors why you were outside this house."

Standing upright, Dante eyed Jones for a few seconds before walking away, tossing, "Leave, Jones," over his shoulder in the process.

"She's going to prison. Since you won't help me, I'll handle this myself. And trust me, you *won't* like what I do."

Between the ominous threat and crisp tone, Dante's feet stopped momentarily. As he continued to his car, he wondered what Jones had up his sleeve.

After Dante grabbed Ava and Barron fried catfish meals from the wing spot up the street, he asked Sade and the twins to join him for lunch. He wasn't worried about things being weird between them. Even though they knew he wasn't their father, they still loved him the same.

A part of Dante was hurt when they asked to stay with their great-grandparents, but he knew that was for the best. What was most important was that they be in a stable environment where they felt loved and safe, and he was sure they were getting that from their great-grandparents.

They ended up going to the twins and Imani's favorite seafood restaurant. Sade was cool with that because she enjoyed their wings. It wasn't that long of a wait before they got a table, which Dante was grateful for. While he and Sade sat beside each other, the twins did the same. They looked at Dante, then Sade, before bursting into laughter.

"What's so funny?" Dante asked with a smile of his own.

"It's weird seeing you two together," Nila answered.

"What do you mean?" Sade asked. "We've always been best friends."

"Yeah, but... This is weird," Mila said before covering her smile.

"Y'all like each other. That's what Mama said," Nila added.

"Oh, did she? When did she say that?" Sade asked.

"When we had to choose where we wanted to live. She said if we chose to live with Dante, you would probably be there too," Mila explained.

"And she said if y'all got married, we can't call you Auntie Mommy because she's our only mommy."

Though Sade chuckled, her leg bounced under the table until Dante placed his hand on it.

Dante asked, "Is that why you two decided to stay with your great-grandparents?"

The twins looked at each other before Nila spoke.

"Kind of. It would be too weird watching y'all be together and not you and Mommy. Plus, we get to do what we want with Nana and Papa. They don't have as many rules."

That caused both Dante and Sade to laugh.

"Very smart choice then," Sade teased as the waiter came to take their order.

Dante was so grateful he was able to spend time with his girls. DNA or not, he'd always show up for the twins, and he prayed they never doubted that.

After getting the twins settled for the evening, Dante prepared to leave. Sade's pout made him want to stay. As he scanned her face, he confessed, "If I had known you planned to return to Memphis, I would have gotten a place here too. Already, I don't like having to say goodbye instead of good night to you."

Sade smiled. "Yeah. I know you can't stay, but I wish you could. It felt so good sleeping in your arms."

"I could always get a room for the night. Just let me know what you want to do."

"I'm kind of tired of hotels, but if the reward of going to one is sleeping in your arms, I'm down with that."

"Cool, go pack a bag."

The happy squeal she released made him smile. While waiting for her, he checked different hotels downtown, opting for a suite at the Peabody Hotel. If he had to take her to a hotel, at least he could afford to take her somewhere nice.

About thirty minutes later, they headed out. The goofy grin she wore, combined with her sleepy eyes, told Dante all he needed to know.

"You're going to sleep as soon as we get here, aren't you?"

"I'm glad you know," she chuckled. "Unless you wanted to make love to me first."

"I'll never turn that down, but I will also let you rest. You've had a long couple of days."

"That's true, but everything's always better with you. I hate how things started when you first got back, but I'm really glad you came home."

"I'm glad I came home too."

Silence found them briefly before they started singing and rapping along with the songs that came on. When they reached the hotel, Dante got them checked in, and they headed to their suite. They showered together and climbed into bed. Even though Dante cut on the TV, it was more for the noise as they drifted off to sleep. He pulled her into his arms, onto his chest, and felt immediate relief.

"I missed you so much, Smiley."

"I missed you too."

She kissed his bare chest—once... twice... before making her way up his frame. Their lips connected as his shaft hardened. Dante flipped her over, hovering over her frame.

So much for going straight to sleep.

His hands slipped under her gown. Her hand wrapped around his wrist, quickly pulling it away from her stomach. Before he could break the kiss and question her, Sade was sliding it between her legs. As he licked and sucked her nipples, quiet moans escaped her. They grew louder when his mouth covered her clit.

"You're s-so good at that," she moaned, spreading her legs wider. "Just like that, Tay."

He continued to apply pressure and licked her swollen bud, fingering her until she came. But he didn't stop. Dante replaced his fingers with his tongue and continued to eat until she couldn't take anymore. As she pulled him up her frame, he wiped his mouth.

He wanted to ask her if Atlas ate her pussy like that. If he made her come the way he did. If she told him that he was good at pleasing her too. Squeezing his eyes shut, he inhaled a shaky breath.

"Hey," she called sweetly, cupping his cheek. "Where'd you go?"

Giving her a soft smile, Dante shook his head. "I'm right here, baby."

He inched his way inside of her, loving the sight of her trembling chin as she tugged her bottom lip between her teeth. His strokes started slowly before shifting to a hard, medium pace.

"You don't have to be quiet here," he said against her ear before licking it. "I want to hear how good I make you feel."

The demand only seemed to intensify her pleasure. She leaked against him, moaning his name as she clawed his back. Her walls pulsed against him as he lengthened his stroke, willing himself not to come at the same time as her. For what he wanted to do to her body, it would take all night.

ATLAS

His eyes scanned the room, settling on her panties and gown that lay on the edge of the bed. Atlas grabbed the silk gown and rubbed it against his face before an even more sinister plan popped into his brain. He went to the closet, picking up the panties she'd worn that day. His body shivered as he inhaled her scent.

Stuffing the panties in his pocket, Atlas went down the hall. He'd need to be quiet; otherwise, her grandparents or the twins might hear him. Slowly, he opened the bathroom door, grateful she showered the same way everywhere—with her back turned and eyes closed as she sang or hummed.

That evening, the song for her shower concert was an unfamiliar tune, but the sound of her voice was entertaining, nonetheless. Sade couldn't sing for shit, but she did so with a passion that he admired, and it always made him smile.

The longer he stared at her silhouette through the foggy shower door, the more aroused he became. He pulled his shaft out, stroking it until his seeds spilled onto the ground.

Before he could grab a hand towel and wipe it up, Sade said, "All right, I guess I've been in here long enough."

Carefully, Atlas slipped out of the bathroom and crossed the hall to her room. He went out of the window just as easily as he'd climbed inside, chuckling at the sound of her squeal. Had she stepped in the surprise he'd left for her?

Hours Later

When he was sure Sade was asleep, Atlas went back through the window. For a while, he stared at her, amazed by her beauty. A point came where he could no longer resist getting closer. Where he could no longer resist her skin. He stripped down to his boxers and gently climbed into bed with her. She stirred slightly, causing him to still.

Atlas waited until her soft snores started back up, and then he wrapped his arm around her. His nose stroked her cheek before he kissed it. She squirmed slightly, muttering inaudibly in her sleep.

"It's just me," he whispered as the pads of his fingers slid down her arm.

"Dante?"

His head jerked as he looked down at her in the darkness. Ignoring her comment, Atlas pulled her closer.

"I love you. You'll always be mine."

Seconds passed before she was asleep again, and Atlas took full advantage—holding her until he was calm enough to sleep. Then he left and went to his home to sleep . . . alone.

SADE

SADE NIBBLED HER bottom lip as she sent Atlas a Facetime request from her computer. She felt like she was silly even to do it. When she first woke up, she thought she had dreamed about a man, her man, the previous night. However, the scent of Atlas's cologne lingered against her sheets and pillow. Her mind took her back to what she thought was a realistic dream—feeling a man's lips, his hands, hearing his voice. When she called Dante's name, he didn't respond.

Was she really dreaming . . . or had Atlas actually been in her room?

She checked the cameras, and he wasn't near the door, but her room was on the side of the house, which was out of the camera's view. If he'd come through her window, it was quite possible that what she thought she'd dreamed was actually real. Sade refused to believe Atlas could do something so crazy, but she wanted to hear him say it anyway.

When Atlas accepted the request, Sade was so surprised by his face and aura that it took her a while to speak. Usually, when he saw her, he would smile with his eyes and his mouth. But now, as he stared at her, his eyes were almost lifeless, and his face was void of emotion.

As she stared at him, his head tilted, and he stared back at her.

Clearing her throat, Sade looked away briefly. "Um, are you okay?" she checked.

"Do you really care?"

"I do, but I didn't call you to argue."

"Then what did you call for?"

"I'm going to ask you something, and I want you to be honest with me." She paused. He nodded. "Were you in my bed last night?"

He grinned with one side of his mouth. "How could I have done that, Day?"

"I don't know. Maybe you came through my window."

"What makes you think I did?"

"I thought I dreamed about Dante, but it was you. . . . . felt you. Heard you. And I smell your cologne."

He released a grunt of a laugh before licking his lips. "Maybe you dreamed about me and smelled me because you miss me."

"So, you're denying that you were here last night?"

"Would you have wanted me to be?"

"No."

"Then no, I wasn't."

"Atlas . . ."

"Unless you have proof, I wasn't, Sade." He sat up with a scowl. "Why don't you love me?"

"What?" she asked, though she heard the question.

"I said, why don't you love me? I tried to make me easy to love."

"Atlas . . . you *were* easy to love. But something changed, and I just . . . It was too much."

He chuckled, but it wasn't one of amusement. "Oh, so, he's worth killing for, but me wanting to watch you and make sure you're always okay was too much?"

With a growl, she slammed her computer down. There was no way he'd admit to it, and worse, he'd riled her up. Now, she would have to get her grandfather or Dante to put bars on the windows. This was getting out of control. Sade couldn't dwell on it at that moment, though. She and Dante were spending the afternoon with Eric and Jessica, his old business partners. Any other day, Sade wouldn't be looking forward to hanging out, but now . . . She was grateful for the distraction.

Sade's Journal

Since I no longer have my phone, I have to write in an actual journal. I thought spending time with Dante, Jessica, and Eric would shake the feeling that's been consuming me. That didn't work. I feel like Atlas was in the room, and being unable to prove it scares me. What scares me worst is knowing I liked how he felt in my bed. I liked the way his lips felt. I liked the warmth of his arms around me. Even if I thought it was a dream of Dante, I liked the way it felt.

What if I would have allowed more? What if we would have had sex? There's no way I would have been able to justify that. There's no way he could have explained that. I would have known it was real, right? The last thing I need is to be paranoid over this. Over him. I know I'll feel better once the bars are on the windows. I can't believe this is my life. I wanted a man who wanted me, but this is a bit too much. And he's acting as if what he's doing is normal. Maybe it is for him. Either way, I'm just glad I dodged that bullet.

DANTE

Three Days Later

LOOKING INTO ATLAS, Dante learned of his background. He was an IT specialist in the army. When he wasn't deployed, he ran his own security system company, which explained why it was so easy for him to watch Sade. His home was in East Memphis, but he spent most of his time at his parents' home in Southaven, about thirty minutes away.

Hacking his phone or social media accounts was impossible because of his training. After Atlas shared a flyer for a neighborhood block party on his Facebook page, Dante figured he'd show up there. He rented a car with tinted windows and pulled up, not bothering to get out and mingle with the community members. Apparently, Atlas's cousin was the one who put the event together, and as Dante suspected, he did show up.

Dante watched his every move. His mannerisms. His expressions. How quickly his mood shifted. Atlas was in his car three hours later, and Dante was a safe distance on his trail. Atlas went to his home, where Dante used a jammer to disable his Wi-Fi. He waited until Atlas turned off the lights before he parked across the street from his home.

Then he put on gloves, a mask, and his hoodie and exited the car. Stuffing his hands in his pockets, Dante crossed the street and casually approached Atlas's front door. Before he could enter, he heard the sound of Atlas's security system beeping and alerting him that it was offline. A light in the far corner cut on, and Dante cursed under his breath. A part of him wanted to kick the door down and still go after Atlas, but the element of surprise would work best in his favor. So, as much as he didn't want to, Dante jogged across the street—determined to finish this later.

Dante was awakened from his sleep by the feel of a thick rope wrapped around his neck. Before he could try to insert his fingers under it, it was used to lift him from the bed.

"Did you *really* think I didn't see you follow me home?" Atlas gritted. "I was waiting for your ass to come in." Atlas shoved him down and straddled him, pinning his arms, making it impossible for Dante to use them to get out of bed. "I saw you fucking her. You were in *my* pussy. Did she tell you she was pregnant with *my* baby?" Atlas tightened the rope around his neck. Dante's eyes watered as he struggled to breathe. "I was going to let you live. Hell, I ran you off the road. Sade wanted us to be . . . *even*. But you fucked it up by not leaving the city when you found out about us. And now, you have to die."

With his energy waning, Dante did the only thing he could think of to do. He lifted his legs and wrapped them around Atlas, using them to push him down onto the bed. Coughing, Dante quickly grabbed his knife from under the pillow and shoved it into Atlas's side.

"Ah!" Atlas groaned, rolling over and grabbing his side.

Hopping up, Dante jabbed the knife into his throat and watched as blood quickly oozed out. He held his neck as he struggled to regulate his breathing. The burning in his throat made the coughing worse. Straggling out of bed, Dante grabbed his phone to call 911 before walking down the hall to wake up his parents and tell them what had happened.

"His family is going to blame me for this too," Sade said as she paced.

After being questioned and having pictures of his neck taken for evidence, Dante made his way to her to let her know that Atlas was dead. He also wanted to ask her about what Atlas said regarding her being pregnant with his baby. Could that have been the truth?

"He broke into my parents' home and tried to strangle me. It was clearly self-defense."

She shook her head. "That won't matter to them. They blame me for Adam's death, and they will blame me for this too."

"Come here," Dante demanded, gripping her hand and pulling her onto his lap on the bed. Her fingers slid across his bruised neck, but they stopped when he asked, "Are you pregnant with his baby?"

Her body stiffened as her eyes flickered. "He said that?" she asked quietly.

"Yeah, he did."

"I'm not pregnant with his baby, Dante." Relief instantly filled him, but before he could fully bask in that moment, she added, "I'm pregnant with yours." For a moment, Dante's heart stopped, and he forgot how to breathe. "*That's* what I wanted to tell you. I'd told Atlas I wanted you and me to get back to our friendship and have a healthy, coparenting relationship. I guess he felt like if you knew I'd been with him, that would get you out of the way." Her chuckle was bitter as she looked toward the ceiling. "He wanted to help me raise this baby, and I didn't realize just how serious he was about that until now."

Dante's hand lowered to her stomach as his forehead rested on hers. "You're having my baby?"

Sade giggled. "Yes. I wanted to wait until a special time to tell you, but . . ."

"Smiley, I don't care about that. You're having my baby. That's all that matters to me."

"Are you . . . really okay with that?"

Dante laughed lightly and released a shaky breath as his eyes watered. "I raised a set of twins that weren't mine, and now the woman of my dreams is giving me a baby of my own. I'm perfectly okay with that. Are you?"

Hesitantly, Sade nibbled her bottom lip and nodded. "I am. I admit that at first, I was nervous and worried about what people would think, but I don't care about that anymore. I love you, Tay, and I'm happy to be the mother of your child."

"Mm." Cupping the back of her neck, Dante planted a kiss on her lips. "You'll be the only one too." They kissed again. "I need to get us a home. Is the baby why you wanted to stay here?"

"Yeah, plus I wanted to be close to the little family I have. I got an apartment. I just can't move in until the first of September."

"Are you sure that's what you want? You can have whatever you want."

"I'm sure. It's a three-bedroom, so the baby will have a room, and I'll have an office. Plus, I need a break from everything that comes from having a big home."

"I feel you. Well, let me know how much the rent will be, and of course, I'll cover it. If you want that to be for you and the baby until we get married, I'm cool with that, but we will be together, Sade, and I'm firm about that."

She grinned and opened her mouth to respond, but heavy banging on the door silenced her. Gently, Dante sat her on the bed next to him and stood. Even though he was at her grandparents' house, he couldn't allow Barron to answer. Those types of knocks never had a positive or pleasant ending behind them.

"Who the hell is that banging on my door like that?" Barron called out, shuffling out of his room. Dante chuckled at the sight of him closing his robe.

"I'll find out."

After looking through the peephole, a frown covered his face as he peered at two police officers. Did they have more questions for him? How did they know where he was?

Dante opened the door and asked, "Can I help y'all?"

"Is Sade Griffin here?"

His head tilted as he looked from one to the other. "What's this about?"

"Is she here?" the taller, buffer one asked.

"Do you have a warrant?"

After pressing the paper into Dante's chest, the tall officer stepped inside.

"Sade Griffin," he called.

Dante's heart raced as he looked over the warrant. This had Jones's name plastered all over it—and these being Vanzette PD police officers was further proof.

"Yes?" Sade asked quietly, twiddling her thumbs.

"You're under arrest for the murders of Patrice Baker and Trina Roe. You're also wanted for questioning in the disappearance of Willow Frank."

"Oh my God," Ava cried as Barron wrapped his arms around her and pulled her into his side.

"Dante," Sade called, tears filling her eyes.

As the officer read Sade her rights, Dante kissed her forehead and said, "I promise I'm going to get you out."

SADE

SADE SQUEEZED HER legs tightly together as she sat on the edge of the cold metal bench. Fights with her sister over the years taught her how to defend herself early, so that wasn't a fear. More than anything, Sade was uncomfortable. It took hours for her to be processed, and that was one of the most degrading things she'd ever encountered. They didn't put much thought into her being pregnant since she was so early in her pregnancy.

Her pregnancy.

What if she had to give birth in prison? Dante would have to raise their child. Just the thought brought tears to her eyes.

Being returned to Vanzette meant being held in a small jail. The holding cell was tiny, with no heat or air. It was muggy and scented with body odor, urine, and blood. She kept her eyes off the other three women in the cell and looked forward to having her own. Sade was fully aware of what she'd done, and though she tried to be as meticulous and careful as possible, there was a chance she'd left evidence behind. If she had to pay for what she did, Sade was fully prepared to serve her time. Her only plea would be to surrender herself and start her sentence after she gave birth.

"Griffin!" Sade stood and rushed over to the metal bars at the sound of her name being yelled. The short, chubby correctional officer leaned against it, chewing gum. "You can have your one phone call."

"Okay."

She stepped back as the officer unlocked the cell. Walking out, Sade followed her over to the phone in the corner of the room. Sade considered if she wanted to call Dante or Ava. Ava would cry or want to ask questions, so she called Dante instead. He answered almost immediately.

"Smiley?"

"Yes. I-I don't have a number yet, so my calls will be free until I do. They said I'll probably get one in the morning, and then you'll have to pay. Is that okay?"

"Baby, I don't give a damn about paying. Call me as much as you need to. What are they saying? I know you probably don't have a bond yet."

"No, not yet. They processed me, and that's it. I'm still in a holding cell with some other women."

Dante sighed heavily onto the phone. "I'm going to get you a lawyer. I have a few options, but I have to make sure it's one who can practice in Vanzette. Are you okay, Day?"

Sniffling, Sade gripped the phone cord tightly. "I'm okay. I don't want you to worry about me."

He laughed. "Do you hear yourself right now? They arrested you for two murders, and you're telling me not to worry about you." She squeezed her eyes shut.

"I-I don't want to get emotional in here, Dante. I'm fine, really. The only thing I'm concerned about is having to give birth while I'm in here. I'll plead guilty and avoid a trial if they can just . . . let me stay out long enough to have and hold my baby." Her chin trembled, and she swallowed hard as her tears threatened to fall. "That's all I care about."

"I'm going to get you out of there . . . by any means necessary. Do you hear me?"

Sade nodded as if he could see her. "I hear you."

"I know it may be hard but try to get some rest. Call me in the morning around nine. I should have some news about an attorney by then."

"Okay, babe. I love you."

"I love you more."

After hanging up the phone, Sade stood there for a while, trying to compose herself.

"Come on," the officer demanded, using her arm to lead her back to the cell.

This was going to be a long, long night.

The Next Morning

By the time Sade got to sleep, she was being woken up and taken to her cell. A woman who gruffly introduced herself as Simone occupied it before turning onto her side on the bottom bunk and returning to sleep. Not wanting to disturb her further, Sade quickly climbed up and tried to go to sleep. Several hours later, they were being woken up by bright lights and yelling about it being time for breakfast.

Breakfast—dry eggs, a banana, and a huge piece of corn bread. She didn't want the eggs, and the cornbread was hard. If she had an idea of what would be offered for lunch, Sade would have only eaten the banana. Since she wanted to keep up her strength, she forced the eggs down but immediately threw them up. Not bothering to take advantage of the free time in the quad with the other women, she went back to her cell.

Simone was curled up on the bed, whimpering.

"Are you . . . okay?" Sade asked, looking behind her, finding no one paying attention.

"Yeah." Simone cleared her throat. "I'm good."

"You don't want breakfast?"

She shook her head. "I can't get up."

"Why not?"

With a huff, Simone ran her fingers over her slightly matted coils. "I'm on my period. I told them last night, but they didn't bring me any pads or panties. I'm bleeding every-fucking-where."

"What? Oh, hell no. That is *unacceptable*." Sade charged out of the cell, heading toward the counter where the officer on duty was seated. She was engrossed in whatever she was watching on her phone, which was evident by her smile. "Hey," Sade called, leaning against the counter.

The officer's smile fell as she looked up at Sade. "Yeah?"

Sade looked at her name badge. Brooks. "My cell mate is on her period. She said she asked for pads and panties yesterday and has not received them. Can she please get those along with some new sheets? She's bleeding through hers and unable to move."

Brooks's eyes rolled. "I'll get it in a few."

"She needs it *now*," Sade rebutted, clenching her fist by her side. "You're a woman. You know how this goes. She's in there, suffering. Help her . . . please."

Standing, Brooks nodded and shooed her away from the counter. "No leaning against the counter." On her walkie-talkie, she requested what was needed from the laundry room. Several minutes passed before a fellow inmate brought everything to the quad. Brooks handed the items to Sade and told her, "Let this be the last time I see your face or hear your voice today."

"Yes, ma'am," Sade agreed before quickly returning to her cell. "Hey, this is for you."

Simone turned her head slightly, her eyes watering at the items Sade held.

"They actually gave it to you?"

"Yeah. Sorry you had to suffer with this all night. No one deserves to be treated like that. I'm going to file a complaint on whoever worked last night. What was their name?"

Simone chuckled as she sat up. "I appreciate the concern, but you'd only be making things worse around here for yourself. These people don't care about us."

"They should," Sade replied, handing Simone everything she needed. "I'll wait out there while you get freshened up."

"Okay, thank you."

Sade made her way back out to the quad and sat in the center of the room. Several plastic chairs littered the floor in front of the TV. Currently, there was a news broadcast playing. It wasn't something she would usually watch, but Brooks had control of the remote.

Sade wasn't sure how much time had passed before Simone tapped her shoulder. Her bright eyes and warm smile made her look completely different. She'd even slicked her hair back into a sleek bun.

"Thanks again. Um . . . Have you had breakfast yet?"

Sade chuckled. "If you want to say that. I'm pregnant and was only able to eat the banana. The eggs came right out."

"Oh no. You can have my banana, and I know a few ladies in here who never eat their fruit. I'll get you theirs too."

"Oh no, you don't have to do that."

"Nah, you did me a solid, and I got you. Hold on."

With tears brimming in her eyes, Sade watched as Simone worked the room. By the time she finished, she'd folded her shirt and used it as a basket to hold several bananas and apples. As she gave them to Sade, she laughed.

"I know you can't live off this forever, but it's a start. You'll get used to the food, and once you get your inmate number, you can get commissary."

"I . . . Thank you, Simone. Seriously."

Sade followed Simone to the table where her food was, and they ate and got to know each other. Simone was serving a twenty-year sentence for killing her abusive husband. They justified the sentence by saying she killed him during a time he wasn't abusing her, which was bullshit to Sade. Having someone to talk to made her first day in jail easier, but Sade couldn't deny how anxious she was starting to feel over never being able to go back home.

DANTE

THINGS WEREN'T ADDING up. As Dante tossed and turned last night, he tried to make Sade being arrested make sense. From what Jones told him, the only way she would have been able to be arrested was if he had proof via DNA that she was at the crime scene. The blood and hair that were found belonged to someone that wasn't in their system.

How could that have changed?

As Dante headed to Attorney Richmond's office, he prayed Sade would call him soon. It was 9:45 a.m., and the more time passed, the more he worried something terrible had happened during her first night there. There was no doubt in Dante's mind that Sade could defend herself, but she'd never been in prison. More than anything, he worried about her physical and emotional state.

When his phone vibrated, he looked down at the dashboard, hoping it was Sade. It was an unfamiliar number but not the one she'd called from last night. Still, he answered quickly with, "Hello?"

"I told you I'd bring her to justice without your help."

Jones?

"What the fuck did you do, Jones?"

Jones laughed. "What needed to be done. Now, this is your last chance, Dante. Either you help me by giving your testimony to help keep Sade behind bars, or I will assume you knew about her plans to kill and find a way to have you charged with murder too. So, what's it gonna be?"

"I have a third option: You can undo whatever illegal stunt you did to have my wife arrested, and I won't have to punish you for it."

"Why do you keep calling her that? You're married to her sister, right? What was her name . . . Imani. She's such a beautiful woman. I see why you wanted to have both."

Jones's laughter grated Dante's ears. Gritting his teeth, Dante gripped the steering wheel as his speed accelerated. He was about to ask Jones how he knew what Imani looked like, then remembered he'd visited her a month or so before they left Vanzette. Was this her doing? Did she renege on their deal and work with Jones to reduce her sentence? Dante didn't want to believe Imani could do something like that, but she'd done worse.

The sisters had been going at each other for years. A little while before the accident, Sade put distance between them, which cut down on the drama. Had the beef been placed back on the stove by his relationship with Sade in Vanzette? And if so, what would it take for Imani to leave them alone?

An incoming call came through, and the number was similar to the one Sade had called from last night. All that was different was the last digit. Not bothering to respond to Jones's comment, Dante ended that call and switched to the other.

"Baby?"

"Hi."

At the sound of Sade's voice, relief immediately washed over him. Relaxing in his seat, Dante smiled. "How are you?"

"I'm okay. How are you?"

"Better now that I hear your voice. I'm headed to Everett Richmond's office now to see about hiring him to represent you. Do you remember him?"

"Hmm . . . vaguely. Was he the scrawny, brown-skinned guy with braces?"

Dante chuckled. "Yeah, that was him. His assistant is now grabbing the affidavit, which will give us more information. It won't have a list of evidence on it, though. He said he won't be able to get that until I hire him for you, and he starts up with discovery."

"Thank you. It keeps me sane knowing I have you working on my behalf."

"I love you, Sade. After everything you've done for me, I'd go to the end of the earth for you."

She released a few sniffles before saying, "Ugh, I'm twice as emotional lately, and you keep putting me in my feelings."

Dante smiled. "I'm sorry about that. How are you feeling physically? Is my baby being a good guest?"

That got a hearty laugh out of Sade. "For the most part. I was already struggling with bloating and gas, plus the morning sickness, and I think it's going to be worse while I'm here. The food is horrible. I'm still having headaches and tired as hell, but they tend to go away after I nap."

"I promise I will get you out of there as soon as possible, Smiley."

"I know. I don't think we'll have much longer, so I guess I'll talk to you later."

"Yeah, call me this afternoon, okay?"

"I will."

"I love you."

"I love you too."

After disconnecting the call, Dante noticed that he had a text. It was from Jones.

901-880-2880: You should have become my ally. Now, you're a target. You're next.

After leaving Richmond's office, Dante was happy he'd agreed to take Sade on as a client. He planned to visit her within the next day or so, hopeful she'd have a bond by then. To keep himself from sitting at home worrying about Sade, Dante went to see Ian Sanders, his friend with a financial firm. He helped put together a few missing pieces while Dante still struggled with his amnesia. By the time the visit was over, Ian had offered Dante the original partner position he'd planned to interview for, and he accepted . . . though that wasn't the point of him stopping by. He would have been okay simply working as a financial advisor, as they'd previously discussed.

Since Sade made it clear she wanted to stay in Memphis, Dante didn't mind working at a firm there so they could remain close to their families. He couldn't wait to tell his parents the good news, but until then, getting Sade out on bail was his primary concern. Barron had called him for an update, and Dante promised to stop by after talking to her again that evening. He knew they would have several questions, and Dante wanted to know how Sade wanted him to answer.

A few hours after Dante returned to his parents' home, he decided to go for a run to clear his mind. It was then that he received a call from Sade. That time, an operator announced the call and confirmed he wanted to pay to accept it. Dante sat on the nearest bench and went through the steps of adding his debit card information to add a hundred dollars before he heard Sade's voice in the receiver.

"Hey, I finally got my inmate number."

The sadness in her tone made his heart ache. "You won't have it for long, Day."

A beat of silence passed before she said, "They aren't going to give me a bond, Dante."

Sitting up, he gripped the phone tighter. "What? What makes you say that?"

"My court date was set with the judge. It's in two days, and where it should have the pending bond amount, it's blank."

Squeezing his eyes shut, Dante massaged his temples as he shook his head. "That doesn't mean you won't get one. That just means the judge will set it when they see you."

Sade released a bark of laughter. "Wake up, Dante. I'm in here on two counts of murder. He's not going to give me a fucking bond." Her voice broke as she said, "I'm going to die in here. I-I'm going to give my baby life in here."

"Okay, all right, take some deep breaths for me, Sade." Dante stood and began to walk. "Breathe for me, baby. You don't need to run your blood pressure up and get lightheaded again."

"You're right," she agreed quietly before taking several deep breaths.

"You'll get a bond, and I'll pay it. Then Richmond is going to get rid of whatever bullshit Jones has against you. Because that's all it is—bullshit. Then you'll be free of this, and we can focus on us and bringing our baby into the world."

"God . . . I hope you're right."

SADE

"YOU NEED TO be careful," Simone warned. "The girls are talking, and Dominique has her eyes on you."

Sade looked up from the sketch of Dante she was drawing. Thankfully, Simone had a notebook she wasn't using. Drawing and writing had become Sade's escape. The quad was curious about her. She was pretty and friendly . . . What could she have possibly done to be arrested? Sade opted against telling anyone outside of Simone what she was in for, but it didn't take much for them to convince an officer to look up her charges.

A double murder charge kept some inmates away, but to others, it seemed to make them gravitate toward her. Sade was used to being a loner, so she didn't care for the attention. She had a decent bond with Simone, and that would be all she needed.

"What do you mean?" Sade checked as Simone sat next to her.

"She likes you."

Chuckling, Sade shook her head and returned her attention to her drawing. "I barely like women as friends. I'm definitely not about to be rubbing coochies with one."

Simone cackled, covering her mouth to silence her laughter as eyes shifted in their direction. "Yo, I don't know what I expected you to say, but it sure wasn't that. Just be careful, okay? I'ma put something under your pillow to help keep you safe. Try not to be by yourself unless you're in the common areas. Dominque has a huge ego and doesn't take rejection lightly—especially if it's public. If she gives you a hard time, find me."

Though Sade agreed, she didn't think it would come to that, but she was quickly proven wrong. The moment Simone went to make a phone call, Dominique and three of her followers made themselves comfortable at the table Sade occupied. She looked at them all and gave them a polite smile before returning her attention to her drawing.

"Who is that?" Dominique asked. "Your man?"

They didn't have official titles, but Dante was her man. He was no longer just her best friend and the father of her child. He'd expressed his desire to be her husband—still. Even after finding out about her and Atlas. Even after finding out about the baby. He didn't even ask how long she knew about her pregnancy . . . if she knew when she left him . . . and Sade was grateful because she'd never volunteer that information.

"My husband," Sade corrected, pulling the picture close. She didn't want to share Dante with anyone . . . in any capacity . . . except their child.

"You think he'd mind if I took care of you while you were in here?" Dominique asked, stroking Sade's cheek. Sade immediately flicked her hand away with a scowl. "I think he might want me to," Dominique continued. "You're too pretty and petite not to have someone in here looking out for you."

"I can look out for myself."

Dominque chuckled and rolled her tongue across her cheek. "Yeah, I heard they think you got a couple of bodies behind you, but I don't believe that. You look too sweet to harm a fly."

Sade swallowed back a chuckle. Leaning forward, she whispered, "Looks can be deceiving."

"Ooh, I like you even more now." When Dominique's hand lowered to Sade's thigh, Sade warned her. "If you don't get your hand off me, you're going to become victim number three."

"Damn!" one of the women who was with her yelled before they all erupted into laughter.

Except Dominique. Dominique frowned. "Did you just threaten me?" she asked, hovering over Sade.

"That's not a threat; it's a warning."

"Break that up over there," the officer on duty yelled, banging her baton against the counter.

Sade didn't bother looking to see if Dominque would leave. Instead, she returned her attention to her drawing. It seemed Simone was right about Dominique. Sade could only hope she would take her charges seriously and not try her in any way.

Just After Dinner...

Sade was uncomfortably bloated. She hadn't had one vegetable since she'd been processed. As much as she appreciated the apples and bananas, they worsened the bloating. Her diet had never been heavy on processed meats and starch, which was what almost every meal she'd been given consisted of. For dinner, they were served corn bread, mashed potatoes, and what was supposed to be hamburger steak. It tasted so artificial Sade didn't bother trying to force it down.

She was glad she was finally able to order commissary because otherwise, she'd die of starvation surviving off jail food. Dante had put enough money on the phone and in her account to order and talk for the rest of the week. He was so confident he'd have her out by then, but if needed, he'd add more money. Her mouth was watering at the thought of the salad and chicken wings she had ordered.

After unsuccessfully using the bathroom, Sade washed her hands and groaned at the sight of Dominique standing at the doorway. She rubbed her palms together with a crooked grin as her minions hung a sheet over the doorway to block anyone's view of what was about to happen inside.

The longer Dominique stalked her, as if she were her prey, the more frustrated Sade became. She wouldn't be in this situation if she hadn't valued Dante more than she valued herself—her freedom. But even that thought made her smile because it felt like he finally loved her more than himself. To have gone through all of that and not be able to be loved by him because she had to spend the rest of her life in prison sent a sharp pain through Sade's heart.

"You gon' give me that pussy . . . or do I have to take it?" Dominique asked, circling Sade.

"You can try."

Dominique's movements were swift as she wrapped her arm around Sade's neck and pressed her into her body. With a roar, Sade leaned forward and flipped Dominique forward, causing her body to crash against the sink. Then Sade straddled her and punched her repeatedly. When one of her friends pulled Sade off her, Dominique quickly shuffled to her feet and put Sade in a headlock.

Sade pulled the shank Simone had given her out of her waistband and used it to slice Dominique's arm, causing her to scream. One of the women hit Sade in the back of her head, causing her to stumble forward on her palms and knees. When she grabbed Sade's hair and tried to hit her in the side of her face, Sade jammed the shank into her side.

The sound of feet shuffling in their direction caused the women to retreat from the bathroom quickly, but it was no use.

Simone rushed into the bathroom, effortlessly taking the shank from Sade to hide. The officer on duty had called for backup, and they immediately pressed the women against the wall.

"Everybody out, *now!*" Office Freeman yelled.

Sade's eyes locked on Dominique's as she held her bleeding arm. The grin that Dominique gave her suggested this wasn't over. But at least she knew now that Sade was no one to fuck with.

DANTE

The Next Day

Dante sat on Barron and Ava's front porch with Barron's shotgun draped over his lap. Apparently, Sade's concerns about Atlas's family were valid. With the news of his death, his family immediately began to draw their own conclusions. When they learned the police ruled it a justifiable homicide because Dante, Sade's best friend and lover, was acting in self-defense... They went crazy. He wasn't sure how they'd gotten her grandparents' address, but they'd gone there looking for her. Dante decided to stay with them as he waited for the security he hired to be available to guard the house until Atlas's family's emotions and tempers lessened.

It saddened Dante to see the web that had unraveled around them. While he wanted to blame it all on Imani and Adam, even Atlas, he and Sade played their roles too. If he had been honest about his memory returning, Sade wouldn't have felt as much pressure to withhold the truth. His Smiley... a *murderer*? Dante *still* couldn't believe it. And because of Willow, he was one too.

The door creaked open, and Barron sat in the rocking chair beside Dante's.

"You plan to stay out here all night?"

"If that's what it takes."

"What have you and my granddaughter gotten yourselves into, son?" Dante's head hung and shook. "Did she *really* kill someone?"

"Sade didn't do anything but try to protect me... from Imani and Adam..." He chuckled, his eyes watering. "From myself. I've made some fucked-up decisions over the years, and Sade has always had my back... just like I have hers. She didn't kill anyone, and even if she did, it was for a good reason."

"You really think Atlas's people will come back here looking for her?"

"I don't know, but I'm unwilling to take a chance. I'm sorry about all this. If I just... would've ignored Imani's advances and attempted to hurt her sister, none of this would have happened. All of this is my fault."

"It's all our faults. Ava and I could've done better with the girls after their parents died. We thought they would grow out of their sibling rivalry and eventually have a healthy relationship. Imani is... different, and we ignored that for a while. She doesn't think and feel the way the rest of us do. I should've acknowledged that sooner."

Barron ran his hands down his face before standing and gently squeezing Dante's shoulder. "Come on in here and fix yourself something to eat."

Two Days Later

Dante's mind was spinning. He hadn't heard from Sade in days. Her court date had passed, but her information had not been updated in the system. As he headed to visit Imani, he decided he had two options: to call and speak with the warden or have Everett do so. He decided to call Everett and see what he could do.

"Attorney Richmond's office. How may I direct your call?" his assistant greeted.

"Hello. Is Attorney Richmond available?"

"He's currently meeting with a client. May I take a message?"

"Yeah, this is Dante Williams. Can you let him know I haven't heard from Sade in three days? I want him to call the warden to see if he can get some information. I wouldn't be as concerned if her bond had been processed online, but from the looks of it, she missed her hearing with Judge Peterson."

"Oh no. Okay. I'll forward this to him as soon as his client leaves. We have your contact information on file, correct?"

"Yes, that's correct."

"Perfect. Expect a follow-up call within the next hour."

"Thank you."

After ending the call, Dante tried to clear his mind for the rest of the drive. That was easier said than done. Between the constant questions from his and Sade's family, Dante was trying not to spiral. The only thing that kept him calm was talking to Sade to let him know she was okay. But the more time passed, the worse the scenarios in his head became.

When he made it to the prison, Dante endured the lengthy process of getting checked in. It took about ten minutes before Imani was making her way into the visitation room. She sat across from him at the cream-colored round table with a smile.

"I'm surprised to see you here."

"Your sister was arrested."

Imani's smile fell instantly. "*What!* For what?"

"That situation in Vanzette," was all Dante offered.

"Shit." Imani covered her face as she shook her head. "She said she was careful."

"She was, which is why I'm trying to make sense of this. Jones had said the evidence they had wasn't enough to convict. They didn't have her DNA in the system." Dante paused as Imani lowered her hands from her face. "That leads me to you. He offered to help you get a reduced sentence in exchange for your DNA, right?"

"Yes, but I said no."

"Did you really? Because Sade and I are the reasons you're in here. Well, you're the reason, but we worked with the FBI to trap you. And you expect me to believe you didn't offer up your DNA in exchange? That would have been the perfect get-back, Imani. You want me to believe you didn't take it? As selfish as you've been . . ."

Imani's head jerked as if his words had physically touched her. She rolled her tongue across her cheek and stood.

"Fuck you, Dante."

"Sit down, Imani. I'm not done with you yet."

"I'd say you are. I'd say you're on to the next . . . who just so happens to be my sister."

"Can we please not go there? Let's not act like you give a damn about me. You cheated on me while we were dating *and* married. You lied to me about our kids. You set me up with the FBI. You used me to hurt your sister. Sit the fuck down and help me figure out how to help her because you know she deserves it."

"She deserves whatever she gets for being dumb enough to kill people over you," Imani said, plopping down in her seat. "But Sade won't survive in prison. She can fight, but that's the only thing going for her. She's used to being carefree and in control of herself and her life. I'd say she could spend her days drawing and painting if you could get those materials for her. Otherwise, she's going to go crazy in there."

"I know. I have to get her out of there, but I need to know what we're up against. If you struck a deal with Jones, I need you to tell me, Imani."

"I didn't. I promise. I told Sade that I wouldn't do that to her. I've done enough fucked-up shit to my sister. I wasn't going to send her to jail too."

Dante considered her words. He didn't bother trying to figure out whether she was sincere. She was a liar and master manipulator.

"A'ight, so if you didn't give him your DNA . . ." Dante pounded his fist on the table. "You *did* give him your DNA, just how you think."

"What do you mean?" Imani asked, her head tilting.

"The attack . . . You still don't know who did it, right?"

"No, I don't."

"I think Jones set you up to be attacked badly enough to have to go to the hospital."

Scoffing, Imani crossed her arms on top of the table and leaned forward. "What makes you think that?"

"He's been here following Sade and met with me to convince me to help take her down. I told Sade, and she said she thought she saw him at the hospital when she visited you. If you didn't agree to give him your DNA . . ."

"He could have easily requested it or stolen it while I was in the hospital," Imani said. "But do you think he'd *really* do that? You don't think it was a coincidence?"

"I think he would. He seems obsessed with making Sade pay, though I'm unsure why. I think he's very calculated and capable of doing something like this."

"Well, I know it might not mean much to you, but I give you my word that I did not willingly give him a hair or blood sample. If he took either, he did it while I was in that coma."

Standing, Dante bobbed his head. "Thanks, Imani."

"Hey," she called as he turned to leave. "If she gets out of this . . . Take care of my sister, okay? And the next time you talk to her . . . tell her to keep her head low and not get into any shit because I'm not there to fight her battles." She gritted her teeth, and if Dante wasn't crazy, he'd swear her eyes watered. But that couldn't have been the case because Imani never cried. She didn't even cry when she was sentenced and had to say goodbye to her twins. If Sade was able to pull tears out of her . . . maybe there *was* hope for Imani yet.

SADE

The Next Day

SADE'S EYES SHIFTED from one side of the hall to another. Her hands and feet were cuffed, which she believed was a bit unnecessary. The officer, however, made it clear that they wanted to take no chances on her attacking anyone—as if she were an unnecessarily violent person. No... Sade had always been a protector and defender of those she'd loved.

Since she had no idea where she was being taken, Sade's nerves were on edge. They didn't subside until she entered a small room with several booths, occupied by inmates on one side of the clear glass and their visitors on the other. Her heart expanded in size at the sight of Dante. Not talking to him for four days had been a prison of its own.

He smiled as he stood, but he frowned when he noticed the restraints. "Is all that really necessary?"

Officer Mitchell chuckled. "Seeing as she just got out of the hole this morning, I'd say they are *very* necessary."

With a roll of her eyes, Sade sat at the small square table across from him. Because she didn't have what the officers considered good behavior, she was unable to meet with him in the main visiting area... where she would have been able to be wrapped up in his embrace.

"You wanna tell me what the hell happened for you to be in solitary for three days, Smiley?"

Though his tone was serious, Sade couldn't help but smile. "Hi, handsome. I missed you."

His eyes rolled playfully. "Don't try to flatter me. I'm upset with you."

"What did I do?"

"I don't know! That's what I'm trying to find out."

"How'd you find out I was in solitary?"

"I had Richmond call for a wellness check since I hadn't heard from you. The warden looked into it and told him you were in solitary."

"Oh."

"Yeah. So explain, and please tell me you weren't fighting while you're pregnant with my baby."

"I didn't really have a choice, Dante," she grumbled, avoiding his eyes. "She attacked me, and I had to defend myself. The baby's fine. They checked me out before putting me in the hole."

"Jesus. I gotta get you out of here."

"Since I missed my court date, I have to wait until next Wednesday."

"Well, I have some really good news. If I'm right about this, I may be able to get you out that day or even before then."

That caused Sade to perk up. Her back straightened as she smiled and sat up in her seat. "What did you find?"

"It's only a hunch at the moment. I'm still working on getting proof... but I think Jones paid someone to attack Imani so she'd have to get outside care. You said you saw him at the hospital, right?"

"Right. Yeah. Well, at first, I didn't think it was him, but when you said he'd been following me, I assumed so."

"If he was at the hospital, I think he was getting your sister's DNA. That's the *only* thing that can explain how they *all of a sudden* have enough evidence to arrest you."

Sade rubbed the center of her chest, her heart, as she sat back in her seat. "If that's the case . . ." She looked around before whispering, "I'm done, Dante. They literally have my DNA at both crime scenes. There's no way I'm coming home."

"If Jones illegally obtained that evidence, it would be inadmissible." Her eyes fluttered, and her mouth went slack. "That would be all the evidence they have; without it, there would be no case. Plus, how would they prove it's actually a match? We could argue that he doctored that too. You'd be free, Sade."

"Don't play with me, babe."

He chuckled and sat up in his seat. "I'm serious, Smiley. I just have to prove that he stole Imani's DNA to match it against yours."

"How do you plan to do that?"

"After I leave here, I'm returning to the hospital to see if I can get that camera footage. If I can't, I've already looped Richmond in. By law, a detective must retrieve and record it as evidence, but I don't want to wait that long. Even if we had to wait, if we can show Jones in her room, that's enough to cast reasonable doubt."

"I don't want to get excited prematurely, but thank you for this. It makes me feel good knowing you have my back."

"Always, bae. Like I told you when you first got here, as much as you've done for me, I'll do absolutely anything for you."

Finally . . . Sade was starting to believe that.

Sade's Journal

On the off chance a guard stumbles across this, I'm going to write carefully so nothing I say can incriminate me. If I get out of here, I'm never doing anything to put myself in a position that takes away my freedom. Not that I have already. I am not saying I killed anyone. I'm just saying if I get to go home, I won't even risk getting a ticket.

I hate being confined. I hate being told what to do. I hate the food. I hate the smells. I hate the people—everyone except Simone. Just a little while ago, this girl pooped in the quad and started tossing it at people. Needless to say, that did not end well for her. She was left a bloody mess and taken to the infirmary.

I don't know what she did to get in here, but they say she has mental issues. If so, I would think she should be in a mental hospital, not jail. My heart broke for her. I wanted to protect her, but there were too many of them. All I can do is pray it doesn't give me nightmares.

Being in here has given me time to reflect. I don't think anyone would ever doubt my love for and loyalty to Dante, but now, I question my love and loyalty for myself. I question if I've ever truly known how to prioritize myself. Even now, I'll have a baby to put first. Is this what I have to look forward to for the rest of my life? Loving others more than I love me? Doing things I don't want to do in their name? Is that love? If so, is it really worth it?

Maybe I'm overthinking and being dramatic. On the bright side, knowing Dante can match my energy feels good. Good and bad. I guess if I had to give up my freedom for someone, I'm still glad it's him.

DANTE

SADE TOLD DANTE about her connection with Reggie, her sister's guard at the hospital. Though she'd discarded her phone when she found out Atlas was watching her, she gave him her computer password so he could contact Reggie through her iMessages. Reggie agreed to meet with Dante, who hoped his plan would work.

Dante's eyes shifted around the café. Ironically, he decided to meet Reggie at the same place he'd met Jones. What was even more ironic was how devoted he was to Sade now compared to how his trust wavered the last time he was here. Thinking that she was capable of working against him made Dante feel horrible about doubting her. Thank God it didn't last long, and he didn't act on it. That would never happen again.

When a lean, dark-skinned policeman walked into the café, Dante stood. He called Reggie's name. Then he bobbed his head and walked in Dante's direction. The pair shook hands before sitting across from each other.

"Everything okay with Sade?" were the first words out of Reggie's mouth.

"No, everything is *not* okay. She was arrested and transported to Vanzette for a double murder charge."

Reggie's head jerked forward, and his eyes bucked before he scoffed. "What? How? There has to be some mistake."

Mistake . . . yes. Wrong person . . . nope.

"I think someone is setting her up, and they used her sister to do it."

"What makes you think that?"

"There's a detective in Vanzette who has had it out for her for months. He threatened to put her in prison by any means necessary. Her sister was randomly attacked, and Sade saw him leaving the hospital. I don't think it's too much of a stretch to believe he was taking some strands of her sister's hair or her blood for a DNA test . . . especially since he visited her months ago and asked her for a DNA sample to put Sade in prison."

"Damn. They must not have a good relationship for him even to think she'd agree."

"That's a long story, but she didn't agree. So, I think he had her attacked so he could get the sample himself."

Reggie thought over all that Dante said for a while, massaging the hair on his chin. "Do you have a picture of him? Maybe I can try to identify him, though I'm sure he wouldn't have let me see him gather any evidence in her room if he did what you suggested."

Dante nodded his agreement. "Yeah, I don't think he would have made himself known. But I do think he could be on some security cameras. Do you think you'd be able to access the hospital footage?"

Reggie's mouth twisted to the side as he shook his head. "I wouldn't be able to get the footage without a warrant."

"Come on, man. I'm sure there's a way for you to get around that. If you can, I'll pay double what my wife offered you."

Scratching his head, Reggie released a hard breath. "The only reason I took that money was because I have a baby on the way."

"And I respect that. Sade and I have a baby on the way too. So you should be able to understand how important it is to me that I get her out of jail."

The seconds ticked by as Reggie considered Dante's words. "Can you promise me that she didn't do what she's being accused of?"

For Sade, a lie would be nothing for Dante to tell. A sacrifice would be nothing for him to give. If he had to, Dante would confess to the crimes himself before letting her be found guilty.

"I promise. She did not kill those women."

Reggie nodded and sat back in his seat. "All right. I'll see what I can do."

Dante's jaw clenched as he watched the security footage that showed Jones entering Imani's private hospital room. He'd been watching footage for hours, but this moment made it worth it. Jones walked to the side of her bed. He looked behind himself to ensure no one else was coming, then pulled a clear bag with *Evidence* written on it out of his pocket.

"You've got to be kidding me," Dante muttered, watching Jones cut some bloody bandages from Imani. He also ran his fingers through her locs as if feeling for loose strands. Jones put the evidence he gathered in the bag, stuffed it in his pocket, and then discreetly walked out.

"Got you."

A crisp laugh fell from his lips before he licked them. "You're coming home, Smiley. You're coming home."

The Next Evening

The excitement Dante expected Ava and Barron to have wasn't there. He'd just shared the news that Sade's lawyer had taken the evidence to the prosecutor over her case, and he decided to drop the charges. She'd be released at any time that night, and Dante stopped to update her grandparents before heading to Vanzette to get her. Instead of a smile covering Ava's face, it was covered with hesitation.

"Either of you can speak at any time," Dante said lightly, looking from one to the other. "I just told you that my wife is getting out of jail, and the charges have been dropped. Why aren't you dancing around this room?"

"She's not your wife," Ava said. "That's a lie you seem to be holding on to."

"She *is* my wife. We'll make it legal the moment we can put this craziness behind us."

Barron chuckled as his hand slipped up and down his leg. "The two of you have unleashed a world of hell since your accident an—"

"The accident that was caused by Atlas, who was working with his cousin and your other granddaughter to have me framed and possibly killed. You two seem more upset by Sade and I finally being able to be together than you are upset over what Imani did. Why is that?"

Ava and Barron looked at each other but remained silent.

"I . . . think it would be best if you kept Sade away for a while," Ava said. "The twins are here, and we don't want anything to happen to them because of what the two of you have going on. Imani and Adam were toxic, but they are no longer present. I think it's best if you and Sade aren't either."

"You think she did this, don't you?" Dante asked.

"Whether she did it or didn't, there's been too much drama over the last eight months, and the two of you have been at the center of it. Is that Imani and Adam's doing? Yes, but they've paid for their sins. Imani, by being arrested. Adam, by dying. But Sade?

She doesn't seem to have to atone for her sins, and that's alarming," Barron said, "The world is crashing down on her, and I fear until she admits to whatever the hell she did to keep your identity a secret, it will only get worse."

"Wow." Standing, Dante avoided their eyes. "I never thought I'd hear something like this coming from the two of you, and I pray you never say this to Sade. Y'all are all she has, and she cares too much about your opinions concerning her life if you'd ask me. She risked her life when Atlas was stalking her to be close to you and the twins, and you want to send her away because of something she's been proven innocent of?"

"She hasn't been proven innocent," Barron said, "Jones did some illegal things, but that doesn't mean Sade is innocent. Even if he got the DNA illegally, it was Sade and Imani's DNA nonetheless."

"You don't know that!" Dante seethed. "He could have forged the results just like he stole the damn blood." He chuckled and took a step back. "I don't know why I'm trying to convince you of something you should already know. Don't worry, I'll keep Sade away . . . and our baby too. If you don't believe in my wife and trust us, you don't deserve to be in our lives."

Dante quickly left, trying to reel in his anger. He didn't blame them for having reservations before, but he expected the charges being dropped would ease their minds. It didn't seem like that would be the case, and as much as Sade wanted to stay in Memphis, he'd kidnap her and keep her away from them before he let anyone make her feel bad about what they thought she'd done.

SADE

Simone's eyes watered as she stared at the picture Sade had drawn for her to send to her daughter. She held it to her chest, releasing a childlike giggle Sade had never heard come from her before.

"She's going to love this, Sade. Thank you so much."

"Of course. You have a beautiful little girl. I know she can't wait for you to leave here."

Simone's expression saddened as she sat on her bunk next to Sade. "Yeah, but she won't be a little girl anymore by then. God, I don't regret killing his ass to protect us. I just can't believe I'm being punished for it. He beat me nearly half to death just because I overcooked breakfast." A bark of laughter escaped her as she briskly wiped a tear. "I made report after report, and they *never* took me seriously. When I finally took matters into my own hands, they do *this* to me."

"Who has your baby girl?" Sade asked, covering Simone's hand with hers.

"His parents. I came here alone, and he used that to his advantage. I can only imagine what they are telling her about me."

Simone's situation tugged at Sade's heart. "Well, if I get out of this, I will help you get out too. Maybe we can get an appeal. It makes no sense that they gave you twenty years with proof of his constant abuse."

"Don't waste your time," Simone grumbled as Officer Brooks stepped into their doorway.

"Pack your shit, Sade. You're out."

"Huh?" Sade stood.

"You want to stay?" Brooks asked with a teasing smile.

"N-no!"

"Then pack up and let's go."

Sade wasted no time packing the few items she'd collected during her time there. She wrote her number down for Simone and told her to keep in touch. As they hugged, she told Simone, "I meant what I said. I'm going hire you a lawyer and get you out of here."

"Just . . . Just pop in on my girl if you can. I don't care if you have to just sit in your car and watch her come out of her school. Take a picture and mail it to me. That's truly all I need."

Seeing as Simone hadn't seen her daughter for the entire five years she'd been there, Sade understood that request. She agreed before they hugged again, then finally, she was on her way out.

Dante figured Sade would want to leave Vanzette when she was released, but that wasn't the case. At that moment, all she wanted to do was rest and be in his arms. He got them a hotel room at the only four-star hotel in town. As they looked around the suite, he told her, "This is cool, but I'm tired of hotels and guest rooms. I want to buy us a home, Smiley. I know you got approved for the apartment in Memphis, but . . ." He hesitated, causing her to look back at him.

"But what?"

"It's not something we need to talk about now. Why don't you get freshened up? I'll order room service, and we can—"

"You're hiding something from me." Sade walked over to him and took his hands into hers. "What is it?"

"Your grandparents . . . They want you to stay away."

Sade's head tilted, and her brows wrinkled as she struggled to process his words. "Stay away?" she repeated. He nodded. "They don't want me around?" He shook his head. "They think I did it, huh?"

"Well . . . They said there's been a lot of drama since we got together. I think they are conflicted about whether you did it, but they don't want us to bring any more issues to them or the twins. I tried to convince them that you were innocent, but they weren't trying to hear me out."

"Oh." Gritting her teeth, Sade released a shaky breath as her eyes watered. "Okay. Then I guess me wanting to be close to them because of the baby doesn't matter anymore."

"Hey . . . You don't need them. You have me."

Though Sade appreciated the sentiment, it wasn't the same. Losing her parents before her last year of high school started and having a toxic relationship with her sister caused her to rely on her grandparents even more. They were her anchor. Without them, she worried she'd feel unsteady.

"Thank you, baby. I'm, uh . . . gonna go ahead and take advantage of having a bathroom with a door and freshen up."

She gave him a quick kiss before scurrying off to the bathroom, trying not to focus on all she'd lost just to gain and help Dante.

One Week Later

Dante had been doing everything he could to make Sade's transition back home smooth. He'd paid for her to have a day of pampering, including a massage, facial, and mani-pedi. He'd paid for her to get her hair done and taken her on a shopping spree. Because she had a few weeks before her next doctor's appointment, he offered to take her to her island or anywhere else in the world, but Sade insisted she was most comfortable in Vanzette with him.

She decided to stay in Memphis, at least until after she gave birth since she liked her new doctor. But Sade didn't plan to return to Memphis until it was time for her next appointment in a few weeks. As she and Dante had dinner at her favorite restaurant, he said, "Can I convince you not to move into that apartment? If you'd prefer something small, I'll find us an apartment that has more space. But I think the one you chose would be a bit tight for us and the baby."

Sade smiled as she wiped the corners of her mouth. Her meal of steak, spinach, and broccoli had been divine. She did try a little of Dante's smoked gouda mac and cheese, but after her brief stay in prison, she'd still been craving vegetables.

"You're serious about us, huh?"

Dante chuckled. "Yeah. Were you not serious about me?"

"I did leave you," she teased, and they both shared a light laugh.

"Nah, that don't count. I feel like you were on some get-back shit with that. Punishing me because of your sister. I know you want to be with me, though."

"Do you?"

"Tell me I'm wrong," he countered, wrapping his hand around his Old Fashioned.

"You're not wrong, Dante."

"Good." He used his fingers to call their waitress over. As she set a plate in front of Sade, she smiled warmly. "This should show you how serious I am."

Sade's heart fluttered at "*Will you be mine?*" written in cursive font with red syrup underneath a slice of strawberry cheesecake.

And under the inscription was a princess-cut ring that caused Sade to gasp.

"It's a promise ring, not an engagement ring," Dante clarified. "But with that ring, I promise to propose in no more than a year if you agree to us committing to each other today."

Sade covered her face bashfully. This was all she'd ever wanted. Even with her convincing herself they were better off as friends because Dante chose Imani over her, no part of Sade wanted to play hard to get.

"Yes, I'll be yours," she cooed.

A low moan escaped Dante as he stood and walked over to her side of the table. After slipping the ring onto her right ring finger, he pulled her in for a kiss that drenched her panties. Sade didn't know how long the peace would last, but in that moment, everything was perfect.

JONES

The Day Sade Was Released...

WITH THE PADS *of his palms pressed together, Captain Bennit released a long exhale. His expression was solemn as he eyed Jones. While Jones had an idea what this was about, he didn't want to assume. He'd been meticulous and careful, casing the hospital from every angle to ensure no cameras were around. It would have been impossible for him to have been caught stealing samples of Imani's DNA.*

"I'm gonna cut straight to the chase," Bennit said. "What on earth would possess you to steal a woman's blood and have it put into the system as evidence on a case we closed months ago?"

Jones's mouth opened... and closed. He shifted in his seat, unsure if he wanted to deny the accusation.

"I'm sorry, Captain, but I'm not sure what you're talki—"

"Dammit, Jones!" Bennit roared, slamming his hand down on his desk. "They have you on camera."

"Wha—There were no cameras. I checked."

"You may have checked, but you didn't do a good job. There was a small camera on the edge of the board that looked like a marker magnet. Because they often use that room for inmates, they go through extra security steps. You would have known that if you were actively involved in the case."

"Captain—"

"But you weren't *involved, because there is* no *case. You aren't a detective for the Memphis Police Department, so how could you have known they increased security cameras to avoid putting someone in the room with inmates around the clock to ensure their and the staff's safety?"*

Jones decided there was no point in denying it anymore. Unfortunately, he'd been caught.

"What does this mean for the case?"

Bennit chuckled. *"There is* no *case. What part of that do you* not *understand, Jones?"*

"Captain, that DNA proved someone in Imani's family was at both crime scenes. That hair, that blood . . . Those were no coincidences. Sade was the only person in Vanzette who knew both victims and had a reason to kill them. How can you sit there and tell me there is no case?"

"Because you stole the evidence without a warrant, the validity of the DNA match is being called into question. Even if the DNA was a match, her attorney is arguing that was a lie and that you had someone change the name in the system to Sade's."

"That's bullshit!" Jones yelled as he stood. "The DNA can be run against what's on file in Memphis for Imani. It will be a 100 percent match for her and a 50 percent match for her sister. She's the killer, Captain."

"That may be the case, but unfortunately, because you did your own thing and took matters into your own hands, the prosecutor will not be able to use the DNA sample and match as evidence."

"Come on," Jones interrupted to blurt.

"And seeing as that was all the evidence we had against Sade, she will be released from prison, and all charges against her will be dropped. Not only that, but I also have to issue a public apology to her and her family on your behalf and pray this doesn't create a snowball effect of people that you've *put away based on DNA asking to have their cases retried."*

That left Jones speechless, so Bennit continued. "I convinced the DA not to press charges against you, but I have to fire you. Effective immediately, you are no longer a detective for the Vanzette Police Department. And might I make clear this is not an invitation for you to continue to go after this woman on your own. You fucked up any chance there was of Sade doing time for this. Now live with it." As Bennit shoved his glasses up the bridge of his nose, he added, "Go empty out your desk and vacate the premises immediately."

"Yes, sir," Jones agreed. "I–I'm sorry."

Remaining silent, Bennit returned his attention to the file on his desk.

As Jones returned to his desk, it felt like all eyes were on him. His body radiated anger. As much as he tried to maintain a composed outward appearance, his insides were hot and shaking, as if they were boiling on the inside. This could not have been happening. Yet again, Sade had gotten away with everything... and Jones had no one to blame but himself.

Once he had all his belongings, Jones was escorted out of the precinct by his lieutenant. His steps froze at the sight of Dante leaning against his car, wearing a smug grin.

"I told you not to fuck with my wife."

"All right, that's enough," Lieutenant Burns said, shooing Dante away from the vehicle.

Dante shot Jones a wink before he walked away, and Jones had to tighten his grip on the box to keep from dropping it and going after him.

SADE

Mid-September

S ADE,
 Thank you for the pictures of Carmen. I can't lie., I thought you'd get out of here and forget about me. I didn't expect you to keep your promise. My baby girl has gotten so big, but I guess that's to be expected. Thank you for giving her back to me in some way.
 Last time we talked, you said you'd be moving back to Memphis. How is that going? Did you find a house yet? If so, make sure you give me your new address so we can continue to write to each other. I know you said I can call you anytime, but at least these letters are cheaper because they only use a stamp.
 Oh! That lawyer you contacted on my behalf came to visit me yesterday. He said you offered to pay for him to represent me, but that won't be necessary. Apparently, his office does pro bono appeals for people they believe have been wrongly convicted. I told him that I did kill Nico, but only because I felt I had no other choice. He said he'd looked into it and believed me . . . thought I had a chance to get out of here soon. Can you believe that? I owe it all to you.
 Thank you for believing in me and not giving up on me. If I get out of here, I don't know what I could do to repay you, but I'll think of something.

Reka is out of the hospital. She was pissed when she got back and saw you were gone. That stab to her side knocked out some of her steam, LOL. She couldn't believe Dominique didn't go after you when you got out of solitary. Dominique gave her a BS excuse about how she could never get you alone before you left, and Reka told her being in the main room had never stopped her from fighting someone before.

So they aren't cliqued up anymore. If nothing else came from your time here except my pictures and you breaking up those rapist bullies, I know a lot of women in here that'll be forever grateful to you for that.

Simone

The sight of Dante's pout made Sade giggle. He was looking forward to finding out the sex of their baby, but it was a bit too soon. Sade was only sixteen weeks pregnant, and her doctor suggested waiting until her next appointment so it would be more accurate. Dante did get excited about the ultrasound and hearing their baby's heartbeat, though.

As they walked hand in hand to his car, Sade teased him with, "Aww, babe, I thought you only cared about having a healthy little one. You said you didn't care about the sex."

"I don't care if it's a boy or girl . . . I just want to *know* if it's a boy or girl."

As Sade chuckled, she lifted his hand to her mouth and kissed it. "Next month will fly by before you know it, and then we'll get to find out."

"You're right. You told me not to get my hopes up about it happening today, so I shouldn't have been surprised." As Dante opened the door for her, his free hand went to her belly. It had rounded and started to protrude, and Dante couldn't keep his hands off it. "I still can't believe we're going to have a baby."

"Neither can I," Sade admitted, covering his hand with hers. "I'm just grateful I'm not dealing with as many symptoms as I was, and my energy is returning."

"Me too. I hate that you had to go through that, but I'm glad you are willing to for our baby."

He gave her another kiss before helping her get into the car. When Sade pulled her phone out to check her notifications, she was surprised to see she had a missed call from her grandmother. After Dante told her what Ava and Barron said, Sade didn't bother contacting them. This was the first time Ava had called, and Sade immediately thought something was wrong.

"My grandma called me," she muttered as Dante started the car.

"Are you going to call her back?" he asked, lowering the volume on the music.

"Yeah, I guess. I'm sure if she's calling me, it has to be something important."

Dante nodded his agreement as Sade returned the call. Ava answered shortly.

"Hello?"

"You called?"

"Yes. I got a calendar reminder about your appointment today. I was supposed to go with you to your appointments, remember?"

"Yeah, well, that's not necessary anymore. Dante's with me. Besides, you made it clear you don't want me around, so I'm not sure why you thought I'd still want you to come."

Ava sighed into the receiver. "Can you come over so we can talk about that? I need to explain where we're going from."

Sade chuckled. "There's no need to explain. You think I'm a killer."

"Sade, please. Just come over so we can talk."

After considering it for a while, Sade agreed with, "Fine. I'll be over later."

She disconnected the call, hoping she wouldn't regret her decision to see them.

"I'll take you over there, but if they start talking crazy, we leave. I will protect you from anyone who means you harm, and that includes emotional and mental harm from them."

Sade hated that it had come down to this, but she was grateful for his protection and support. "Thank you," she mumbled, taking his hand into hers.

Maybe Ava wanted to apologize. Even if she did, Sade wasn't sure what that would change. In the back of her mind, she would always wonder when the next time she'd do something to make them disappointed or upset and cause them to want her to go away. She was an adult and could handle their rejection, but that was something she refused to introduce to her child.

Sade's Audio Journal

"Something is off with my grandparents. I'm going to go talk to them, but I still don't know if I will have peace when it comes to them. I don't know if it's the hormones or not, but I feel more sensitive than usual. I want to be on good terms with them, but I feel like something is going on that they aren't telling me about.

"Do they know what I did and are just waiting for me to confess? Is that why they've been so against me lately? But how could they know? Who could have possibly told them? I don't think Imani would. What could she get out of that?" Sade chuckled. "Well, maybe that would make her look like less of a screwup in their eyes. I don't know. Something's going on with them, though, and until I figure out what it is, I'm not sure if they will be the secure, stable presence they've always been for me."

"If you feel uncomfortable at any time, we can leave," Dante said as he rang the doorbell.

"Okay, but I don't plan to be here long anyway. We agreed to tell your family after the next checkup, so I want us to still do that."

"All right, Smiley," Dante agreed as the front door unlocked and opened.

Barron smiled at his granddaughter, whose mouth remained slack. His eyes lowered to her protruding belly.

"You're really pregnant, huh?"

"Oh, so you don't just think I'm a killer, but you think I'm a liar too?"

"That's not . . . I was only saying that because this is my first time seeing you with this belly, Sade. I know you weren't lying about being pregnant." Barron opened the door wider as he told them, "Come in."

They followed Barron into the living room as if they were unfamiliar with the home. At the sight of Ava seated on the textured couch, Sade asked, "Where are the twins?"

"With their other grandparents." Before Sade could question why they allowed Adam's parents to have the twins, Ava added, "It was somewhat of a truce. Having some time with the girls keeps the peace between both families. If we hadn't agreed, they would have sought custody anyway. This way, we get to decide how often they can get them and when."

"You do realize Samantha blames me for his death and has tried to fight me, right?"

Ava shrugged and released a low breath. "Yes, but that really has nothing to do with the fact that those are her grandbabies.

Regardless of how she feels about how Adam died or you, we can't keep them from her."

With a roll of her eyes, Sade crossed her arms over her chest and asked, "Why did you want me to come over?"

"You'll want to be seated for this," Barron said, pointing toward the space next to her grandmother.

Sade sat there while Dante sat in the recliner that was on the opposite side of her, and her grandfather sat in a similar chair.

"The reason we had such a harsh reaction to you getting out of jail is because we were triggered by you going to jail to begin with," Ava said.

"Triggered over what?" Sade asked.

"The fact that your parents' love story was a hell of a lot like yours," Barron answered. "Your mother, Andrea, had a best friend, who she claimed as her sister. Her name was Tonya. They both were friends with your father, Martin. Your mother had feelings for your father, but she didn't go after him. Instead, she told Tonya. Tonya, then, went after your father."

"Like me and Imani," Sade said.

Ava nodded. "Yes. Now, the difference was that your father turned Tonya down because he had feelings for your mom." Ava's eyes shifted toward Dante, who inadvertently avoided them. "Andrea and Martin talked; they agreed to date, and we thought that was the end of it."

"But it wasn't," Barron said. "Apparently, Tonya's advances continued over the years. Eventually, Martin surrendered to them, and they had a longstanding affair. During this time, Tonya got married and had a daughter. Even still, she wanted your father. Andrea and Martin hit a rough patch in their marriage, and he agreed to a divorce pact with Tonya. Well, Tonya actually divorced her husband, but your father decided he wanted to work things out with your mom."

Ava's hand covered her mouth as her eyes watered. Though Sade had no idea where they were going with this, her emotions also began to unravel.

"The car accident that killed your parents ... That wasn't an accident," Ava said. "It was a double murder, and Tonya was behind it. After she was convicted of tampering with their brakes and causing the accident, she was sentenced to life in prison. Her daughter suffered the most with that decision, and because of bullying at school, she committed suicide."

"Oh my God." Sade clutched her chest.

"So when you and Imani started bickering over Dante, we feared things would become volatile," Ava shared. "That's why I always tried to get you to see you couldn't share him. I didn't want either of you feeling so possessive of him that you tried to get the other out of the way."

"I can understand that, but I'm not sure why that would make you believe I killed those women."

"Love can make you do crazy things," Barron said. "We lost your mom because her best friend wanted your father. It wasn't too far off for us to think you killed someone to keep Dante's identity a secret. When you were first arrested, we didn't think that. After we looked into the case and learned some of the details, we started to become triggered over what happened to Andrea and Martin."

"Thanks for telling me this." Sade paused. "Why didn't Mom ever tell us? I get why she didn't bring Tonya around, but still."

"I think she wasn't too proud of how they behaved over your father," Ava answered. "That's the only thing I can think of."

With a nod, Sade stood. "This is a lot to take in. All this time, I thought it was truly a horrible car accident that took my parents away from me, and now, you're telling me they were murdered. Does Imani know?"

"No, she doesn't."

Sade rubbed her hands together, needing to be able to direct the nervous energy that filled her in one place.

"Okay. I guess she doesn't need to know. I, uh... We're gonna go."

Ava stood. "I never wanted to tell you this, but I needed you to know why we reacted the way we did." She took Sade's hand into hers. "I don't want you to stay away, baby. I just don't want anything to happen to you in the name of love."

"Well, you don't have to worry about that. Adam is dead, and he's the one who wanted Dante dead. Atlas went a little crazy, but now he's dead and no longer a threat. And Imani doesn't give a damn what we do. Those charges against me have been dropped and will never be an issue again." Sade released her grandmother's hand and grabbed Dante's. "We're finally getting to our happily ever after. I'd like you to be included, but I will also be at peace if you're not."

"We want to be in your lives," Barron said.

"And our new grandbaby," Ava added.

Sade looked at Dante, and when he nodded his approval, she agreed.

Sade sat between her parents' graves. She'd been there long enough to clean them off and put out new flowers. Before she arrived, she had a million thoughts and questions in her mind. Now that she was here, she only wanted to sit in silence and feel close to them. Learning this new truth felt like the scab had been ripped off the wound, and she was grieving her parents all over again. Except this time, she wasn't mad at God for taking them from her—she was angry at Tonya—and wanted her to pay.

JONES

Jones shot a dart into the picture of Sade that hung on his wall.

She looked just like her mother. Just like the woman who ruined his marriage. Andrea Griffin. Depending on who you asked, Andrea was the victim. She . . . and her cheating husband, Martin. But not to Jones. To Jones, they were the reason his wife was in prison, and his daughter was dead.

Even while dating Tonya, Jones knew her heart belonged to someone else because of how difficult it was for him to get inside. Still, he'd chosen her—fallen in love with her—and had no intentions of letting her go. So, imagine his surprise when Tonya told him she wanted a divorce to be with the *real* father of her child . . . Martin.

The heart that Jones had fought so passionately to make his way inside of was officially closed off to him, and Tonya had no regrets. Not even when Martin told her he wanted to stay with his wife.

By that point, the damage had been done. Not only did Martin not want to be with Tonya anymore, but because she lied to him about her daughter, he also wanted to make her suffer. Before Tonya could receive full custody of the child that had never been his, she was convicted of killing Martin and Andrea Griffin. For a while, framing his wife for the murders was worth it . . . until the daughter he'd schemed to keep committed suicide.

Jones didn't think he'd ever fully grieve Dena. Nor did he think he'd ever get over what her mother had done. He tried by burying himself in his work. For a while, that worked—until two murders happened, back-to-back, in his town. Others quickly wrote them off as unconnected coincidences, but Jones's gut told him that wasn't the case.

When he looked into Patrice and Trina's phones and history, he was slapped with the past. Sade was the spitting image of her mother. Their having the same last name led Jones down a rabbit hole of research until he confirmed what he had already believed to be true—Sade and Imani were the daughters of Martin and Andrea Griffin.

It gave him great pleasure to learn that Imani was already in prison, and it enticed him to know he could put her sister there too. They may not have been responsible for the tangled web Tonya wove, but they would be proof that a child had to pay for the sins of their parents. They had to pay for Andrea catching the eye of the man Tonya wanted, locking her heart away from her own husband. They had to pay for her having a child by Martin and leaving Jones for him. They had to pay for Dena killing herself because she couldn't take the bullying and missing her mother.

Andrea and Martin were gone . . . and so were Tonya and Dena—leaving Jones all alone.

To see Sade convicted of Patrice and Trina's murders felt like the final piece needed for Jones to receive closure. But that closure was now gone. All that remained were the drudged-up feelings he'd experienced when Tonya told him the truth about Dena and left him over ten years ago.

DANTE

Two Weeks Later

Confusion quickly turned into anger as Dante stared at his car. All four tires were slashed. His evening out with Ian and Eric gave him relief from the stress of moving into a new home, but now, the high he was on had grounded him. This was intentional, and Dante needed to figure out who had done it and why.

After requesting a tow truck, he returned to the bar and grill and asked the manager if he could review their security footage because someone had slashed his tires. Unfortunately, their cameras didn't work and were merely used to try to keep people from causing trouble just from the sight of them. Dante checked the surrounding restaurants, and they said the same thing, which only frustrated him more.

Since he was having his car towed to the tire shop near his new home, he called an Uber instead of asking one of his friends to come back or asking Sade to get him. She'd gone to bed earlier than usual because of a dizzy spell. Though Dante offered to stay home with her, she insisted he leave because of his scheduled plans.

On the ride home, Dante wondered who could have slashed his tires. He was not involved with any road rage incident on his way to the bar and grill. He couldn't recall seeing anyone looking familiar and wanting revenge while there. And without that camera footage, Dante had absolutely no clues to follow. To that end, he convinced himself that maybe they had mistaken him or his car for someone else. He would, however, keep his eyes open and be alert in case something else happens any time soon.

The Following Monday

All eyes were on Dante as he headed across the lobby toward the elevators. Whispered tones piqued his curiosity, but he ignored them since they weren't speaking up. After having his tires slashed, Dante chilled for the rest of the weekend with Sade. He tried not to obsess over it and hoped it was a random occurrence.

Working at Ian's financial firm was nice, especially because he was a partner, but Dante missed the old days—working with Imani, his closest male friend Eric, and his wife Jessica. A part of him was broken, knowing he'd never be able to return to those days again.

When he made it to his floor, Dante saw why he'd received stares ... why people were whispering as he walked. The floor assistants fervently ripped pictures of him from the walls. He stepped forward, snatching the eight-by-eleven photo.

Hi, my name is Dante, and I cheated on my wife with her sister. Don't trust me with your money or your credit ... We steal.

After reading the caption under the picture, Dante crumbled the paper in his fist. He ripped down one picture after another, noticing they trailed every wall down the hall.

Ian rushed out of his office, his body relaxing at the sight of Dante.

"Ian, man, I'm so sorry about this."

Ian gave him a dismissive wave of his hand. "Whoever did this taped these flyers all over the building. We've been trying to get them down, but it's a lot."

"This has to be the same person who slashed my tires," Dante said, more to himself as he continued to walk and tear down flyers.

"What? When did this happen?"

"The night we went out."

"Why didn't you say anything? How did you get home?"

"I didn't want to inconvenience either of you. At first, I thought it was a case of mistaken identity. Now, I know it was for me."

"Damn. Well, security is checking footage from last night, so we'll see who did this."

"Good."

"But with that being said . . ." Ian squeezed the back of his neck and briefly shifted his eyes. "Until you get this under control, we're gonna need you to work from home. I know the situation, but it's not something I want to have to explain to our clients."

Though Dante was frustrated by Ian's decision, he respected it and planned to take accountability.

"I get it, man. Thanks for giving me grace in a situation that's beyond my control. I'm cool with working from home. But when security gets a hit, please text me the photo."

"For sure. I got you."

The pair shook hands before Dante went to his office to grab a few of his files. He did have three meetings scheduled for that week and questioned whether he should reschedule them. For now, he'd focus on one thing at a time, and his biggest priority was finding out who was responsible and making them pay.

Dante stared at the picture Ian sent him. He didn't recognize the man dressed in all black. Not only did he have a hood tossed over his head, but he also wore a mask and gloves. Dante was impressed by his ability to bypass the alarm system. If Atlas were still alive, Dante would have assumed it was him. But this man—the short stature and slim frame—Dante didn't recognize him at all.

"This is so frustrating," Sade seethed, rubbing her belly. "I don't recognize anything about this man, baby."

"I don't either. I'm trying to think if he could be an old client affected by what Imani did. But they were compensated, so no one should have a reason to want revenge."

"Hmm... What if they lost something that being compensated couldn't fix?" Dante remained silent, so Sade continued. "They got their money back, but what if someone's credit being affected had a lasting effect?"

Dante massaged his chin as he sat back in his seat. "That's a possibility. If they were trying to get a house, car, or business loan and Imani didn't come through, the application could have been rejected."

"For some people, that kind of thing makes them spiral."

"That's a possibility, but I don't know. Maybe I'll review the affidavit that lists the victims' names. If I can find them online, I can see if anyone has his frame. But I'm not sold on this."

"While you do that, I can check their files individually and see if anyone was waiting on a large loan or credit repair for something life changing."

"You sure?"

"Of course. My creativity is a bit low with everything going on, so it's not like I'm painting or working on a new coloring book."

"I'm sorry about this, Sade. I feel like it's one thing after another. Maybe your grandma was right. Are we crazy thinking we'll be able to live a normal life?"

Straddling his lap, Sade affirmed him with, "I don't mind being crazy in love with you."

His hands lowered to her ass, and he squeezed it. "And I don't mind being crazy in love with you, either."

SADE

"NERVOUS" WASN'T THE best word to describe how Sade felt. Though she was unsure how her sister would respond to the sight of her belly, Sade wanted to visit her anyway. That morning, she took the twins out for breakfast before they had to go to school, and she was grateful for the time spent with them. Just a little while ago, she believed they'd be ripped from her life again because her grandparents wanted her to stay away.

Learning that her parents had been murdered instead of it being an accident had completely devastated Sade. It made so many things make sense. In her youth, she wondered why her parents seemed to favor or spoil Imani more. Saying it was because she was the baby of the family didn't make sense. And when things got even more toxic between her and Imani over the years, her grandparents were cautious yet adamant about Sade being the one to be the bigger person and cut Dante off.

Knowing that her mother and father were in a similar situation made it feel like missing pieces of a puzzle had been returned. While Sade was confident things wouldn't have turned murderous between her and her sister, she could admit how rage could turn deadly by accident—and there had been a lot of times Imani's actions filled her with rage.

Like Sade, Tonya had to watch the man she loved want to be with someone else. Someone close to her. Someone like a sister.

Had Sade been a trigger for her grandparents for all those years? And if so, why didn't they just tell the truth? Sure, they said the reason was because they didn't want their granddaughters' perspective of their parents to change, but that sounded more like an excuse than the truth. If she had known that her parents were targeted because of their love and her father's affair, it would have completely changed the way Sade handled the situation with Dante and Imani.

It seemed silly to wonder if she and her sister could have had a healthier relationship with that knowledge, but Sade had decided to tell Imani even though her grandparents didn't want her to.

With her hands crossed on top of the table, Sade twiddled her thumbs and nibbled her bottom lip. At the sight of Imani, she smiled. Her sister walked with an air of confidence, even in prison. Sade stood, and Imani's eyes immediately lowered to her stomach. Chuckling, she shook her head as they both sat down.

"Is that Atlas's baby?"

Sade shook her head. "No. It's Dante's."

Imani's head tilted, and her jaws clenched. She released a slow, long breath. "I guess you're finally happy now. Not only did you get Dante, but you're also having his baby too."

Sade shrugged. "Yeah . . . honestly . . . I am. I didn't come to throw my happiness in your face, but I won't lie about it, either. More than anything, I just wanted you to know."

"I'm not upset about it. I feel like it's second nature for me to give you a hard time, but I don't care. You're the one who wanted him and . . . I guess it's good that you finally got him."

"So, you're okay with this?"

Imani chuckled. "If I wasn't, it wouldn't change anything. But yeah, it's cool. I really don't care."

"Good." Sade sat up a little straighter in her seat. "There's something else you should know. Grandma and Grandpa wanted me to keep it to myself, but I can't do that."

"What's going on?"

Sade told her everything about her parents and Tonya, and Imani followed up with, "Are you fucking kidding me?" as she leaped from her seat. The guard yelling her name caused her to sit back down. "Our parents were murdered, and they *didn't think* that was something we needed to know?"

"That was my thing. I can understand why they wouldn't have told us immediately, but there was no reason for them not to tell us by now. I know they meant well and didn't want us to hurt over what happened even more, but that could have been a lesson for us to learn from."

"I agree. I'm not telling the twins about what I did to get me in here until they're at an age where they can process and make sense of it. So, I get them not telling us while we were still in high school. But let's be honest—you and I were a hell of a lot like Mama and this Tonya lady. Now, I don't think we would have actually ever killed each other, but you did threaten to kill me a time or two."

Sade smirked. "That was a heat-of-the-moment threat, Imani."

"I don't know now. After what happened in Vanzette . . ."

"Anyway," Sade stretched with a wave of her hand, causing Imani to laugh. "I feel like if we would have known about that, then we would have been more aware of how we treated each other. I spent a lot of time being resentful because they gave me a harder time about Dante than you, and you were the one who did wrong to me. If I would have known they feared I'd snap like Tonya, it would have made things make sense."

"Well, there's nothing we can do about it now. Tonya is in prison, right?"

"Right. I didn't look up her and her husband, though I was really tempted to. But I felt like that would send me down a rabbit hole, and I'd want to punish her even though she's already being punished."

"Same. She's lucky I'm serving fed time. Otherwise, I'd find and handle her if we were in the same place."

Sade chuckled, though she knew her sister was serious. "Does this . . . change anything for you?"

Imani's mouth twisted to the side as she thought it over. With a shrug, she hummed. "It makes me feel a little bad about what I did, how I baited you over the years. It shows me how serious and deadly things could have turned out. I would have never wanted things to get to that point. I can't imagine how what I did over the years made you feel mentally and emotionally. What if I had made you snap?"

Sade scratched and tugged her ear. "I'd like to think I wouldn't have given you that much power over my emotions. That's why I stayed away and moved to Vanzette. But I honestly don't know. I'm just glad we'll never have to find out."

Imani licked her lips as her eyes watered. "I know I've said it before, but I really am sorry. Being here has caused me to do a lot of reflection, and I'm becoming more self-aware. I've always been selfish and uncaring when it came to the feelings of others. I never cared how my actions affected them. . . . . . I want you to be happy with Dante and my little niece or nephew. You deserve it."

The sisters continued to talk, and by the time Sade left, she felt lighter.

After spending time behind bars herself, Sade decided to put together a care package for her sister. She remembered how good it felt to not only have Dante put time on the phone and on her books but also to order her food as well. So, she did the same for Imani. When she finished adding the funds online and ordering her food to be delivered for the next three weeks, Sade decided to write her sister a letter. It was crazy how their relationship was being strengthened while they were apart, but Sade was grateful for it, and she hoped by the time Imani was out, they could treat each other like normal sisters.

DANTE

THE SMILE ON Sade's face made the effort Dante put into their home date worth it. Since she mentioned being in a creative slump, Dante tried to think of what they could do to pull her out of it. There was an unfurnished room in their five-bedroom home. It was supposed to be a guest room, but Dante used its emptiness to his advantage. He covered the hardwood floor and taped canvases to the walls and in the corner of the room.

Dante undressed Sade and covered her body with paint. She made art with her body, and it was the most unique, sexy, and intimate thing he'd ever seen. Though he insisted it was her moment, she undressed him as well. Unlike her, he used only his hands and feet, amused at his creations. Sade told him they were beautiful.

After they made love, they dressed and prepared to do a grocery store run when Dante got a camera alert on his phone. The doorbell sounded shortly after. He headed down the hall to open it while Sade grabbed her purse.

Dante eyed the deliveryman skeptically.

"Hello. I have a package for . . ." He looked down at his clipboard. "Sade Griffin?"

"Williams," Dante corrected, though they weren't technically married yet.

"Oh. Apologies."

"I'll sign for it," Dante offered, extending his hands for the pen and clipboard.

The deliveryman gave him the box, and Dante was curious about what was inside. He stepped back outside when he saw the name "Atlas" written on top of the box. There was no reason for Sade to be getting a package from a dead man.

"Day!" he called, setting the box on the ground. After grabbing a pair of scissors from the kitchen, he met her in the hallway. "Someone just dropped a package off for you. 'Atlas' is written on the top. Have you heard from anyone in his family lately?"

She shook her head as she stood at the door and looked down at the box. "No, I haven't. I'm not sure why anyone would be sending me something in his name."

"Do you mind if I open it just to be safe?"

"Not at all."

Dante opened the box, revealing a card on top of a smaller box. He lifted the card and read it aloud. *"Such a pity. The lives lost because of you. Atlas was the last... How long will that be true? You've kept your hands clean, and now, it seems Dante is doing your dirty work. Who will be the next person he hurts?"*

"Baby, don't open it." Sade placed her hand on his shoulder, but that didn't stop Dante from opening the top of the box.

The moment he did, flies flew out. Sade covered her mouth but to no avail. She vomited in the bushes at the sight of the mound of poo and crawling maggots.

"This has to be Jones," Dante said. "Who else would be bringing up alleged murders? Plus, me killing Atlas was self-defense." He finished closing the box and walked it over to the garbage, not bothering to wait for Sade's response.

He found her in their bathroom, brushing her teeth. Dante washed his hands three times before starting to feel a little cleaner.

"Why won't he just leave us *alone*?" Sade seethed. "You'd think losing his job would have brought him to his senses. Why can't he just . . . let it go?"

"I think losing his job is ammunition for him to keep coming until we stop him."

Sade shook her head as she closed the space between them and wrapped her arms around him. "I know what you're thinking, but we can't."

Dante scoffed. "Why not? Do you think I will just let him stalk and taunt you like this? To what end? You're pregnant. You don't need to deal with continued stress."

"You're right, but I don't want us to respond and bait him to do more. Maybe if we ignore it, he'll stop."

"It's clear he's still watching us. That needs to be handled. We'll try it your way, but we're doing it my way if it doesn't work."

Sade nodded in agreement, and Dante kissed her forehead. He never thought there would come a day when he'd be able to consider taking a life so casually. But for Sade? He wouldn't give it a second thought.

DANTE

OLIVIA SWOONED OVER the ultrasound Dante showed her. Knowing the twins weren't his biologically left a huge hole in all their hearts. Even though Dante still did what he could for them and tried not to treat them any differently when they were around, it stung every time he saw them and was reminded they weren't his daughters. That pain overflowed onto his parents too. Because he was an only child, all their grandchildren would have to come from him. Olivia cried when she learned Imani's infidelity had taken that away.

"When are you going to find out what you're having?" Deandre asked his son.

"The next checkup, I believe. I was hoping it would be the last one, but Doctor Smith said it was still a bit too early, and she didn't want to risk not being able to see and getting us excited or telling us an incorrect gender."

"That's understandable. Well, I just want to know what my grandbaby will be," Olivia said. "This baby is truly a gift. It won't replace the twins, but it sure makes their loss easier to handle, knowing we'll have this little one."

"And you're sure there's no chance this is that other man's child?" Deandre asked.

Dante was always open with his parents because he often asked them for advice. He'd shared with them how Sade had been involved with Atlas, and that was the reason Atlas entered and died in their home.

"She said it's mine, and I believe her."

"Will you get a DNA test just to be sure?"

"I trust her, so I don't think there's a need for one."

Deandre sighed. "I love Sade, and I'm not saying she could be as heartless and conniving as her sister, but if you know she was involved with a man around the same time as you, I'd get that test to be sure."

"Nah." Dante shook his head. "He wasn't around when we were doing our thing in Vanzette. I get where y'all are coming from, but I'm 100 percent sure the baby is mine."

"And if that's the case, what's wrong with taking the test just to confirm it?" Olivia asked sweetly.

Dante's phone vibrating in his pocket stopped him from responding. He pulled it out and sat up in his seat at the sight of two new messages from a blocked number. The pictures of Patrice and Trina's dead bodies made his heart stop, along with the caption, *You're next.*

Chuckling, Dante stood, absently telling his parents he had to go. They asked if he was okay, and he wasn't sure he even responded vocally. Those crime-scene photos were just the evidence he needed to prove Jones was behind everything happening to him and Sade lately, and even though he told Sade he'd ignore it, that was no longer an option.

For a while, all Dante could do was stare at Captain Bennit. He'd taken the three-hour drive to get to Vanzette and was sure the captain would be of assistance. After he'd run down everything that had been happening, Bennit's response was, "There's nothing I can do."

"Excuse me?" Dante sat up in his seat, tilting his head so that his ear was more aligned with Bennit's mouth—because he refused to believe what he was hearing. "If Jones didn't send me these crime-scene photos, who the hell else did?"

"Even if he did, I can promise you we won't get a trace back to him on that blocked number. He could argue that several other people with access to their files could have sent you that." Dante couldn't deny that. "There's no camera footage to show who slashed your tires. The footage you have of the person who put the pictures up doesn't match his description."

"He could have easily paid someone to do that for him."

"I don't deny that, but again, you have no proof. And I can make a safe bet that if you called the delivery company, Jones will *not* be the name of the person who placed that delivery."

"Are you saying you don't believe he's behind this or that I can't prove it?"

"I'm saying that you can't prove it." Bennit released a loaded sigh. "Before the truth came out about what he did in Memphis, I would have said it was impossible for Jones to do any of this, but now, I'm not sure. What I can say is that without proof, neither we nor the Memphis Police Department would be able to press harassment or vandalizing charges against him. I'm sorry I can't be of more help. If you get some proof, come back and see me, and I'll get someone on this."

"So what? That's it?"

Bennit shrugged. "I mean . . . yeah. Honestly, we have no way of proving that Jones has been logging into our software to get those photos or do anything else, for that matter. Even if he was following the two of you, we can't prove that unless you see him and take pictures. If he is doing something, he's doing it without leaving proof, which is what you'll need for us to help you."

Dante chuckled as he stood. "Don't worry, I'll handle it myself."

"I would advise against that," Bennit said, "If anything were to happen to Jones, I wouldn't be able to ignore this threat. You'd be the prime suspect."

"Ask me if I give a fuck," Dante tossed over his shoulder, opening the door to leave.

SADE

SADE STARED AT the pictures that were screenshots of Patrice and Trina's discussion about her with the caption, *The police may have stopped... but I won't.*

She tossed her phone onto the bed and walked over to the window. Though it was her idea to ignore Jones, she didn't know how much more she could take of this. Guilt hadn't gnawed at her because of what she'd done, but Jones's taunting made her anxious. It didn't seem to matter that the police had released her as a suspect and kept the cases closed. Jones wanted her to suffer, and though she may not have said vocally that she was, his actions were weighing on her mind heavily.

Suddenly, her phone vibrated, regaining her attention. Sade's eyes widened when she opened it and saw one spam email after enough pop up. They came back-to-back so fast she couldn't block one without another notification. With a growl, she powered off her phone and plopped down on the bed. Boisterous laughter escaped her before she screamed. Being on the receiving end of Jones's actions started to drive her insane. She'd need to be on the offense to get ahead of this.

Sade grabbed her computer and went to the kitchen, setting it up on the island. She did a brief search on the Vanzette Police Department's website. They didn't have a list of their detectives, so that didn't lead her to anything. A search of his name only led to cases he'd worked on in the past. There was no personal information or reports of him having this type of behavior with anyone else.

Stumped, she tried to think of a way to contact him. Then she remembered he'd called Dante. Sade Facetimed him from her computer, hoping he still had Jones's number.

"Hello, Smiley."

"Hey, babe. Do you have Jones's number?"

"I have the number he called me from, but it's no longer in service."

"Damn."

"Why? What's wrong? Did he do something else?"

Sade massaged her temple. "He's spamming my email and sent me some screenshots of conversations between Patrice and Trina."

"Send that to me. I'll start collecting everything he sends and keep a record of what he does. Even if he doesn't slip up and do something that will tie it back to him, I'm going to take care of him, and this proof will explain why."

"I take it things didn't go well with the captain?"

Dante chuckled. "Not at all. He said they can't do anything with solid proof."

"Of course they can't. What more proof do they need than him stealing my sister's damn DNA?"

"I don't know, bae. I know I told you I'd try to ignore him, but when I find him, it's over. I can't stand around and not do anything. That's not the kind of man I am."

"There has to be more to it than this. What about this case could have made him snap? I'm looking into it, but I'm not seeing any news reports or articles about him ever doing anything else like this."

"Hmm . . ." Dante massaged his chin. "Just because you don't see it doesn't mean it hasn't happened. I doubt if this is the first time he's gone rogue like this. Maybe I should hire a private investigator. If this is a pattern for him, that'll help us build a better case against him. And at the least, hopefully, they will help me track him down."

"That sounds like a good idea, baby. I can look up some since I'm already on the computer, and we can go through them together when you get home."

"All right, Smiley. Do you need me to bring anything home?"

"Home . . . I love the sound of that." Dante bit down on his bottom lip and moaned at the sight of her smile. "All I need is you."

"Then I'll be right there."

Sade,

That lawyer you got me is amazing! He said there's a really great chance I can leave here soon. Instead of going to a board, I'll be going straight in front of the judge. I think that's a good thing, right? That it's just one person who will make the decision. Either way, I'm really excited about the possibility of getting out of here.

The court date hasn't been set. He said it could take up to ninety days. I don't mind waiting. Hell, I've waited this long.

I reached out to Carmen's grandparents. Not sure why I thought that would be a good idea. I guess a part of me thought if they knew there was a chance I was getting out, they'd realize I wasn't the monster their grief made me out to be. I hoped they would have some mercy and remember what their son had done to me. But they don't care.

They don't care that I had to fight for my life almost every night. They don't care that he subjected Carmen to the beatings. They didn't care that I was so traumatized that I felt that was the only way to stop him. All they care about is that it was their son, and I took him away.

They are going to make getting my daughter back hard for me. I already know. But she's worth that upcoming battle, and I won't stop until I have her. I didn't mean to burden you with that. You know I don't talk to anyone in here about personal stuff. Thank you again . . . for everything.

Simone

DANTE

Dante peppered kisses along Sade's neck and arm. Her giggles egged him on. She shifted slightly, lying on her back. He took in her features—that brown skin, thick hair, and beautiful smile. Being pregnant gave her a glow that Dante loved seeing every day. Her confidence was a little low that morning because she'd broken out, but Dante made sure he made love to her body and mind to remind her of how beautiful she was.

Now, he was supposed to be heading to the office to grab some files, but he found himself back in bed with her.

"If you don't stop, you're never going to leave," she warned, wrapping her arms around his neck. "Not that I'm complaining."

"Mm . . ." Sade's hand slipped into his boxers. As she stroked his growing length, Dante released a sizzling breath. Just when he was on the verge of exploding, he slipped inside her wet walls.

Her back arched as she made room for him, digging her nails into his arms as he came inside of her. His hips rocked against her, and the sight of her trembling chin as she whimpered was almost his undoing. Dante buried his face in her neck, trying to focus on anything except how good she felt. He wanted her to come before he released a second time.

Dante upped the ante, whispering in her ear, "I love the way you feel." Her whimper made him moan. "This was what you wanted, right?"

"Yes, baby," she almost purred, wrapping her legs around him tightly.

"Then make a mess for me."

And that's exactly what she did. By the time they were done with their second round, there was a puddle underneath her. They showered together again before he begrudgingly dressed to go to the office. Since they'd been having a few days of peace with no communication from Jones, Dante had thoroughly enjoyed making their home into their personal cocoon. He hadn't left for a thing and loved every minute of the solitude.

"Do you need me to bring you anything back?" he asked as Sade fixed his tie.

"Can you bring me more canvases? Veronica wants me to create some custom pieces for her new office."

"You sure you up for that?"

"Yeah. I'm inspired. I think it'll be fun. She wants lots of babies of all different shades to line the walls."

"That sounds dope, Smiley. I got you."

After a few kisses and their declaration of love, Dante headed out. He was looking forward to returning to the office, even if only for a brief moment. But more than that, he was looking forward to getting back home to Sade.

It took Dante about an hour to update things on the company software and grab a few new files. After what happened with Imani, he was meticulous about record keeping and used password-encrypted software only installed on his work computer. When he finished, he stopped by Ian's office to catch up with him.

As they headed out, they talked about their weekend plans. Dante agreed to go out but made it clear he'd need to check with

Sade first. She'd always been a loner, and being pregnant made her want to do even less. To his surprise, she'd been talking to Jessica and Veronica more, though, and he hoped she had something planned to do with Jessica for the weekend.

When they stepped into the lobby, Dante saw Jones, and he had to keep himself from snapping. Jones leaned against the window by the revolving doors, his ankles crossed, with a smug grin. Dante ran his fingers down the corners of his mouth and took a deep breath. Ian was still talking, but his words went in one ear and out the other as Dante set his files down and headed in Jones's direction.

"Give me one good reason why I shouldn't lay your ass out right now," Dante demanded through gritted teeth.

"That wouldn't be a very professional thing to do."

"You want to talk about professionalism after you had a woman attacked so you could steal her blood? Why in the hell aren't you in jail anyway?"

Jones pushed himself off the wall. "I guess that's something me and Sade have in common . . . getting away with things."

"This is the only warning I will give you: stop with the antics. No more text messages, shit gifts, spam emails . . . Stop all of it."

"And if I don't, what are you going to do? Kill me?"

Dante scratched his nostril. "Try me and find out."

Jones passed him, looking over his shoulder, and said, "Sade's getting bigger and bigger. You know I was watching her while you were away. Are you sure that baby is yours?"

Before Dante could stop himself, he was turning Jones around and punching him—repeatedly. Had it not been for several sets of hands peeling him off Jones's unconscious body, Dante would have beat him to death.

Ian shoved Dante out of the building, using his body to keep Dante from going back inside.

"Are you out of your mind!" Ian yelled, gripping Dante by his neck and shoving him backward. "We had clients in the lobby that saw that shit! What were you thinking?"

"I was thinking he's been taunting my wife and needs to be stopped. *That's* what I was thinking!"

"And you had to do that here?"

"Where else? He's been a ghost!"

Ian released a shaky breath and squeezed the bridge of his nose as Dante paced. "Look . . . I've loved having you back, man, but this is too much. This isn't a good look for my firm and—"

"Save it," Dante interrupted. "You don't have to fire me. I quit."

Ian's body crumbled. "Let me terminate you. At least that way, I can give you a severance package and bring you back when you take care of this."

Dante scoffed. "I didn't come here because I need the money; I came here to do what I love. But I never intended this man to be a menace and not let me and my wife move on. So, I quit. I know this isn't a good look. I apologize for doing this in front of clients, but I will never apologize for knocking him out."

"Get this taken care of so you can come back," Ian pleaded, extending his hand for Dante to shake.

Dante shook it, nodding his agreement. However, even when Jones was out of the picture, he wouldn't return. The last thing he wanted was to be a stain on anyone's reputation. Money would never be an issue for him and Sade, and he didn't have to work if he didn't want to. Maybe he'd take some time off until after the baby was born. Hopefully, by then, Jones would be out of the picture, and he and Sade could finally settle into a life of normalcy.

SADE

SADE'S PHONE DINGED. She opened the text, her heart dropping at seeing a picture of her and Atlas when they first returned to Memphis with a caption that said, *You would have been better off with him. The other one is violent.* A second picture came through, and it was of Jones—beaten badly. Sade gasped, then laughed. She called Dante immediately, refusing to believe he'd finally caught up with Jones.

"Yeah?" he answered, the wind whipping against the receiver.

"Uh-oh. You sound mad."

"I'm letting off the rest of my steam with a run."

"So the picture Jones sent me of himself was real?"

"It was."

"What happened?"

"He was at the office talking shit about the baby not being mine, and I snapped. Ian wanted to fire me, but I quit. He told me I could return once this is resolved, but I won't. If anything, I'll start my own firm like I should have done to begin with."

Sade sighed and stood, needing to walk around herself. "I'm sorry, babe. He deserved that ass whupping but not at the expense of your job."

"It was worth it. I'm glad he felt confident enough to think I wouldn't touch him because we were in public. Money's good, so I'm in no rush to start working again. I want to get things ready for the baby and enjoy having you to myself as much as I can before he or she gets here."

That made Sade smile as she slipped into her shoes and headed outside. "I love the sound of that. I wish I could have seen the house in Decatur, but I don't want to fly when I get bigger. I don't want to feel uncomfortable."

"We still have time. It's just a short flight away. Whenever you want to go, we can leave."

"And you're sure you're up for that right now?"

"Absolutely. If you want, I'll book a flight for us when I get home. Might as well make it a weeklong trip and see the penthouse in New York too. I think if you see the beach house in San Diego, you won't want to come back home."

Sade's heart fluttered, and she smiled as she locked the door behind herself. "I think you're right. You know I love being near water. But I might need to wait until I have the baby to go there." She paused. "I love that we can do whatever we want when we want. I wish we could just spend the rest of our days traveling and giving our baby a taste of different cultures."

"Who says we can't? We can remain planted until the baby is old enough to travel and experience what we'll be doing and then get to it. Let's get a nanny too. That way, we can have some alone time."

"You thinking homeschool?"

"Absolutely. Maybe not for high school, but definitely elementary. I know those are fundamental years, so we can revisit this conversation when the time comes, but you know my cousin Briscoe was an army brat and was homeschooled because they traveled so much."

"Yeah, and it worked in his favor too. That man was never in Memphis."

Dante chuckled. "At all. He's paid and living his best life, experiencing one amazing country after another. That's what I want for our kids."

"Plural?" she replied with a grin.

"Yeah. You didn't think we were stopping at one, did you?"

She giggled. "I feel like we had this conversation and agreed on a number, but I'm not sure."

Dante was silent for a while. "You're sure there's no way the baby is his? If you tell me there's not, I will believe you."

Sade sighed. This seemed like the time to be honest with him. "I'm 100 percent sure the baby is yours because I was pregnant when we were in Vanzette." She clicked her tongue. "I was pregnant when I left you."

"What?" he almost whispered.

"I felt like you were with me because of what I'd done for you. You'd never chosen me before, and . . . I didn't really believe how you felt for me."

"So what? You were going to keep my baby away from me and create a readymade family with Atlas?"

"I said that was what I would do, but I regretted it as soon as I was away from you. There was no way I could have kept this child from you, especially after telling you about the twins."

"Damn, Day. I'm going to need some time to process this."

Sade nodded. "I understand."

"It's not going to be an issue, though. I know, so I won't hold this against you."

"Thank you, Dante. I'll let you go. I love you."

"I love you too."

Dante disconnected the call quickly, and Sade hoped it wouldn't take him long to get over the truth. If it did, she would be patient with him because he had the right to feel however he felt.

Several Hours Later

When Dante made it home, he didn't seek her out like usual. That was a sign to her that he still felt some type of way over what she'd shared with him. Still, she went looking for him and found him leaning against the door frame of the baby's nursery.

"Are you still mad?" she asked quietly. "If so, I'll leave you alone. But I'm glad you came home."

"I'll always come home to you, and I'm not mad." Dante turned to face her. "I was hurt. Thinking you could keep my baby from me . . ." He chuckled. "But I feel like I don't have the right. I mean . . . I got your sister pregnant and married her. Well, we *thought* I got her pregnant. So, do I really have room to be upset about anything you do?"

"Dante, you'll always have the right to feel how you feel. This will never be a tit-for-tat kind of thing. Yes, you got Imani pregnant, but we didn't start being honest with each other about how we felt until after that. These things don't compare, and you being with my sister first doesn't give me a lifetime pass to do things that might upset or hurt you." She wrapped her arms around his neck. "That was me being bitter and proud. I wasn't trying to hurt you intentionally, but I'm sorry I did."

"It's okay. I'm just glad you told me, and I can experience this with you."

"Thank you for forgiving me and for being understanding. I would have accepted if you harbored hurt or anger over this, but—"

Dante chuckled and interrupted her to declare, "We have too much time to make up for, Smiley, for me to waste time being upset over something as minuscule as this. You told the truth, we're here together, and that's all that matters to me."

"Good, because that's all that matters to me too."

Their lips connected, and they shared a tender kiss before pulling away and heading to their room to plan the trip they were about to take.

DANTE

One Week Later

When they returned to Memphis, Dante wasn't expecting the police to be waiting for him at the airport. He could only laugh when he heard the charge—assault. This was nothing but Jones making his next move. Even if Dante had to do time for it, beating him was still worth it.

The tears in Sade's eyes broke Dante's heart. As she sniffled, he told her, "You know the password to my computer. My attorney's information is saved in my contacts 'list' on Gmail. Shoot him an email to let him know what happened, and he'll give you a call."

"Is it the same one that handled my situation?"

Dante shook his head. "No, but he's just as good. Come here and give me a kiss."

Sade did as he told her, hugging him as best as his cuffed hands behind his back would allow. He was glad he'd taken her to Georgia and New York, giving them a chance to rest and have some fun before having to deal with Jones's new bullshit.

Three Days Later

"Is this a joke?" Dante asked his attorney.

"No, and I don't need you to say anything to make the judge question why you're so surprised."

"But I *am* surprised," Dante admitted. "What the hell is going on?"

When Dante was transported for his court date, he wasn't expecting the charges to be dropped, but that was precisely what had happened.

"Give me a second, and I'll find out."

Dante nodded as Attorney Dennis made his way toward the judge next to the prosecutor. They had a whispered conversation before Dennis went back and stood next to Dante.

"Apparently, Jones is dropping the charges against you. He said he had you mistaken with someone else, and you're not the man who attacked him."

"What? Isn't that something they should have confirmed before arresting me?"

"Seeing as this works in your favor, pipe down with the questions," Dennis said low enough for only Dante to hear. "Because he didn't have any eyewitness testimonies, and the police didn't bother to get any security footage, you're free to go."

"Is there a chance he can change his mind and press charges again?"

"Yes, but that won't make him look credible. If you can, get any footage erased and make sure no one who was there will testify against you. That way, if he does, it'll be more difficult for the prosecution to make their case."

Dante nodded his understanding, hanging his head as he chuckled. He didn't know what kind of game Jones was playing. Was this supposed to be a show of power? Was this supposed to make Dante relax before Jones did something worse? Was it a ploy to make him anxious and keep him on high alert? Dante wasn't sure, but he'd be prepared either way. At that moment, he was just grateful to be going back home to Sade.

Dante got into bed as delicately as he could. He wanted his kisses to wake Sade up, not his body weight. A part of him wanted to be upset that she hadn't answered his calls, but she was in such a deep sleep that he could only smile when he walked in and saw her.

When he wrapped his arm around her, a quiet moan escaped him. Home wasn't the structure that surrounded him; home was Sade. The moment she was close, he instantly relaxed and felt at peace. She shifted against him but didn't wake up completely.

"It's just me," he whispered. Suddenly, Sade pulled in a deep breath and hopped up in bed. "Relax, Sade. It's me."

Clutching her chest, Sade took ragged breaths as she gripped his wrist. "Jesus, Dante. You almost made me pee on myself."

As serious as she was, Dante couldn't help but chuckle. "Who else would be in the bed with you, Smiley?"

"Hell, I thought I was having another dream where I thought it was you, but it was really Atlas."

Dante scratched his head, trying to process what the hell she'd just said. "Huh?"

She shook her head and gave him a dismissive wave of her hand. "Nothing. You're home! How did this happen?" She hugged his neck, and *that* was the greeting he'd hoped for.

After he ran down what happened in court, Sade said, "Is he playing a game we're unaware of? What reason would he possibly have to drop the charges? You don't think he has something worse up his sleeve, do you?"

"I considered that. Or, he could want me to owe him. I know his target has been on you, and that's mainly because he doesn't know I killed Willow. Maybe he thinks that because he didn't send me to jail, I will help him with you. Either way, letting me out will be an error in judgment for him before it ever becomes an issue for us."

"I hope you're right about that, but I'm just so glad you're home!"

As she straddled him and began to cover his face with kisses, Dante laughed as he confessed, "I'm glad to be home too."

SADE

Two Days Later
Mid-October

THE FEEL OF Dante's hand on Sade's thigh soothed her. After Jones's last stunt, they decided to go to their local FBI office. Jones had somehow maxed out her credit cards and emptied every one of her bank accounts except the offshore one with the money she'd taken from Dante. He'd texted her and said the money would be given to the families of her victims. That made Sade hesitate to go to the FBI. She didn't want to risk them looking into why Jones was on a rampage. After Dante assured her she didn't have to worry about that, she agreed.

"I'm going to keep you updated," Agent Foster said. "If anything pops up from us tracking the text messages and where the money was transferred, I'll call you as soon as possible."

"Thank you," Sade replied as she and Dante stood.

They shook Foster's hand and headed out of his office. "A part of me feels relieved that Jones went to such an extreme because now, someone is finally taking this seriously."

"I agree," Dante said, "I'll put back the money he took, bae. You know you don't have to worry about that."

"Thank you." She sighed, tightening her hand on his grip. "Do you think we still need to get a private investigator?"

"Let's see what Agent Foster will be able to do first. I'd rather Jones suffer in prison before he dies anyway."

As Dante opened the passenger door for her, Sade was briefly distracted by the feel of her phone vibrating. She waited until she was situated in his car before she pulled it out, smiling at the missed call from her grandmother.

She returned the call, and Ava's first words were, "Baby, I am *so* sorry."

Sade's brows wrinkled as she sat up in her seat. "For what, Grandma?"

"That detective from Vanzette stopped by here. He tried to convince us that you'd killed those women and—"

"Wait . . ." Sade chuckled, but it immediately turned into a frown as her nostrils flared. "Jones came to your *house*?"

Her words caused Dante to look in her direction.

"Yes, but it doesn't matter. I know why he's been harassing you. It's not because you killed those people."

Her heart palpitating, Sade swallowed hard. "Then why?"

"Jones . . . his first name is Terry. Terry Jones. That's *Tonya's husband*. Well, *ex*-husband."

Sade's shoulders went slack. "The woman who killed my parents . . . Jones is her ex-husband?"

"He is. I wouldn't be surprised if that's why he's after you."

"I get the connection, but that doesn't make sense. Why would he want to punish me? It's not like I had anything to do with his wife leaving him. Hell, if anything, it should be the other way around. I should have been going after him to get to her."

"Some people don't need a reason, but maybe one day you can ask him. My gut tells me he's holding you responsible for your father's actions. To him, maybe Martin is the reason he lost his wife and daughter, so he wants to make *his* daughter suffer."

Sade massaged her temple as she sighed. "That would explain why he's been hyperfocused on me. Thank you for telling me. This makes me feel a little better."

They talked for a while longer before Sade ended the call and let Dante in on what her grandmother had shared.

"You know what?" Dante said. "I agree. That would explain why he's obsessed with you. I knew it couldn't have been something as simple as him not wanting someone to get away with murder. And that's why we hadn't been able to find information about him doing this to anyone else in the past. This isn't normal behavior for him, which is why he wasn't arrested and his captain wasn't more helpful. This is strictly because of his wife and daughter, and he's seeking revenge."

"Son of a bitch," she muttered through gritted teeth.

"If this is personal, he's *not* gonna stop, baby."

"I know. I'm hoping the FBI can find something. It would serve him right to be in prison just like his wife. I didn't think anything could top finding out she killed my parents. Now, I have to deal with her psycho ex-husband trying to exact his own unnecessary revenge." Dante chuckled, causing her to ask, "What?"

"I don't know. It was different when I thought this was something random. Knowing about his daughter committing suicide because of the bullying she sustained . . . I kind of get why Jones is going after you. It's not like he can go after your father. If someone did something to you or our baby, I'd want revenge too, and I don't think I'd care where and from whom I had to get it." He sucked his teeth as he shook his head, a clear representation of his inner conflict. "Granted, this is all Tonya's fault. But she's already being punished, and he wouldn't punish her for the daughter's suicide anyway. So, who's better than the man who his wife cheated with?"

"And he's gone, which makes his children Jones's next victim. Wow."

Silence engulfed them, leaving Sade with the quietness it took to process the information she'd just received.

A Few Days Later

The goofy grin that had been on Dante's face since the appointment made Sade laugh every time she looked at him. He was happy and proud they were having a boy, and Sade was too. They'd spent the last two hours looking at clothing and bouncing around ideas for the nursery now that they finally knew the sex of their baby.

"I can't wait to start decorating now," Sade cooed, wrapping her arms around him.

"I can't believe we're having a boy. I'm still stuck on that. My dream girl is giving me my first child, a junior." Dante pushed her hair out of her face and off her shoulders before cupping her cheeks. "I never thought this would be our reality. A part of me is glad Imani tried to frame me. It finally led me to you."

"I don't regret not one thing we've had to do to get to this moment, babe—at all."

A low hum escaped him, but before he could connect his lips with hers, Dante was pulling out his phone. A frown quickly covered his face.

"He's at the house," Dante said, quickly grabbing her hand and leading her out of the store.

"Jones?"

"Yeah."

Sade pulled up their camera app, but an incoming call from their neighbor kept her from opening the feed.

"Hello?"

"Sade, I wanted to let you know a man just kicked your door in. I had my husband to call the police. He's wrapping up with them now."

Relief filled her, knowing Jones couldn't do too much damage before he was stopped. He'd better damn well hope the police got there before they did.

"I see him on the camera. Thank you for calling, and tell Yancy thank you for calling the police as well."

"Of course."

Felicia ended the call, and Sade opened the living room camera. She watched Jones spray paint their sofa before ripping paintings off the wall. Unable to watch anymore, she closed her eyes and tried to take some deep breaths.

Dante's speed was so fast it seemed they made it home in no time. When they arrived, the police were there; Jones was not. Sade allowed Dante to handle the police report. She was too jaded to talk to anyone. After they left, he joined her in their bedroom. Dante sat on the edge of the bed next to her and took her hand into his.

"What do you want to do?" he asked. "I can clean up what he damaged in the living room and dining room. Thankfully, he couldn't go further before he heard the sirens and fled. If you're uncomfortable staying here, we can go to a hotel or one of the other houses."

"I'm tired of hotels," she whined. "I'm not scared. I don't think it was a coincidence that he came while we were gone."

"Yeah, he wouldn't have done this if we were here. The good thing is, this now opens a case against him in Memphis."

Sade nodded and palmed her face. "I need to go to my island. That'll make me feel better."

Dante kissed her temple. "Then that's where we'll go. I have something to handle real quick, so I will have Eric and Jessica come over. When I return, I'll take care of the living room and dining room."

"You don't have to, baby, I will."

"We can do it together before I leave then."

"What're you about to do?"

"Pay Jones a visit."

Sade's Audio Journal

"My mind has been so scattered, I haven't been able to process a coherent thought or even record it. I've never hated a person more than I hate Jones. Well, maybe my sister when we were kids, but that's another story. This man is diabolical. What makes it so frustrating is he's slippery. He knows the law and how to evade it. He also knows how to mess with us without actually touching us. Jones being so out of reach is driving me crazy. I can't wait for him to be caught. This needs to be over soon."

DANTE

Several Hours Later

Dante didn't want to mention it to Sade until he was sure it would lead to something. Because Vanzette was a small town where almost everyone knew everyone, it didn't take much for Lathan and Veronica to ask around for information on Tonya and Terry. Dante cared less about their marriage and more about whether anyone knew where Jones currently lived. It just so happened that Lathan's barber knew exactly where Jones lived because his brother's landscaping company cut his grass.

As it neared midnight, Dante figured Jones wouldn't return home soon. He probably wouldn't come back if he were in hiding because of what he'd done. Dante headed to the front door, knocking, though he was sure no one was inside. After waiting a few minutes and not getting an answer, he prepared to pick the lock but didn't have to. It was already unlocked.

Chuckling, Dante made his way inside. Vanzette was truly a safe place. So safe, most of the citizens didn't feel the need to lock their doors. He was surprised Jones kept his doors unlocked, though, and a part of him wondered if it was a trap. Taking the risk, Dante figured he couldn't be arrested for breaking and entering if the door was unlocked.

He went room by room, not finding anything unordinary—until he reached Jones's bedroom. There, he had a wall covered with pictures of Sade, Patrice, Trina, and Willow and facts about their cases. To the side of that was a dartboard with Sade's picture taped on it. Dante took several photos to show Agent Foster before looking in Jones's closet.

Instead of clothes, he found pictures of him, Tonya, and Dena. There was a letter written in red, promising Dena justice. Candles lined the floor in front of pillows as if he sat there for hours. Dante took pictures of that too before leaving. Finding that had creeped him out. If he needed proof that Jones had gone off the deep end, that was it.

The Next Afternoon

Dante entered the kitchen, where he found Sade shuffling around in his T-shirt. Despite the circumstances, she looked beautiful with her puffy ponytail and glowing skin.

"Hello, Smiley."

"Good afternoon, handsome."

He held her waist, giving her a few pecks on the lips before pulling away.

"I missed you last night and this morning."

Dante sat at the island as she poured him a cup of coffee. Last night, she was asleep when he got in bed and still asleep when he got up and left this morning.

"Thank you," he said, accepting the coffee. "I need this."

"Did you get any sleep at all?"

"Not much. What I found at Jones's house disturbed me. I was too anxious to sleep. When Foster returned my call, I headed to his office."

"You were at his house yesterday? What did you find?"

Sade moved the cutting board from the counter to the island so she could look at him while he talked. She eyed him as she chopped the onions for her greens as he spoke.

"Yeah. He had a shrine to his daughter and a wall dedicated to you and the shit that happened in Vanzette." Dante pulled out his phone and handed it to her after a few swipes. "I shared this with Agent Foster, and he suggested we use this to get a restraining order against him. He said they weren't able to track the money to an account that is attached to him, so that was a dead end. They tracked the phone to someone in China, which was a bust too. At this point, he thinks the restraining order, breaking and entering, and vandalizing will be the things that he can be charged with, which will stick."

Sade had to tear her eyes away from the pictures on Dante's phone.

With a nod, she cleared her throat. "I want to be happy because this is progress, but I can't lie and say this isn't bothering me."

"Same. It really creeped me out. I didn't want to tell you, but I felt you needed to know."

"Thank you for not keeping this from me. If all else fails, at least we have his address now. I don't want you to have to kill him. We have enough blood on our hands."

"I agree, but if he does something else, I'm going back to his house, and I'm not leaving until he's dead. I know we said he deserves to suffer, and prison will be the best place for him to do that, but this needs to end, Sade—now."

Not bothering to disagree, she told him to rest while she prepped their dinner for later. But Dante wouldn't be able to rest until he knew Jones would be out of their lives for good.

Four Days Later

The only downside to being at Sade's island was that you had to wait for the ferry to enter and leave. They had to wait three days before the ferry would be available, but now that they were there, it was more than worth the wait. Dante understood why the island was her place of peace. Completely secluded, she didn't have to worry about anything or anyone. She had the kitchen fully stocked, so they decided to cook together after a brief rest.

They agreed not to talk about Jones or anything else happening in Memphis. Their ex parte hearing would be held in six days, which was the only reason Dante was looking forward to returning. The restraining order was a start, though Dante wasn't sure if Jones would even take it seriously.

Dante started his Kem playlist. His arms wrapped around Sade from behind, and as Kem sang about sharing his life with his woman, Dante serenaded Sade. She turned in his arms, wrapping her arms around him. They swayed around the kitchen, singing and staring into each other's eyes. By the time the song was over, Dante was sure he loved her a little bit more.

SADE

As THEY STARTED their third movie of the evening, Sade snuggled up against Dante's chest. She fed him a handful of popcorn and jalapeño peppers from the bowl in her lap. The last two days had been so peaceful, and Sade was grateful for that. Her phone had been off, and being able to detach from the world worked wonders for her soul. When Dante's hands went to her belly, she smiled.

"I can't believe I thought I could do this without you."

"I can't believe I hadn't shown you how real my love for you was, and you felt like you had to."

"Well, you've definitely shown me now."

Her eyes lowered to the beautiful ring she'd been wearing ever since they made things official. If Dante had gone that far out to ask her to be his woman, she couldn't wait to see what he'd do when he asked her to be his wife.

"And I'll never stop." He kissed the top of her head. "I'm going to court you for the rest of our lives. I never want you to doubt how I feel about you." He kissed her cheek. "How much I love you." He kissed her neck. "How happy I am to be with you."

"Even with all the drama?"

"Even with all the drama. I love you, bae. Nothing will ever change my commitment to you."

Sitting up slightly, Sade put the bowl of popcorn on the side table behind his head. She straddled him, then lowered her lips to his. With all the hell happening in Memphis, Sade found solace in going through it with Dante by her side.

As his hands lowered to her ass, Sade circled her hips against him. It wasn't long before their bodies were connected as one. The slow ride she took them on had her toes curling as she moaned his name. The moment wouldn't last forever, but Sade was grateful for the pleasurable, climactic escape.

The Day Before the Return to Memphis

The day had started perfectly. They swam in the ocean. While she painted, Dante read. They grilled chicken and fish with corn on the cob and salad as a great day turned into a great evening. Now, Sade was so uncomfortable she didn't even want to get in bed.

Her stomach seemed to have grown while they were away, and she was having more issues with her back. The cramps in her stomach made it difficult for her to breathe. She gripped the island in the kitchen, opting for short, choppy breaths that only intensified the pain.

"What's wrong, Day?" Dante asked, walking over to her. Absently, he tossed his water bottle into the trash.

"My back is killing me, and these cramps came out of nowhere."

"Try to take some deep breaths with me."

She shook her head and squeezed her eyes shut. "I-I can't."

"Yes, you can, and you'll feel better too. Breathe through them with me."

Dante took her hands into his, guiding her through deep breaths until the cramps subsided. He helped her get into bed and surprised her when he pulled her heating pad out of his bag. Sade laughed as her eyes watered.

"Figured you might need this."

"You're a lifesaver."

"I'll give you a massage and put you to bed."

"Thank you, baby."

Sade rolled over onto her side and allowed Dante to put the heating pad on her back. She used it for about twenty minutes before he removed it and massaged her back until she fell into a peaceful sleep.

Back in Memphis

As soon as Sade took her phone off airplane mode, the notifications started to pop up. She stared at the text from an unknown number. Knowing it was from Jones made her want to ignore it, but a part of her was curious about the video attachment.

"All right, Smiley. The bags are inside. I'm about to go for a run. Do you need anything before I leave?"

Forcing a smile, Sade shook her head. "I'm good, Tay. Enjoy your run."

He gave her a kiss on the forehead before heading out. Sade showered and climbed into bed, where the urge to watch the video consumed her. Finally, she surrendered to her curiosity and opened it. The first thing she saw was her mother's tombstone, which caused her to sit up in bed.

When Jones came into view, he said, "I wonder how your mom would feel if she had to grieve you like Patrice, Trina, and

Willow's moms are grieving them." A slow smile lifted the corners of his lips. "Too bad she's already dead."

A clipped scream escaped her before she slapped her hand over her opened mouth. Tears flowed from her, but they weren't sad tears. They were *angry* tears. *That* was the final straw. Now . . . Sade wanted him dead.

DANTE

After the Hearing

SOMETHING WAS WRONG. The judge granted them a temporary restraining order until their hearing in fifteen days, and Sade didn't seem to care. She seemed to be in her own little world as the judge told them Jones would be served as soon as possible. What Dante thought was a win and their getting back in control only seemed to drain her further. He waited until they were in the car to ask, "What's wrong, Sade? That was a win back there."

"I don't think it's going to matter."

"Why not?"

She shrugged, looking out of the window. "I don't think he's going to stop. He has to die."

Her statement caught Dante so off guard he didn't respond immediately. Shifting slightly in his seat, he took her hand in his and used it to pull her attention to him.

"Talk to me. Tell me what happened."

Sade used her free hand to get her phone out of her purse. She handed it to him after pulling up a video. Dante's calm was replaced with anger as he watched it.

"When did he send this?"

"The day we came back."

"Why didn't you tell me, baby?"

"I didn't want to even think about it. I just . . . had to shut down to keep from being consumed by anger and sadness. I wanted to go to Jones's house and put a bullet between his eyes." She scoffed and wiped a tear that had slipped down her cheek.

"He hasn't been back home since he broke into our home."

Finally, Sade looked at him. "How do you know he hasn't been back?"

Dante hadn't told her everything he'd done the day Jones violated their home. He also didn't tell her about his visit to see Imani the next day before returning home. Imani gave him the information about a man who took anyone's life for the right price. As much as he wanted to kill Jones himself, what Captain Bennit said was true—if anything happened to Jones, Dante and Sade would be the prime suspects. On the off chance the emergency temporary restraining order wasn't granted, Dante had a backup plan in place to have Jones killed.

"He's been watching the house," Dante continued to share, "waiting for Jones to arrive. I was supposed to call him after the hearing today and tell him what to do. He texted me before court and told me that Jones still hadn't arrived."

"If he doesn't go home, how will they serve him? The no-contact clause won't matter if he doesn't get the papers. He can still send us texts and emails if he wants to."

"Well, they are aware that he was a detective in Vanzette. I won't be surprised if they try to utilize their services. The judge did tell us to work with them directly to receive confirmation from the sheriff that he was served. Hopefully, they will have other contact information for him and will know where he could be hiding. If not, we'll handle this our own way as soon as he pops back up."

"I'm just ready for this to be over," she grumbled, putting on her seat belt.

Dante was too.

A Few Days Later

Dante wasn't sure what Eric wanted to discuss when he asked him to join him for an early afternoon round of golf, but it certainly wasn't an invitation to go into business together. Though Dante appreciated the offer and the fact that he and Jessica trusted that he had nothing to do with Imani's schemes, he didn't plan on saying yes. It seemed Jessica and Eric were doing well for themselves, and after what happened at Ian's firm, Dante didn't want to risk anyone else getting caught up in his mess.

As they rode to the next hole, Dante expressed just that.

"I appreciate the offer, but I'll have to decline. After what happened with Ian, I want to go into business alone. I don't want my name to be synonymous with drama in our industry."

"I feel you. Do you think that would be the case, though? How much more can he do?"

Dante chuckled. "I'm not trying to find out. That's why I'm not opening the business until he's out of the picture. Plus, I want to be there as much as possible for Day. I can't imagine how hard this has been for her. This is her first baby, and she's having to deal with all this bullshit."

"Man, I've been praying for her. Both of y'all. She seems to be handling it well, though."

"By grace," Dante said, pulling his phone out of his pocket. "I want to give her whatever she wants and needs for all that she's gone through. Now and when the baby gets here. After that, I'll get back to my business." He accepted the call from Lathan with, "Lathan, wassup, man?"

"Hey, uh . . . I'm going to send you a Facebook link to watch a video Jones posted. It's gone viral."

"A'ight, thanks."

"You good?" Eric asked.

"I'm not sure. Give me a sec." Dante hopped off the golf cart and clicked the link to the video.

"I hate it has come to this," Jones said, "but I have no other choice. Earlier this morning, I was served a restraining order at the request of Dante Williams and Sade Griffin. This happened while I was temporarily staying with my old captain, who advised me not to make this video, but desperate times call for desperate measures."

Dante steeled himself, unsure what Jones would say next. *"I've been staying with Captain Bennit of the Vanzette Police Department because I didn't want to return home. I did something illegal in Memphis and knew the police would be after me. They want to arrest me for breaking into Dante and Sade's home."*

Jones chuckled. *"Why did I do it? Well . . . I've been trying to make their lives as miserable as I possibly can. See, before they went back to Memphis, they stayed in Vanzette. There, two murders were committed, and a woman went missing. While I don't think Dante was involved in the murders, Sade committed them because of him. The charges brought against her were dropped because of a bad choice by me, but I am 100 percent certain Sade Griffin killed Patrice Baker, Trina Roe, and maybe even Willow Frank.*

"Since the police are unwilling to make Sade pay, I tried to. Unfortunately, I've reached the end of my rope. With the restraining order, it's out of my hands. I'll probably be arrested soon and will be unable to get justice for her victims. If you want to pick up where I left off, their address is . . ."

"Are you fucking kidding me!" Dante roared, exiting out of the video to call Sade. As he hopped back onto the golf cart, he told Eric to take him back toward the entrance so he could head home because not only had Jones told thousands of people he believed Sade was a murderer, but he'd also given them their address too.

JONES

"YOU'RE HOPELESS," BENNIT complained. "I agreed to let you stay here because you promised to stay out of trouble. You do understand if people harass or try to harm Sade at her home, they can add doxing to your list of growing charges?"

Jones tried to sip his beer, but Bennit ripped it from his hand.

"You have to go, Jones. You're doing too much."

Jones chuckled as he stood. "I wouldn't have had to do that if you hadn't let MPD convince you to serve me."

"What did you expect me to do? Lie and say I didn't know where you were?"

"Yes! That's *exactly* what you were supposed to do."

"No." Bennit shook his head as he placed his hands on his hips. "I let you stay here because of the warrant. I knew they'd be looking for you at your place. So, I only let you stay because you said you had some things you wanted to get in order before you turned yourself in. Now, I feel like you said that just to get me to agree. You never planned on going back to Memphis and turning yourself in . . . did you?"

Not bothering to respond, Jones headed to the guest bedroom he'd been occupying to pack his things. Yes, he may have lied about his intentions, but he had no choice. He couldn't go home and figured the police captain's home would be the last place Memphis officers would look for him. While that may have been true, Jones hadn't considered how easy it would be for Bennit to snitch on him.

When he finished packing his things, he grumbled, "Thanks for nothing," in Bennit's direction as he headed for the front door.

"Ungrateful bastard," Bennit replied. "Go to Memphis and do the right thing!"

Jones was going to Memphis, but it *wasn't* to turn himself in.

SADE

SADE'S BLADDER WOKE her up. When she got back in bed, she saw that she had received several missed calls and text messages from Veronica. Fearing something had happened to her or Lathan, she called her back immediately.

"Sade!" Veronica yelled into the receiver. "I've been trying to get in touch with you."

"I was asleep. Are you okay?"

"I'm fine. I was worried about you. Look at what I sent you."

"O-okay." After disconnecting the call, Sade went to their text thread and clicked on the Facebook link Veronica had sent.

The longer she watched Jones's video, the more infuriated she became.

"Shit. This is *not* good," Sade mumbled, hopping out of bed. She checked the time to see when Jones posted the video. It had only been up for an hour and already had thousands of shares. As she packed both her and Dante's bags, the sound of glass shattering gained her attention.

Her phone vibrated, and a part of Sade didn't even want to answer. She grabbed it from the bed as loud chatter from outside permeated the room. Dante's name and picture on her phone brought tears to her eyes, but that wasn't the time to be emotional.

Sade answered with "Baby," as she crept down the hall.

"I need you to get out of the house. I'll meet you at—"

"It's too late. People are here. They..." Her eyes widened. "There's like ten people outside. They broke the window, and now, they're trying to kick down the door."

"Okay. Listen to me. I'm on my way, but I probably won't get there in time. I need you to go to the garage and leave. Even if they try to find you, you should get someplace where other people are around."

Sade shook her head as she grabbed two knives from the kitchen and headed back to their room. "No. I'm tired of running and being uprooted. I'm tired of hotels." She laughed. "I'm tired of Jones." As she grabbed her 9 mm, Sade told him, "If anyone trespasses and enters our home, I'm going to kill them. And I pray to God that Jones is out there too."

Dante sighed and cursed under his breath. "All right, Smiley. I'm doing one-twenty. I'm trying to get there as quickly as I can."

More glass shattered as Sade nodded her agreement. Voices spilled, and footsteps pounded on the tile.

"Okay, Tay. I love you."

"I love you too."

"If anything happens to me..."

"It won't. *Please*, bae."

"If you come in here, I'm going to shoot!" Sade warned, ending the call and extending the gun.

She heard laughter before three women rounded the corner and entered her room.

"You killed my sister, bitch?" The woman with wide eyes and curly hair lifted a bat. "Now, I'm going to kill you."

As the woman charged in Sade's direction, Sade fired. The other two women screamed and fled the room—bypassing bullets in the process. Sade hopped over the woman's body, making sure no one else was in their home. She released more bullets, causing everyone else who was outside to flee. Her entire body trembled as she slid down the wall. Ragged breaths escaped her as her grip on the gun loosened.

"Fuck!" she roared before finally releasing her tears. Cramps caused Sade to grab her stomach as she groaned. Her baby's discomfort only increased her pain—emotionally and physically. "I'm sorry, little one," she whispered, inhaling a sizzling breath. "Mama's *so* sorry."

Resting her head against the wall, Sade continued to breathe deeply. When the cramps subsided, she called 911.

DANTE

Dante barely got his car in park before hopping out and rushing to Sade. She was seated on the back of an ambulance, bobbing her head to whatever the officer said. A car came to a slow creep, rolling the window down to toss bottles in their direction as they yelled, "Murderer!"

As the car swerved down the street, Dante cupped Sade's cheeks and stared into her eyes. "Are you okay? The baby?"

"We're fine. My blood pressure was up, and my stomach was killing me, but we're fine."

A sigh of relief escaped him as he pulled her into his arms. "What happened?"

Sniffling, Sade buried her face deeper into his chest. "I killed her."

"Who?" Dante tilted her face with her chin.

"Trina's sister. She came at me with a bat. I warned them if they came in that I would shoot. She didn't believe me."

"Mr. Williams?" Dante turned at the sound of his name being called. "I'm Detective Tate."

With one arm still wrapped around Sade, Dante shook his hand.

"We're advising the two of you to vacate the property. I'll have Officer Murphy escort you wherever you want to go to ensure no one follows you. That post has gone viral, and people have been riding by nonstop since we arrived. Do you know where you can go until this dies down?"

Dante looked at Sade, and he could tell by her distant stare that she was starting to disassociate.

"Yeah, uh, I'm going to take her to our beach house in San Diego."

"Okay, good. Just as a precaution, the bedroom is an active crime scene. I'm sure you'll need to pack some things, but be mindful of what you'll see. Murphy will lead you back inside when you're ready."

Dante nodded, cupping Sade's cheek. His touch caused her to breathe again as she looked into his eyes.

"I'm going to pack us a couple of bags before we head to the airport."

"I had already started," she told him, her eyes shifting again.

"Hey," he called softly. She blinked her eyes but remained distant. "Smiley." Dante lowered his hand to her stomach, rubbing it until she looked at him.

"Hmm?"

"Are you okay? Seriously."

She nodded her head as she gritted her teeth. "I'm just tired, Dante."

As much as he wanted to hold her, Dante gave her a quick kiss and headed inside with Murphy. The sooner he got their bags packed, the sooner they could leave. And at that point, Dante was sure getting as far away from the house as possible was the only thing that would help Sade.

Two Days Later

The light had begun to return to Sade's eyes. Like Dante knew it would be, the beach house was her favorite of the three homes he'd purchased for them. She sat out on the beach all yesterday—coming inside only to use the bathroom. She ate out there, talked to herself and God, and stayed well after the sun had gone down.

The next morning, they started their day walking a couple of miles along the beach after breakfast. Now, they were at the farmers' market, where Sade got her fill of fruit, flowers, and dainty jewelry.

Her thumb stroked his hand as she sipped her tea. "This is perfect, Tay. The beach, this market, the normality of no one knowing us here. This is exactly what I needed."

"We can stay for as long as you want to, baby."

"Maybe until my next appointment. That's the only thing I care about."

"That works. I can do a grocery order and have it delivered to make sure we'll have everything we need." She gave him that beautiful smile he'd fallen in love with when they were kids. "There's that smile. I missed that."

Sade licked her lips and laughed softly. "You know I'm always smiling and happy when I'm with you."

"Nah, shit's been rough, Sade. I can't romanticize the fact that us being together has been . . ." He shook his head. "A magnet for drama. Sometimes, I wonder if Grandma Ava was right. And I know I've said that to you before, but I feel like I'm failing you. I feel like I can't protect you from this. I'm sorry, Smiley."

Sade sucked her teeth before smiling and wrapping her arms around him. "If anyone should apologize, it's me. I'm the one who lied when you had amnesia. I did what I did to them. This is the snowball effect of my actions. So, if this is your way of preparing to say I'm better off without you, save it. There's no doubt your life would be a hell of a lot more peaceful if I hadn't . . . You know. So, if you want to end things to return to a normal state, I'll accept that, but I love you, and I don't blame you for any of this. If it's up to me, you're not getting rid of me."

Pulling her closer, Dante lowered his lips to hers. As long as she was willing, he'd put forth the effort. But if at any point it seemed she would be better off without being attached to him, Dante would end things . . . no matter how hard that would be.

A Few Days Later

"Where is my sister?" Imani asked.

Dante crossed his arms over his chest, wondering if he wanted to bring Sade the phone. They had spent the afternoon in Balboa Park, and she was so inspired they went to CVS and grabbed several sketchbooks for her to fill. Now, she was on the beach drawing until it was time for them to leave for the dinner cruise.

Dante looked at the phone on the table as if he could see Imani. "Why?"

Imani sucked her teeth. "I've been calling y'all for days since Grandma told me what happened. I want to make sure she's okay." Dante was so caught off guard by her statement he couldn't respond. "Hello?"

"Y-yeah, I'm here." Clearing his throat, he chuckled. "Since when do you care about anyone other than yourself?"

Imani huffed. "Where is my sister, Dante?"

"She's on the beach drawing."

"Why hasn't she been answering my calls?"

"Our phones have been in airplane mode. I check mine once a day to make sure our families are good. Other than that, I'm keeping her as stress free as possible. Which means . . . no phones."

"That's good, I suppose. But I want to talk to her myself, so I'll know she's okay. It won't take long, I promise."

"A'ight, but . . . What's gotten into you?"

Dante took the call off speaker and put the phone to his ear as he headed off the patio toward the beach.

"Things are changing between us. I don't know. She's . . . tolerable to me now."

Dante chuckled. "That sounds more like you, but it also sounds like a compliment. Regardless, I'm glad y'all are getting along better."

"Mhm. We don't have to talk while you take her the phone. I like *her* better. Not you."

Imani's playful tone couldn't be ignored as he released a howl of laughter. "Yes, ma'am. Trust me, I don't like you either."

She snickered, and it felt like they'd made good progress for some reason. Progress toward what, Dante wasn't sure. But progress, nonetheless.

"Smiley," Dante called as he neared her.

She looked back, and he was temporarily speechless between her glow and the sun highlighting her gorgeous smile.

"Your sister wants to talk to you. Are you up for that?"

"Ooh, gimme!" Her hand extended for the phone as she wiggled on her beach towel.

"What the holy hell is going on?" Dante said to himself, but both sisters heard and laughed.

"Hi, sissy," Sade almost cooed into the phone. "I'm fine. I am, I promise."

At the sound of her laughter, Dante took backward steps to return to the patio. He wasn't sure when the shift had happened between them, but he meant it when he said he was grateful for it.

SADE

As SHY AS Sade felt, she didn't ask Dante to stop taking pictures of her. Somehow, their playing in the sand turned into a mini photoshoot with her as the model. Her head flung back as she laughed, her hand resting on her sand-covered belly.

"Babe, that's enough!"

"Nah. I'll never have enough pictures of you."

Dante took a few more snaps before sitting next to her. Sade rested her head on his shoulder. They'd been in San Diego for two weeks, and each day that passed decreased her desire to return home.

They planned to drive to Malibu, Pasadena, and Los Angeles over the next week. Sade was most looking forward to shopping. As much as she missed her small family, she wished she didn't have to return to Memphis. Almost daily, her peace was being robbed there. First, by the turn her relationship with Atlas had taken, and now . . . Jones. A part of her wanted just to stay in California and never return. But that felt too much like running away and allowing Jones to think he'd won. That was something Sade could *never* do.

"Is it still trending?" she asked.

"The video? Nah. It was finally taken down."

"Good." She paused. "Um . . . Trina's family. Have you seen—"

"Sade, I thought we agreed—"

"I know. I just . . . I can't imagine how that family feels. I can deny Trina, but I can't deny that I killed her sister."

"They shouldn't have come into our fucking home. No charges are being pressed against you because you have every right to defend yourself. If they feel some type of way about that, they can take it up with Jones for sending them out like that."

"Woof," Sade chuckled, placing kisses all over his face. "Someone's upset. Calm down, baby."

Dante sucked his teeth, but his expression softened the more she kissed him. "I don't want you to feel bad over that. You did the right thing. If you hadn't shot her, you'd be dead. And I care far more about your life than any of theirs."

Deciding to change the subject, Sade asked, "Are you bored with not working yet?"

"I'm getting there," he admitted with a smile. "I love traveling with you, but it's that part of me that thrives when I'm working and doing my purpose that feels lacking, you know?"

"I understand. I felt the same way when I couldn't paint. Being inspired by the job Veronica commissioned me for was my saving grace. Why don't you go back to work, babe?"

"I've been thinking about starting up online. Everything I do is online anyway. I don't need a building or staff. That would just cut into my profit. I was thinking about renting some office space by the hour when I needed to meet with clients in person, but other than that, I can do everything else virtually."

"That's good, Tay. I think you should definitely go for that."

"Yeah . . . Eric and Jessica took all the clients when that mess with Imani went down, but they want to give me ours when I reopen. So, I won't have that awkward stage of finding new clients."

"Yay! When do you plan to start?"

"Maybe once we get back home and get settled. I want to make sure you're good first, though. I had one of my old homeboys fix the window and pull up that carpet to replace it. How are you feeling about going back? I think we should move."

Sade sighed as she looked out toward the ocean. "Unfortunately, I think we will have to move too. I don't think I'll ever feel safe there knowing our address has been blasted all over social media."

"Yeah, I'd be too paranoid. I know you're tired of staying in hotels, so how about we stay here until I find us something there? You said you wanted to stay in Memphis until after you had the baby, right? Is that still the case?"

"Yes, I guess. I don't want to have to change doctors. I am tired of hotels, but if we have to stay in one, I'm okay with that."

"As much as I hate to say this, maybe we do need to stay in an apartment for now. One with a doorman and security. One that will require guests to check in. I don't like the idea of people being able to get to you when I'm not around. If we get a house, I'd always want a guard there with you."

Sade shook her head as she moved it from his shoulder. "I don't want a guard. I know they'll be for my protection, but I like my freedom and space. I think an apartment with security and a doorman is good, especially if we plan to travel more after the baby is born."

"Cool. I'll go ahead and do an application for those new luxury apartments in Germantown. They will probably be best. We can view them when we get back to Memphis."

"Okay," Sade agreed before standing and heading to the water to dip her toes in. Moving again so quickly would have been too much to handle on her own, but she was grateful Dante was taking the lead.

With all the craziness happening with Jones's doxing, Sade and Dante almost forgot about their hearing. They rushed back to Memphis, just to be held up by TSA. What should have been a quick run through security turned into them being held separately for hours. As frustrated as Sade was, she tried to remain calm. Clearly, they would miss their hearing, and Sade hated waiting until the day of to fly back out. Granted, she never had issues with TSA before, but . . .

When she'd had enough, Sade stood from the white bench and walked over to the locked door. Beating on it, she yelled, "Hey! I have a court date! Let me the hell up out of here!"

A minute or so passed before the TSA officer who had initially asked her to follow him came and unlocked the door.

"All right, Ms. Griffin. You're free to go."

With a roll of her eyes, Sade exited the room. "I told you I didn't have any drugs in my bag. This was a total waste of time."

"Hey," he called, causing Sade to look back at him. "If you make it to court in time, make sure you tell my uncle Terry I said hello."

Like Sade thought they would, they missed the hearing. Thanks to Jones's nephew holding them up at the airport, the judge did not extend the temporary restraining order, and they would have to start the process all over again.

"I can't," Sade said, feeling defeated as they walked to the car. "I can't go through the waiting period again. Yes, it was great not getting texts or emails from Jones while we waited for the hearing, but I can't go through this again."

"You won't have to," Dante assured her. "I still have my man sitting on his house. As soon as Jones shows up, he will hold him there for me."

"I just can't believe the judge didn't even hear us out about his nephew holding us for hours. How is that fair?"

Dante chuckled. "Fairness doesn't matter when it comes to the law. We tried to do it the right now, and now, we'll handle it *our* way."

"And Jones wasn't even here," she continued, half-listening to Dante as he opened the car door for her. "He gets to not be present with no punishment, yet because we were late, the order is no longer valid? That's dumb!" With a growl, she plopped down into the seat and crossed her arms over her chest with a pout. "I'm ready to go back to San Diego already."

Amusement filled Dante as he closed the door and walked to the driver's side, but Sade didn't care if he laughed at her. She'd grown weary of trying to do things the right, peaceful way. If Jones wanted a war, they'd give him one.

Sade stared at her grandparents' home. She had no urgency to go inside. She decided to stay with them because she didn't want to stay at a hotel. But as she sat outside their home, her gut told her she'd be better off at a hotel. She called Dante. Hours ago, it seemed like a bearable plan for them to part ways until they moved into the apartment. While she stayed with her grandparents, he'd be with his parents. Now, she was missing the peace from being with her man already.

"Hello, Smiley," he answered, and like always, it made her smile.

"Hi. Are you still at the house?"

"Yeah, we have everything packed up now. I think the moving company will have one more trip to the storage unit, and then, that will be it."

"Good. I'm just glad they were able to help with the move since it was such short notice."

"Money talks with all things."

"Have you heard back from the apartment?"

"Yeah, the lease agent called. The application was approved, and we can look at a unit whenever you want. She said we can move in in two weeks."

Sade sighed as she nodded. "Okay. I guess I can make it two weeks here."

"Has something happened?"

"Not yet. I haven't even gone inside yet. I just feel like they will give me hell about Trina's sister. Even though it was self-defense, you know they are kind of hard on me."

"Yeah. Well, you don't have to stay there, Day. My parents are more than okay with you being there, and we can always get a hotel suite. It's up to what you want to deal with less—being in a hotel again or hearing your grandparents' mouths."

She laughed. "You're right about that. I'm gonna try with them first. Hopefully, not seeing me for two weeks will soften them toward me. If it doesn't, we can go to a hotel."

"I'm cool with that. I'm going to miss sleeping with you, though."

"Same. I've gotten the best sleep of my life in your arms."

"How about I call you when we're done here? If they are going to give you a hard time, it will happen as soon as you walk through the door. Then you can let me know you've changed your mind about staying there, and I'll get us a suite downtown."

That made Sade chuckle. "You act like you know me so well."

"I do. So, I'll call you in about an hour so you can tell me to get the suite."

"Okay, okay. I'm going to prove you wrong, but call me anyway."

They shared declarations of love before Sade headed to the front door. She knocked then let herself in with her key. After going to the twins' room to speak to them, she temporarily got caught up with helping them find an outfit to go to the movies later that evening. When she was done, she headed to the kitchen, where she found her grandparents reading and sipping coffee at the table.

"Hey," she spoke, looking from one to the other.

Her grandfather's eyes lifted from his book. As he peered at her over his glasses, Barron smiled. "You look refreshed."

"I am. The time away was exactly what I needed."

"How did the hearing go?"

"We were late, so it was dismissed. Jones's nephew works for TSA and kept us at the airport for hours," Sade shared as she sat at the table.

"So, you'll have to start the process all over again?"

"Yes, but I don't think we're going to."

Sade stared at her grandmother, who had yet to say a word. "Hey, Grandma."

Ava set down her book, crossing her hands on top of it. Sade sighed as her head tilted because she knew what was about to come.

"You killed that girl."

"She and ten other people were in my home. She had a bat and was about to hit me. How else do you think I could have handled that?"

"You could've shot her in the leg and let the police handle her."

With a chuckle, Sade shook her head. Her fingers tapped the table as she looked from Ava to Barron.

"That's easy to say, but when you're in that moment and your life is in danger, you're not thinking about shooting them somewhere to spare their life. I can promise you, she wasn't going to spare mine."

Ava's tongue clicked against her mouth. "I keep trying to tell you it will only get worse. You lied to your sister and Dante while he was there with you. You slept with him knowing he was married to someone else."

"Will you stop!" she yelled, slamming her palm against the table. "Yes, I lied, but I wouldn't have had to if Imani hadn't tried to blame him for her crimes. I lied to save his life and to keep him free, and you're not going to make me feel bad about that. What I'm going through isn't Karma; it's the effect of a deranged man who is after me because of something that I had nothing to do with. And maybe, just maybe, this could have been avoided if either of you had told me and Imani the damn truth!

"Had I known about my parents and the Joneses, I could have recognized him while I was in Vanzette and been prepared for this. I could have gone to his captain and let him know he would be biased because of my parents and gotten him off the case before he had time to focus on me. But because the two of you decided I didn't need to know that my parents were murdered, you left me with a huge blind spot! So, I don't want to hear you say anything about this being what I 'deserve' because of Karma because it's *not* Karma, Grandma.

"It's me paying for my dad's cheating. It's me paying for you not telling me the truth. If anyone should feel bad about what the hell is happening in my life, it should be you! Now, I've tried to keep the peace between us, but I'm not doing this anymore. Since you can't seem to accept the fact that this is not a conversation I'm going to have every time Jones does something crazy, I'm staying away like you wanted me to weeks ago."

"Sade, wait," Barron said as he stood from his seat, but she ignored him.

She was more upset by her grandmother's words than what happened in court. Sade was tired of her grandmother's pessimistic attitude. She missed the days when, even when Ava didn't like what she was doing, she tried to guide her positively and with love. The advice she gave was often a life lesson Sade appreciated because it was something she believed she could benefit from. As Ava aged, she was starting to become looser at the lip, and most of what she said when she didn't agree with Sade led to a disagreement.

Tears blurred her vision as she walked through the living room. As much as she hated admitting it, Dante was right. She should have known Ava would make this difficult for her.

Sade was so focused on wiping her eyes and opening the car door that she didn't notice the figure standing behind her until a scarf was put over her mouth as she was picked up and carried to a waiting car.

DANTE

Something wasn't right.

It wasn't like Sade to not answer his calls... especially knowing he'd be calling in an hour. A part of him thought she was asleep, so he called Barron before heading that way.

Barron answered with, "Hey, son."

"Hey, Grandpa. Where's my baby?"

"I'm not sure. She left here a while ago."

"Hmm. That's odd. I've been calling her, but she hasn't answered."

"Maybe she's taking a nap."

"I thought that too, but if she's not there, I don't know where she'd be taking a nap. She's not here at my parents' house. Did she decide to stay with you all, or did she say she was going to a hotel?" Dante asked.

"Well, after what happened with her grandmother, I'm pretty sure she's not staying here. They had a little spat. I can't really even call it that." Barron chuckled. "She put your grandmother in her place, and I was a little proud of her for that." He released a low sigh. "I've been telling Ava to ease up on Sade. Her temperament with Sade is up and down lately, depending on what's happening. I thought she'd gotten past the past after we told you all about Martin and Andrea, but the Trina girl's sister dying has traumatized my wife all over again. I get that, but I don't agree with what she said, and Sade didn't either. She's pregnant and has a lot going on, but Ava just kept poking the bear."

"Was she upset when she left?"

"Oh yeah."

"God, I hope she didn't have an accident or something. Let me track her location."

"All right, Dante. Call me back when you know something."

Dante agreed and ended the call. As if his nerves weren't bad enough, seeing that Sade had turned off her location only worsened matters.

"Okay, Day. Where you at, bae?"

As he headed to his car, he received a call from Barron.

"Hello?"

"I went outside to smoke a cigarette. Her car is still here. The door was open. She'd dropped her keys."

Dante's feet temporarily froze in place as his heart dropped. "Jones has her. Have you called the police?"

"N-no, but I'm about to now."

Dante ended the call and rushed to his car. He called Wicked, the man watching Jones's house, to see if he'd shown up, but Wicked had yet to see Jones. If he had Sade, where would he have taken her? Time couldn't be wasted on a wild goose chase. He'd need to remain logical and stay in his head, not his heart if he wanted to find his woman.

By the time Dante arrived, the police were already there. He watched their camera footage, grateful they still had it active even though they'd cut the notifications off after Atlas died and they came to a truce with his family. Dante didn't have to see the face behind the mask. He could tell by the body shape that it was Jones.

Even with the Memphis Police Department putting out an APB for Jones and Sade, Dante knew he'd have to handle this himself. He called Captain Bennit, who told him Jones hadn't returned to his place in weeks. Standing around doing nothing was driving Dante crazy, so he left with no clear destination in mind.

As he drove, he thought back over the last several months, trying to find a clue in Jones's words and actions. Would he be at Sade's parents' graves? Dena's? Then it hit him. This, to Jones, was about Patrice, Trina, and Willow. Dante didn't know where he'd taken her yet, but he was sure they would be in Vanzette.

JONES

JONES WATCHED AS Sade's head bobbed. Groggily, she groaned. Heavy lids fluttered before they focused on him. When she realized who he was, she tried to stand, but he had her tied by her wrists and ankles to a chair.

"What did you give me?" she asked through gritted teeth. "If anything happens to my baby because of you . . ."

"Spare me the threats. Do you think I care about that baby? Both of you will be dead soon enough."

Sade chuckled, licking her dry lips. "Actually, you're a dead man talking. Dante's going to kill you—and that's *only* if I don't get free and do it first. Now, what the *fuck* did you give me?"

Sitting back in his seat, Jones lit a cigarette and crossed his ankles. "Something to make you sleep so I could transport you here without any issues."

"What was it? I'm not supposed to be taking sleeping medicine unless it's a certain kind. That could send me into labor prematurely. Are you ready to deal with that? If not, I suggest you let me go."

"Nice try, but you're not getting out of here that easily."

"Where are we anyway?" Sade's eyes shifted around the room, and Jones saw the exact moment she recognized where they were. "Is . . . this . . ."

"Your old shed?" Jones grinned. "It is. I got pretty close to your renters and told them this house wasn't the family home you presented it to be. I told them the woman who lived here killed three people, and they wanted no parts of that." He chuckled. "They moved out. You didn't get the notice?"

"No, I didn't. You've been spamming my email to the point where I can't even open it without getting hundreds of notifications daily."

"Yeah, well, they left two weeks ago. Willow's dead, though I have no proof. And the older neighbors to your right are on vacation. That means for miles on this stretch, it's just me and you. No one will hear you scream. No one will come to your aid."

That didn't get the reaction Jones was hoping for. Her eyes remained the same size. Her nostrils didn't flare. Her mouth didn't twitch. She didn't momentarily stop breathing. There were no jerky movements within her body. She seemed genuinely unfazed by his words, and that only pissed him off more. Before he could stop himself, he was leaping from his seat and backhanding her.

Her jaws clenched as she glared at him. "I'm going to enjoy killing you, Terry."

Jones smiled as he sat back down. "Strong words when *you're* the one tied to that chair."

"And that was a weak action by a free man. Why don't you untie me and make this a little fairer?"

"Cut the shit!" he roared, spittle spewing from his mouth. "Enough of the back-and-forth. I'm done with this."

"You at least owe me an explanation," she baited. "This can't be because of two women you don't even know. Why have you been so obsessed with me, Terry?"

Jones rolled his tongue across his cheek. "It is about them. Patrice, Trina, Willow . . . They deserved justice. And since the Vanzette Police Depa—"

"Cut the shit!" she yelled, mimicking him. "Tell me the truth. Why have you been stalking and harassing me?"

"Fine," he agreed, "It's not *just* because of them, but they were a big part of it."

"What else?"

"You're a seed that has come from bad soil. Your parents were evil, just like you and your sister. They might not have been murderers like you, but they were selfish, and they killed something else too."

"And what did they kill, Terry?" She smiled as her head tilted. "Your marriage? That's what this is about, right? Tonya?"

It took Jones a while to respond. He wasn't expecting her to know about his past. He'd put great effort into sealing documents that included his personal information online.

"Yeah, I know about that," Sade continued. "I know about your daughter too. How she killed herself because of Tonya." She chuckled. "I have to say, though . . . if I were stuck with you for a father, I probably would have killed myself too."

Like lightning, Jones was out of his seat, squeezing her neck until her eyes watered and turned red, and she passed out.

Jones tossed water onto Sade to wake her up. She choked and coughed, almost toppling over in the chair. He drew close to her, leaving them just a few inches apart.

"I want to make you suffer," he said. "I thought about slicing your throat like you did Trina or strangling you like you did Patrice. What did you do to Willow? How did you kill her?"

Sade remained silent, staring at him with fiery eyes.

"Cat got your tongue now? You were so talkative before." Jones chuckled as he remained silent. "I'll make you a deal. If you tell me what happened to Willow, I'll make your death quick and easy." He pulled his phone out. "In fact, if you confess to all three murders, I'll send a bullet into your head and kill you instantly. You won't feel a thing."

Jones pressed record and waited for her to speak. He huffed and ran his hand down his face. Placing his Glock on his thigh, Jones told her, "If you're not going to confess, do you have any final words to share with your family?" Sade kept her silence, further infuriating him. "Fine, have it your way."

He stopped the recording and looked down to put his phone in his pocket. Then standing, Jones aimed the gun at her.

"You really don't care about the people you killed . . . do you?"

"Did you care about the people your wife killed? If you did, you wouldn't be doing this to me. Stop drawing this out and just kill me already."

He lowered his head as he paced. "This is no fun with you acting like this. You won't admit to what you did. You don't seem to be scared. What am I going to do with you?"

Sade chuckled and looked toward the ceiling. "You don't get it, do you?"

"Get what?" he asked, aiming at her again.

"There's nothing you can say to rattle me. I don't care."

"How about this . . ." He sat back down. "The sixteen-year-old who killed herself . . . that was your *half sister*." Her mouth went slack. Finally . . . a reaction. "Yeah. Turned out Dena *wasn't* my child. She was your father's. She was the only good thing I had left, and Tonya tried to take her from me because she wasn't mine."

Sade licked the corner of her mouth before nibbling her cheek. "I know you didn't take that lightly."

"I didn't. I set her up."

Her lip twitched as if she were putting the pieces together. "Set her up how?"

"She didn't cause the accident that killed your parents; I did." He chuckled. "What? You thought I didn't make her suffer too? Oh, I did. Trust me."

Sade's chest expanded as her breathing escalated. That was it. *That's* what he'd been waiting for.

"You killed my parents?" She shifted in her seat.

Jones stood. "I did. And now, I'm going to kill you too."

The door burst open just as Jones fired. However, instead of the bullet hitting Sade, it went into the wall. Jones pointed the gun toward Dante, but it was too late. Dante's bullets ripped through his center. He fell onto the ground, gasping for air as fire surged through his core. Dante stood over him with a smile before firing one last time.

SADE

SADE SAT IN the middle of the floor in her old living room while the police talked to Dante outside by the shed. Jones was right about her tenants. They'd moved out and notified her with an email she hadn't seen. As she stared into the distance, tears streamed down her cheeks. Learning that Jones had killed her parents caused Sade's heart to burst. But thanks to Dante, Jones was dead, and it was finally over.

JONES

*T*ONYA,
 This is letter one of two. If you receive this, it's because I am dead. This letter will be the key to your freedom. Now that I am gone, you can roam the earth again. I couldn't stomach the idea of you being happy and free, falling in love with another man like you hadn't done what you'd done to me. To Dena.
 You destroyed us.
 For what? Lust? Was what you had for Martin real *love*? Even if it was, he didn't love you. If he did, he wouldn't have chosen Andrea over you. I hope that truth eats at you for the rest of your life.
 Dena deserved a better mother than you. I deserved a better wife than you. And you deserve to spend the rest of your days miserable. But at least you'll be able to be miserable as a free woman.
 Call Attorney Robert Hitchum. He has a signed statement and video recording of me admitting to tampering with the brakes on Martin's car and being responsible for the accident that took their lives. With that, they should release you.
 I hate you, and I can guarantee you I died with hate in my heart over what you did.

Jones

DANTE

The Next Morning

"Authorities say ex-detective Terry Jones *had a personal vendetta against Sade Griffin because of her parents. Sources say Jones's ex-wife was romantically involved with Griffin's father, and the affair had a deadly end. At any rate, Griffin has yet again been cleared of all charges. Captain Bennit released a statement this morning identifying Jones as the killer behind two murders that happened earlier this year. Willow Frank, once presumed missing, is now considered deceased, along with Baker and Roe. We will keep following this case. For now, I am Zella—*"

Bennit muted the TV and returned his gaze to Dante and Sade. He'd asked them to stop by his office so he could apologize in person on Jones's behalf.

"When you came to me, I should have done more," Bennit said. "I didn't want to see how much he was spiraling. I failed him and the two of you. But we're righting that wrong. Every news station in Vanzette is airing this story repeatedly for the next three days to make sure everyone in the town knows it was Jones who killed those women, not you."

Dante looked over at Sade, who gave him a small smile. Because of Jones's confession of framing his wife, it wasn't a far stretch for the police to believe he was trying to do the same thing to Sade. It helped to know he had a shrine dedicated to his daughter and a wall full of information on Sade and the victims. Dante had to keep himself from laughing at the fact that Jones, in death, was being blamed for the crimes he was obsessed with proving Sade did.

"We sent the press release to Memphis as well," Bennit added. "I don't know if they'll run it, but I'm sure they will. I hope this allows you to get back to your life and find some peace."

"Thank you," Dante said as he stood. After shaking Bennit's hand, Dante helped Sade stand from her seat. "I appreciate you calling us in, but I want to get her home so she can rest. Yesterday was a lot."

"Yeah, no. Of course. Call me if you guys need anything."

"Thanks," Sade replied with a small smile.

She'd been quiet and in her head. As happy as she was that Jones was dead, Dante felt she wouldn't return to herself until after her emergency appointment. Though Doctor Smith tried to assure her over the phone, Sade insisted on an appointment. Dante didn't mind the extra precaution and hoped he could take her mind off things until the appointment tomorrow.

"How are you feeling?" Dante asked as they walked out of the precinct hand in hand.

"I feel okay. I'm glad this is finally over. How do you feel?"

"Same. How are you physically?"

"My feet and ankles are swollen. I don't know if that's the baby or being tied up."

"I was wondering if that was the case. Looked like you were wobbling a little bit."

She gave him a genuine smile as she rubbed her belly. "I'll feel better when the doctor tells me he's okay. I know I only had one dose of the drug, but not knowing what it was is really bothering me. Plus, the last time I fainted, they warned me of the side effects of doing it too often. Now that it has happened again because Jones choked me, I just want to make sure our little one is okay."

"You don't have to explain, Smiley."

They got into the car, listening to music instead of talking. When they arrived at the hotel, Dante gave her a massage and held her as she drifted off to sleep. Suddenly, with a gasp, Sade sat up and looked down at her stomach.

"What's wrong? Are you in pain?"

She shook her head and blinked her eyes rapidly. "He . . . He moved."

"What?" Dante sat up as she put his hand on her stomach. "Oh, wow," Dante mumbled at the feel of his son kicking.

Sade giggled as her eyes began to leak with tears. "He moved. He's okay."

"Wow." Dante lowered himself to her stomach and kissed it. "Hey, little one. Thanks for letting us know you're okay in there."

He moved again, causing them both to laugh as Dante's eyes watered. Feeling their baby move was the perfect ending to their day.

The Next Afternoon

After the appointment, Dante treated Sade to ice cream. She hadn't stopped smiling since Doctor Smith confirmed their baby boy was okay. He watched her eat the strawberry ice cream with pure joy. It finally felt like they could relax and breathe. Her phone vibrated on the table, and at the sight of her grandmother's name, Sade rolled her eyes.

"You know if you don't answer, she will call me."

Sade shook her head as she sighed. "Quite frankly, I'm not in the mood to hear her apologize because she heard about what happened. She can stand on the last thing she said to me."

Dante tilted his head before shaking it. Her phone stopped ringing, and not long after, his started.

"Baby..."

"Just answer it," she told him, wiping the corners of her mouth.

He did and put the call on speaker. The weather was warm enough for them to enjoy their ice cream at an outside table, and Dante was grateful for the privacy.

"Hello?" Sade said, and the dry tone she used made him chuckle.

"Sade... hey. How are you?"

"Fine."

"We saw the news. They're saying Jones killed those people and tried to frame you. I'm glad the truth came out."

Sade chuckled. "Are you? Because the last time we spoke, you said what he was doing was my Karma."

Ava sighed. "Sade, I didn't call you to argue."

"Honestly, I'm not sure why you called at all."

"I just... I wanted to apologize."

Sade's eyes rolled. "That's unnecessary, but I want to tell you two things. One, Jones killed my parents, not his wife. Tonya will probably be out of prison soon. Two, I would like for us to remain in no contact. The bulk of my pregnancy has been one source of stress or suffering after another, and I'm not willing to waste any more time doing things that make me unhappy, and that includes this back-and-forth thing I've been doing with you."

"Wait. He what? All this time, I thought it was Tonya."

"That's what Jones wanted. He framed his wife. The truth is finally coming out, though."

"Wow. . . . . I don't know what to say."

"Say you won't call me until after I've called to let you know I've had my baby."

"I can do that if you promise to let us be in your child's life and yours."

"I'm not promising that, but I'll be more willing to try with you after that."

"Okay. I love you, baby, and I really am sorry."

"It's okay. I love you too."

When she disconnected the call, Dante asked, "Do you ever feel guilty about lying to them?"

Sade released a long exhale as she shook her head. "I did initially, but I felt less bad about it when she started judging me without proof. I don't ever want them to find out that I really killed them, but I also won't make her suffer because it's the truth. As long as she can talk to me respectfully and not be so negative, I don't mind going around them after I have the baby."

Dante could accept that, so he didn't bother responding. They'd been having a great day, and he didn't want anyone, especially Ava, to ruin it.

SADE

Late November
Sade's Audio Journal

"*I* FEEL LIKE I *haven't recorded one of these in a while. That makes sense. For the first time in a really long time, life is so, so good. Since I've been using this method to vent and get the bad things out of my head, I can finally put this to rest. I'm healthy, my baby and my man are healthy, and our relationship is going strong. Hopefully, I won't need to record again. Hopefully, life can stay this good.*"

"You didn't have to deliver these yourself, but it was so good to see you!" Veronica exclaimed, hugging Sade a third time.

She'd finished the canvas paintings for Veronica's clinic and decided to deliver them herself.

"I don't mind. It was nice coming back to Vanzette and not feeling like I had a target on my back, you know?"

"I get it. Do you have time to stay for a little while so we can catch up?"

"Sure!"

Sade took her time going inside Veronica and Lathan's home.

"How are you feeling?" Veronica asked, leading Sade to the sitting room.

"I'm feeling good. I'm peeing a lot, and the baby is moving like crazy. But other than that, it's been pretty good lately."

"Good. Can I get you some water or something? Have you been staying hydrated?"

"I've been trying. Dante literally makes me drink water every hour." Sade's eyes rolled as she smiled. "Especially if I do a light workout. He treats me like I'm fragile."

"Aww, that's cute."

As they continued to talk, Sade relaxed more and more. After years of not feeling connected to women because of how toxic things were with her sister, she finally had a genuine friendship with both Veronica and Jessica.

"So, what are you working on next?" Veronica asked.

"I finally have an idea for my next coloring book. It'll be for expecting moms. So, it'll have bellies and babies for each trimester they can color."

"I'll definitely need to order those in bulk for my clinic. I'm bummed you're not coming back to Vanzette so I can be baby boy's pediatrician, but this will make up for it."

Sade laughed. "Listen, I honestly don't know where me and Dante are going to end up. I wanted to stay in Memphis to be close to family, but this whole ordeal with Jones kind of ruined that for me. We've moved on and have peace now that he's gone, but . . . I don't know. A part of me still wants to leave."

"No one will blame you if you do. But I also understand your desire to stay and be close to family. Especially since things are getting better between you and Imani."

"I know, right? She's starting to understand just how long she will be gone. The twins will be in their midtwenties when she gets out, and her nephew will be a preteen." Sade sighed as sadness consumed her. "Adam and Atlas are dead, and she's still here being punished. I know to some, death is the ultimate punishment, but somehow, that doesn't seem fair."

"It sounds like you're feeling compassion for your sister, and that's something I never thought I'd witness."

Sade smiled. "You and me both. I know she was terrible to you too, and I apologize on her behalf. I won't make excuses for it because it was wrong. But I don't know . . . she's . . . maturing. I just hope she keeps it up so that she can make the most of her freedom when she gets out."

They continued to talk for several hours before having lunch. Then Sade headed back home to Memphis. She was grateful for the brief trip and visit with her friend. It finally felt like life was back on track.

After a day of getting the nursery together, Sade decided to unwind, watching *Breaking Bad* and eating fruit. The show had never caught her interest before, but Jessica mentioned how good it was when she first watched it, so Sade decided to give it a chance. She was only on the second season but had been pleasantly surprised.

"You forgot your phone in the nursery, Smiley," Dante said, handing it to her.

Sade looked at her phone as it lit up with a missed call from Attorney Thomas. She'd hired him to look into Simone's case. Since it was just after five in the evening, Sade hoped he was calling with great news. She sat up in bed, paused the episode, and then returned his call. Sade exchanged pleasantries with his receptionist, and then she directed Sade's call to his office.

"This is Attorney Thomas."

"Hi, this is Sade. I was just returning your call."

"Sade, hey. How are you?"

"I'm well. How are you?"

"I'm well. I know it's kind of late, but I couldn't wait until morning to give you the good news. Simone's court date was today, and the judge agreed that based on the evidence and her ex's history of domestic violence, she should have received a lesser sentence. She's being released tomorrow with time served."

Sade squealed as she hopped out of bed. "Oh my God, you just made my day! I'm *so* happy to hear that! Are you going to see her tomorrow?"

"Normally, the family would have the pleasure of picking her up, but she expressed that the only family she has in Vanzette is her daughter, so I'll pick her up."

"Yes, that's correct. Well, please, give her my number and tell her to call me as soon as she's settled. Thank you so much, Attorney Thomas."

"I will, and you're welcome. Thank you for moving on her behalf."

As Sade ended the call, she wiped her eyes.

"What was that about?" Dante asked, stealing a slice of apple from her bowl.

"That was the lawyer I had working on Simone's case. A judge overturned her sentence today. She's going home tomorrow!"

"That's great, baby. You said she did five years, right?"

"Right, and that was more than enough. Really, it was too much, in my opinion, but I'm just glad she's finally going to be able to go home. Hopefully, Nico's parents won't make it hard for her to get custody of Carmen once she's settled and stable. I got a feeling they will, though."

"Yeah, that's going to be tricky. I get they are hurting over losing their son, but if it was his life or hers . . . What did they really expect her to do?"

Sade could only shrug as she got back into bed. She didn't want to think too much about that. For now, she was just glad Simone would be free come morning.

DANTE

THE GLOW, THE smile, the peace, the belly—Dante could not keep his hands off Sade these days. She was twenty-eight weeks pregnant and the apex of his world. Dante was filled with pride as they shopped for things for themselves and the baby. They were finally living the quiet life Sade had been craving.

Her creativity was back, and she was painting like crazy. Dante had opened his online business, and it boosted his confidence to have his old clients glad to be working with him again. He offered them the chance to stay with Eric and Jessica if they wanted, and their choosing him solidified Dante's expertise and purpose in his mind and heart. To him, the only thing that would make life better was the arrival of their baby boy.

"I have to pee," Sade told him, using his hand to tug him in the opposite direction. "After this, can we have lunch?"

Dante nodded his agreement as he chuckled. "Yeah, we can. What do you have a taste for?"

"Korean barbecue. Can we go to the hot pot place in Bartlett?"

"Whatever you want, Smiley."

As she squealed and clapped her hands, Dante laughed lightly. These days, all it took was a good foot rub and food to make her the happiest woman on earth.

He pulled his vibrating phone out of his pocket, confused at seeing Barron's name. Dante's eyes shifted toward the bathroom, making sure Sade had gone inside before he answered.

"You good, Grandpa?"

"Yeah, son." He paused. "Uh . . . I know Sade wants to keep her distance until she has the baby, but y'all need to stop by. Today, if you can."

"I'll see what I can do. What is this about?"

"We have a message from Vanessa, Atlas's mom."

"Aw, hell. This can't wait until after she has the baby?"

"It's . . . concerning the baby, Dante."

"What do you mean?"

"Just stop by. We'll explain everything."

Barron disconnected the call, and Dante groaned. A part of him wanted to forget what he'd heard and not tell Sade, but he couldn't do that. It would be best if they took care of this now. He hated that after weeks of peace, it felt like they were about to step into some drama that the man he killed was somehow at the center of.

As Sade approached him with a comfortable smile, Dante hated to tell her something that might wipe it off her face.

"What's wrong?" she asked, wrapping her arms around him.

"Why do you think something is wrong?"

"You're frowning," she noticed, rubbing the space between his wrinkled brows.

"Oh. I just got off the phone with your grandpa. He wants us to stop by." Her eyes rolled as she sighed. "He says it's important. Something about Vanessa."

"All right. We can stop by before we eat. I don't want to obsess over what it is and not be able to enjoy my food."

"We wouldn't want that, would we?" Dante teased, grabbing their bags off the nearby bench before leaving the mall.

"Thank you for stopping by," Ava said with a smile. "It's good to see you."

"You too," Sade agreed, sitting next to Dante on the couch. "What's this about?"

Ava and Barron looked at each other, and then Barron spoke first.

"You know we reached a sort of truce with Adam's family. Because the twins are his only children, we've worked out an agreement so that they can spend time with his family."

"Right," Sade said.

"Well, when Samantha came to get the girls, her sister was with her. Vanessa would like you to take a DNA test just to prove the baby isn't Atlas's."

Sade stared at them for a while before bursting into laughter. She leaned forward as much as her belly would allow, gripping Dante's thigh. As serious as the situation was, her level of unbothered amused Dante.

He licked his lips, trying to hide his smile.

"Wow. Are you serious?"

"Very," Ava said.

"But Atlas told them the baby wasn't his before he died."

"Apparently, they are questioning that because he started saying it was," Ava clarified. "I think they are grasping at straws. He's gone, and they want this baby to be what they have to remember him by."

"I get that . . . especially since the twins are around more. And I can admit that Atlas started to become possessive of the baby and call it his, but it's not, and they know that. However, I'll agree if they need a test to put this to rest."

"Good," Barron said. "They said you can get it done now. Is that safe?"

Sade smiled. "Yes, Grandpa. They have noninvasive prenatal paternity testing. I'll talk to Doctor Smith about it and see when I can schedule it. Tell Vanessa and Clay I'll get the test done as soon as possible."

"We will," Ava agreed as Sade stood, causing Dante to do the same. "Are you leaving so soon?"

"Yeah, I'm hungry," Sade admitted with a smirk.

"I can fix you something," Ava offered with hopeful eyes.

"Thanks, but I kind of had my mouth fixed for Korean barbecue."

"Oh. Okay. Well . . . Maybe another time."

Sade's mouth twisted to the side as she considered her grandmother's words. "Maybe . . . next week?"

Ava's eyes widened as she grinned. "Next week would be perfect."

"Okay. I guess I'll see you then."

"Okay."

They said their goodbyes, and as Dante opened the car door for Sade, he told her, "I knew you wouldn't be able to stay away."

ATLAS

Back on the Island

ATLAS WATCHED SADE *as she sliced a yellow and red watermelon. She hummed and floated around the kitchen in a flowy, oversized dress. With bare feet, she was the epitome of perfection. The epitome of beauty. The epitome of femininity.*

He shook his head as he thought about how Imani and her minions spent years trying to break Sade down and crush her confidence, how she felt unworthy because she wanted the man who chose her sister. They were all damn fools. Any man who had Sade would be one of the lucky ones. And at that moment, Atlas was glad it was him.

He walked over to her and wrapped his arms around her, kissing her until her giggles made it hard for him to do so.

"What has gotten into you?" *Her cheery voice and bright eyes made his heart skip a beat.*

"You're beautiful. You know that?"

Biting down on her bottom lip, Sade nodded.

"Yes, but it's always nice to hear you say it."

"You know I'd do anything for you, right? If anyone hurts you . . . I'll make sure they never have the chance to again."

Pressing her palms into his chest, Sade stared into his eyes. She looked deeply, like she was searching for something. Since he was telling the truth, Atlas hoped she would find it.

"Are you okay, baby?"

"I am. I just want to make sure you understand that."

"Where is this coming from?" she asked sweetly, caressing his chest.

"I wish I would have been around when you were in school. I would have protected you."

Her brows lifted, and her mouth opened slightly as realization filled her. Her chuckle was soft as she nodded.

"Oh . . . I see. You're thinking about Imani and Dante?"

Atlas nodded. *"He said he was your best friend, but he wasn't. If he was, he wouldn't have let them do that to you. He didn't deserve you, and he doesn't deserve this baby."*

"We were kids," Sade reasoned, wrapping her hands around his wrists. *"Do I wish things would have been different? Yes. But I can't dwell on that now. My life is better with you in it. That's all I care about."*

Atlas lowered himself to his knees and hugged her waist. He rested his head on her stomach and said, *"Thank you for this gift. You and the baby . . . You give me hope. You keep me grounded. Steady. You're my anchor. I don't know what I'll do if I lose you."*

Sade ran her hand down the back of his head, then used his chin to lift his head. *"It's a good thing you don't have to worry about that."*

SADE

The Christmas Cabin Trip

S ADE SWIRLED HER spoon around her spiked coffee as she stared at the falling snow. All things considered, she'd enjoyed her time at the cabin . . . with Atlas. As upset as she was at Imani for manipulating her into the trip and causing her to lie to her best friend, Sade had developed a connection with Atlas that made it worth it. She kept telling herself it was just about the sex and temporary companionship, but Atlas's desire for her was melting her.

"Mornin'," Imani grumbled, shuffling into the kitchen. She looked bougee as ever in her white sheer robe with fur and matching fur kitten heels. Her locs were pulled up into a fat bun, providing an unobstructed view of her beautifully sculpted face. It always bothered Sade to witness such a beautiful woman act so ugly.

"Mornin'," Sade responded, heading out of the kitchen.

"Wait. Are you still mad at me? You've been avoiding me this whole trip."

"That's what you wanted, right? Time alone with Adam."

Imani huffed and rolled her eyes. "Yes, that's what I wanted, but without the attitude from you."

Sade chuckled. "I'm not sure how you thought that was possible. You brought me here under false pretenses, and you're putting me in a horrible position with Dante."

"Look, let's not bring him into this. It's our last full day here, and Adam wants to do something as a group. I don't want you having an attitude to ruin it."

"Oh, so that's what this is about? You don't really care about how I feel or us not doing anything. This is about Adam and what he wants."

Her jaws clenched, Imani stared at her sister, and Sade laughed with a shake of her head.

"Enjoy your day, Imani," Sade said as she left the kitchen.

"Be ready to go in an hour!"

"Whatever," Sade grumbled under her breath, not even bothering to look back. She took small sips of her still-hot coffee, almost dropping the cup when she entered her room and saw Atlas placing something on her bed.

"Jesus, you scared me." Sade clutched her chest, trying to slow her palpitating heart.

"Sorry, I was trying to surprise you with this gift."

With a tsk, Sade walked over to him. "You didn't have to get me anything, Atlas."

"I know, but I wanted to." He lifted the gift bag and handed it to her. "Merry Christmas, Sade."

"I can't take this. Not until I go get you something."

He gave her a sexy smile and licked his lips. "I don't want you to get me anything. Now, take this."

Sade accepted the bag and then set her mug on the dresser. She removed the tissue paper and pulled out a leather-bound book. As she opened it, Atlas said, "I got this from the vintage shop in the town square. It has little dotted pages inside. The lady said that it was good for artists. Was she right?"

With watery eyes, Sade slipped her hand over the aged leather. "Yeah, she was." Sade laughed in disbelief. "This is . . . beautiful, Atlas. I'm going to keep this forever. Thank you."

"You're welcome. I'm glad you like it."

Sade pulled him in for a hug as she told him, "I love it."

Her eyes squeezed shut as tears threatened to pour. It was such a thoughtful gift, and she wasn't expecting it to come from him . . . Someone she'd known on such a shallow level. Maybe it was the holiday season, but the gesture had definitely opened Sade's heart to Atlas just a little bit more.

SADE

Just After Christmas

WHEN TEARS DROPPED and landed on the notebook Atlas had given her, Sade quickly wiped them away. She didn't think getting the DNA test results would bring up old feelings and memories of Atlas, but that was what had happened. She tried to pinpoint where things started to go wrong between them.

The move to Memphis?

Being with his family?

Her agreement to let him father a child that wasn't his?

With a sigh, Sade stood and grabbed her phone off the charger. She hadn't even bothered to open the DNA test results because she knew what they would say. As she went down the hall searching for Dante, she wondered how Vanessa and Clay would feel when they saw the results. Would they be relieved? Or would their grief be doubled?

Dante was seated in a recliner in front of the projector, which played a crime movie that Sade was unfamiliar with. She handed him her phone and said, "The results are in."

He looked at the phone before taking it from her. "Why are you giving it to me?"

"I figured you'd want to see them too."

His eyes rolled toward the ceiling. "I told you if you said the baby was mine that I believed you."

"Still . . . I want you to see it for yourself."

Dante opened the email, smiling when he saw the results that Sade already knew in her heart. He stood and wrapped his arms around her, dropping a kiss on her forehead.

"Smiley, I already believed you. But it is nice to see this in black and white."

"Good."

As she removed herself from his embrace, Dante asked, "Are you okay? You seem . . . sad or disappointed. Did you want this to be *his* baby?"

Sade scoffed and crossed her arms over her chest. "Of course not."

"Then what's wrong with you?"

"Nothing's necessarily wrong. I was just thinking about Atlas and how things started to go so wrong."

Dante tilted his head. His tongue rolled over his teeth as he eyed her. "You regret what happened?"

"No. It was either him or you, and I'm happy you're still here with me." She released a nervous chuckle. "This really isn't the kind of thing a person wants to discuss with their partner."

"So, this is about you missing him then? Or, at least, missing the way things *used* to be with him?"

"It's about saying goodbye to something and someone I thought I'd have a future with. I didn't go to his funeral, and even though I told Atlas we were over, I never really got closure. I feel bad." Sade sat on the arm of the recliner. "All Atlas wanted was to love me and be with me." She chuckled bitterly. "To be there for our child. And he . . . went a little crazy with it, but he was the first man to make me feel worth the pressure he was putting behind me. So, I guess I feel guilty because he'd still be alive if it wasn't for me."

"He'd still be alive if he wouldn't have tried to kill me."

"You know what I mean, Tay."

"I do." He sat back down and pulled her down to his lap. "Is there anything I can do to convince you this wasn't your fault?"

"Honestly, I'm not sure. I know that logically. Like I didn't make him start acting crazy. But in my heart, I feel responsible. And I know Vanessa will probably be hurt because the baby isn't his. As much as I hate her and her sister, I feel bad about that too. They blamed me for Adam, and I know they blamed me for Atlas. Now, she will blame me for never having any grandchildren."

"Even if she did, again, that's not your fault, baby."

Sade sighed as her phone vibrated. "Uh-oh." It was Vanessa. "I kind of hate I told Grandma to give her my number. I wasn't actually expecting her to call me after the results were delivered."

Dante chuckled as he gripped her thigh. "Answer, Day."

Sade pulled in a deep breath before answering with, "Hello?"

"Sade, hi. Is now a good time to talk?"

"Um, sure. What's up?"

"We saw the results. Thank you."

"You're welcome. At least you don't have to worry about dealing with me for the rest of your life."

Vanessa chuckled like Sade hoped she would. "Silver lining, and I'm sure you can say the same." They both shared a laugh. "Can you come over? No funny business, I promise. You can bring anyone you'd like. It will just be me and Clay. There's something about Atlas that I'd like to share with you."

Sade looked at Dante, and he nodded. "I would only feel comfortable with Dante being there with me."

"The man who killed my son?"

"The man your son tried to kill. The man who defended himself. Can you just . . . tell me over the phone?"

Vanessa sighed. "I probably will never be ready to face him. I don't care about the logic of him defending himself against Atlas and that being the reason he's dead. That was still my baby."

Vanessa's sniffles tugged at Sade's heart.

"Vanessa, I'm not sure this is a good idea. How about we just discuss this over the phone?"

"How about I go and just sit in the car?" Dante suggested. "I'll be outside if you need me."

Sade thought it over before agreeing. "Okay, I can do that."

"Good," Vanessa said. "Can you come over in two hours?"

"Yeah, I'll be there."

"Thank you, Sade."

With a nod, Sade disconnected the call. Her mind raced with ideas of what could be so important that Vanessa wanted to tell her in person. She didn't feel comfortable around Vanessa after what happened at the restaurant and would have preferred to meet her with Dante, but Sade understood her plight. She didn't know how she'd feel if she had to sit across from the man who murdered her child, whether it was self-defense or not. That took a level of maturity, forgiveness, and spirituality that Sade wasn't sure she'd ever have.

SADE

Two Hours Later

"I'D FEEL MORE comfortable sitting outside," Sade said as Vanessa held the door open.

"It's kind of chilly out here. Are you sure?" Sade nodded. "Okay. Clay! Come out here."

While they waited, Sade leaned against the pole on the porch. Resting her weight on the bottom step, she looked back at Dante. Though she couldn't see him through the tinted glass, there was no doubt in her mind that his eyes were on her.

When Clay stepped onto the porch, his eyes shifted from Sade to the car. His Adam's apple bobbed as he forced himself to look at Sade.

"What's this about?" she asked, wanting to get their meeting over with.

"I wanted you to know that I never hated you; I hated the idea of Atlas *being* with you. He really liked you, and I feared it would lead to him having an episode," Vanessa said.

"An episode? What do you mean?"

"Atlas had schizophrenia," Clay shared, completely knocking the air from Sade's lungs.

She gripped the pole and looked from Clay to Vanessa.

"What? H-how did I *not* know that?"

Vanessa smiled as her eyes watered. "Because he was taking his medicine. When he takes his medicine, the symptoms are under control. I think he stopped taking them when you returned to Memphis."

"I noticed a little difference in him," Clay said. "But I didn't take it seriously. He hadn't had an episode in a while. I thought he was just depressed and not handling his emotions well."

"And I was in denial," Vanessa added. "I'd just gotten him back home, and I didn't want to believe he had stopped taking his medicine. If I questioned him about it, he'd pull away." She wiped a tear before it could fall. "I didn't want to lose him again."

"So the schizophrenia is why he started to spiral?" Sade asked.

"It was," Clay answered. "The delusion, the detachment, inability to control his emotions or not having an emotional reaction when needed. All of those things were signs that he'd stopped taking his medicine."

"The minute he started fixating on your baby, I should have known he'd stopped," Vanessa said. "I'm so sorry. We should have caught it sooner."

"You don't have to apologize for that, but I really appreciate you telling me. I'd been trying to figure out where we went wrong for things to get so crazy between us, and this makes it make sense. He was like a completely different person toward the end . . . and now I know why." Sade blinked back her tears, guilt sitting on her heart for a different reason now. "How didn't I notice the changes? Why didn't I say something? Instead, I just . . . pushed him away."

"Oh, please, don't do that," Vanessa said. "We're carrying enough guilt over this situation. You don't need to. The truth is, Atlas was a grown man, and he chose to stop taking his medicine."

"How'd you find out that was what happened?"

"We noticed the pill bottle in his bathroom when we went through his things. I checked the date he'd gotten it, and he hadn't taken any of the pills."

"Wow."

"So, it's not your fault. None of this was. We'll probably never know why he chose to stop taking his medicine, but that was his choice. We just wanted you to know."

"Thanks again for telling me," Sade said, unsure what else could be said.

"Of course, and good luck with your delivery."

Sade waved at them both before turning and going to the car. Dante got out and opened the door for her, and she was glad Vanessa and Clay went inside without saying anything. The moment Dante drove away, Sade started to tell him everything.

By the time she finished, his response was, "Damn. How do you feel about that now?"

"This gave me some peace, but it also made me feel bad. Like I'm able to now say I know why things changed, but I feel a little guilty because I didn't try to help him figure out what was going on. And I know that wasn't my responsibility, but it makes me feel like I should have been more concerned about someone I said I cared about. He was exhibiting abnormal, unstable behavior. What if I would have just tried to figure out why?"

"Might I offer a different perspective?" Sade nodded. "I don't think he wanted you to know, Smiley. If he did, he would have told you. That's not something you just forget to tell the person you're seeing. He intentionally kept that from you. So, I don't think your asking would have made a difference. It was his choice to keep that from you, and it was his choice to stop taking his medicine."

"That's what Vanessa said."

"And I agree. I also don't want you to feel guilty over this. It wasn't your battle. I don't want you taking this on and making yourself upset. This was a very unfortunate situation all the way around, but it wasn't your fault at all."

"Thank you, baby. I needed that."

Dante took her hand into his and kissed it. His words and Vanessa's assurance made Sade feel a little better, but she knew it would take some time before she shook away the lingering guilt.

DANTE

New Year's Eve

WHILE JOY AND laughter permeated the room, Dante was stuck in his thoughts. His parents had invited the family over to bring in the new year, and Dante agreed to come, but he planned to return home before midnight to celebrate with Sade.

Since learning about Atlas's condition, Sade had been a pang in his heart. Even with her trying to release the guilt, he knew her well enough to know the moments she sank into it. The moments she'd disassociate and become trapped by the thoughts in her mind. Every time they happened, it made Dante feel a little worse.

She might not have said it, but he questioned if she resented him for killing Atlas. If she'd created a story in her head that excused his actions . . . would it no longer justify Dante's reaction? As he swirled his glass around, Dante stared at the brown liquor. His father sat beside him, and Dante tried to prepare himself for what he was about to say.

"If you ain't want to party, you should've stayed home," Deandre teased, nudging Dante's shoulder.

That got a smile out of him. "I'm trying to stay locked in. Just got a lot on my mind."

"This is about that boy?"

Dante had already shared what happened with his father. He thought talking about it once would get it off his mind, but that wasn't the case. The thoughts lingered, triggered every time Sade seemed to be triggered by her own.

"Yeah. I'm watching her grieve the man I killed. I don't know what to do."

"Is she really grieving him, or is she grieving that situation?"

"Is there a difference?"

Deandre chuckled and took a sip of his drink. "Oh, there's a big difference. If she's grieving the man, that'll take longer for her to process. And there's a chance she never will. If she's grieving the situation, she'll heal from that with time. It'll just take her mind connecting with her heart and shutting some of those negative feelings off."

"She says she needed closure and that learning about his condition gave her that, but she also said she felt guilty over not questioning what was going on with him."

"That sounds like she's grieving the situation. Give her time. She'll come out of it eventually. There's nothing you or anyone else can say to her. I'm sure you've already said it all."

Dante nodded his agreement with a smile. "Yeah, I have. She said it helped and that she heard me. So, I guess I just have to wait and see."

"Just give her some time. One day, she will wake up and not think about it at all. And when she does think about it, it'll be processed in a healthy way. One that won't make her feel responsible in any way. Until then, just continue to give her grace."

"I will. Thanks, Pops."

"You're welcome. Now get out of this corner sulking and come socialize with ya people. You know you'll be ready to go soon."

Dante laughed as he stood and followed his father, not even bothering to disagree.

SADE

WHEN DANTE FIRST started spoiling her, Sade didn't think he was up to something. Now, she wasn't so sure. He'd paid for her to get a massage, mani-pedi, and her hair done. Now that she'd made it back home, he'd laid out a dress for her to wear but didn't tell her where they were going. Because she trusted him, Sade showered and dressed in the form-fitting, pale pink, off-the-shoulder maxi dress she'd gotten from Meshki.

"Wow," Dante muttered as he took her in. "You look absolutely stunning, Smiley."

"I think this is the first day I feel fat."

His robust laughter turned her pout into a smile.

"Baby, you are *not* fat. Even if you did gain some weight, it's for a good reason."

"Mhm." Her smile widened when his hands molded against her waist as he kissed her.

"You've never looked more beautiful than you do right now."

"Thank you, Tay. Now, tell me where we're going."

Dante chuckled as he took her by the hand. "You'll see in a moment. Let's go."

For the entire ride, Sade's nerves got the best of her. She calmed down when they pulled into the parking lot of her favorite restaurant. "This really is just a date that you spoiled me to get ready for?"

"Would you be disappointed if there wasn't a surprise?"

"No, just surprised."

"Good."

Dante got out and opened the door for her, then led her to the restaurant. As soon as they stepped inside, Sade's hands covered her mouth, and her eyes watered.

"Surprise!" was yelled from everyone in the dining room.

The area was decorated in pink and blue for the surprise baby shower/gender reveal.

"You did this?" she asked as Dante's hand went to the small of her back.

They walked farther into the dining room, where their family and friends were waiting.

"Nah. This was Veronica's idea. She and Jessica put it together. You know Mama and Grandma Ava helped, but this was all your friends' doing."

That only made Sade more emotional. She went around the room, giving everyone hugs. For a while, she was so in shock she barely talked. Once she accepted what had been done for her, she warmed up to everyone in the room. What put her more in her feelings was Imani calling Ava when it was time for them to reveal the gender of their baby. A cart with a blue and pink cupcake was rolled from the kitchen.

"All right, Dante," Olivia said. "You feed Sade the cupcake. Pink for a girl, blue for a boy."

Dante lifted both with a wide grin. He licked his lips and asked her, "You ready, bae?"

"Yes, I'm ready."

She opened her mouth slightly, laughing when cheers erupted as he fed her the blue cupcake. He waited until she swallowed to give her a kiss that Sade happily accepted.

"This has been perfect," she said after wiping her mouth. "Thank you to Veronica and Jessica for planning this. Thank you, Grandma and Mama Olivia, for the assist. And thank you all so much for coming to celebrate me and Dante's little one. We truly appreciate you more than you'll ever know."

Her heart was light as she sat down and prepared to open the gifts everyone had brought. At the beginning of her pregnancy, Sade was sure she'd spend it stressed and upset. Now, she could finally enjoy her pregnancy, and she was looking forward to her little one entering the world even more.

Two Weeks Later

As Sade soaked her feet in water, she beamed over Simone's good news. Nico's parents surprised her by agreeing to give her full custody of Carmen once she had a job and a stable living environment. Sade couldn't have been happier for Simone. After they made plans to see each other that weekend, Sade ended the call and dried her feet. It was Dante's and her date night, which happened to be her favorite night of the week.

She didn't know what he had in store, but he told her she could dress casually. After slipping into a sweatsuit, Sade made her way down the hall slower than usual. Being in her final trimester had been bittersweet. She was excited it was almost over, but the extra weight and less energy made her days longer.

The breath she released gained Dante's attention. His head lifted from his phone, and he smiled.

"You all right, mama?"

"Just a little tired, but that's nothing new."

"Normally, I'd ask if you want to stay home, but . . ."

"Oh no. I want to leave the house. I love our date nights."

"Okay, good, because I think you're going to really, really enjoy this."

"Well, I really enjoyed the last surprise. That's gonna be hard to top."

"Hmm . . . We'll see." He gave her a soft kiss that caused goose bumps to cover her arms. "You ready?"

"I am."

When they were seated in the car, Dante asked, "What's your fondest memory of me?"

It didn't take Sade long to think about it. Her eyes misted at the memory. "How you reacted to my parents dying. As soon as I called, you came over. You spent two weeks with me until Grandpa put you out." Sade chuckled and took his hand into hers. "I don't think I would have made it through that without you. Imani was out with her girls, avoiding it. My grandparents were . . . too jarred and busy with funeral preparations and getting adjusted to having us with them to really focus on me. But you did. You gave me space to grieve, but you didn't let it consume me. You'd always been my best friend, but after that . . . That's when I decided I was never going to let you go no matter what anyone said."

Dante lifted her hand to his mouth and kissed it as he often did.

"I was glad I could be there for you. It was like second nature. You've always been my heart. When things aren't right with you, they aren't right with me. I love you more than anything and anyone else in this world, Smiley."

"Ugh, you're about to make me cry."

"You do that a lot lately."

They shared a soft laugh as she wiped her eyes. "These darn hormones. I was never this much of a crybaby."

"Hmm . . . Now, I don't know about that, Day."

"I wasn't! . . . Was I?"

Dante laughed. "I mean, I guess you have average emotions. I don't have anyone to compare you to. Your sister didn't emote like a normal person, so I can't use her."

"She's getting better. What about Mama Olivia?"

"Nah, Mama was always emotional. She believes tears cleanse the soul and express joy, so there's always a reason to cry to her. You're like that now, but you weren't before you got pregnant."

Sade chuckled. "I'll take that as a compliment."

They continued to talk until they pulled into the parking lot of an event venue. At first, Sade thought their date night would be a party or concert, but no cars were parked there.

"Is everyone else parked in the back?" she asked.

"Yeah."

"So, what is this? A concert?"

"You'll see," he said, opening his door.

Her excitement grew as she stared at the venue entrance, trying to make out the movement. As they made their way inside, she had to keep from skipping. Usually, Sade didn't like surprises, but she'd been enjoying them lately.

She immediately recognized the blue and white color scheme when they walked inside.

"Kirby High School class of 20—ah!" With a gasp, Sade gripped his arm and bounced from one leg to the other. "You re-created our prom!"

"I did," he confessed, giving her a sexy smile and wink. "Come on, let's go inside."

They entered the double doors, and Sade felt like she'd gone back in time. Everything looked almost exactly the same as their high school prom—the white and blue décor, round tables for seating in the back, light bites and refreshments to the left, and a dance floor in the center of the room. Her eyes zeroed in on the blue and white strobe lighting and silver chandelier.

"Oh my God, Dante. This is absolutely perfect. I can't believe you did this."

"I felt like we both needed a redo after what happened at the first one." He clapped his hands, and several women came from the right. "So, I got everything you'll need in the back. Dress, shoes, all that. They'll do your hair and makeup. I'll see you in a while, beautiful."

Dante kissed her cheek, and before she could thank him, he headed in the opposite direction to get ready himself. As happy tears raced down her cheeks, Sade walked to the small group of women waiting for her with broad smiles.

Sade stared at her reflection in the mirror and tried not to cry. The night of their prom, when Imani doused her with punch, she ruined their mother's dress. It was Sade's most prized possession from their mother. Nothing Ava tried could fully remove the stain. Sade was so disgusted that she never wanted to see the dress again. Years later, Dante had the fabric turned into a pale yellow silk shawl that she draped over the white gown he'd gotten her for the evening. The longer she caressed the fabric and looked at her reflection in the mirror, the harder it was for her to maintain her emotions.

For a brief moment, she felt like that eighteen-year-old girl all over again—weak, bullied, taken advantage of, no confidence. Quickly, she reminded herself that was never an identity she should have taken on. Regardless of how her sister tried to dim her light, Sade had no choice but to let it shine. Then and now.

When Kem began to play, Sade knew that it was her cue to leave. She took one final look at herself before leaving the dressing room. A giggle escaped her at the sight of Dante in a chocolate suit, just like years ago.

"Well, don't you look handsome."

"And you look beautiful as always."

"Than—Dante . . ."

As he lowered to one knee, Dante took her hand into his. "I've loved you since before I even knew what love was. I made some horrible decisions in my youth that almost cost me you. I'm grateful to God that during the most horrible time in my life, I was finally blessed with the chance to make things right with you. We have a lot of years to make up for as husband and wife. I want us to start now. Sade Griffin, will you marry me?"

She nodded her head rapidly before she laughed a hearty laugh. "Of course, I'll marry you. For real this time."

Dante laughed as he pulled the pear-shaped diamond out of his pocket and slipped it onto her ring finger.

"I love the sound of that."

Once he secured the ring, Dante kissed it, then stood and pulled her into his arms. The tender, deep kiss he gave her made Sade moan as she held him close. Their bodies swayed to the music in the background as her heart processed what had just happened. Dante Williams had just proposed to her. He would soon be her husband—not just in her head, but from his heart.

They spent the rest of the evening dancing until her feet started to hurt. Then they returned home, where they made love well into the morning.

DANTE

A Little Under Two Months Later

As SOON AS their son's cheek touched Sade's, his crying stopped.

"Hi, little one," she said before kissing him.

"You know your mama's voice, huh?" the nurse asked.

Dante blinked back tears at the sight. He couldn't wait to hold his baby boy. The nurse took him away briefly to get him checked out and cleaned up.

"He's here, Smiley. You did it," Dante said before kissing her forehead. "I'm so proud of you, and I love you. Thank you so much for him. God, I love you."

Sade's eyes fluttered as she gave him a lazy smile. "I'm just happy he's here. I'm so tired."

"I know, baby. The hardest part is over. You'll be able to rest soon."

He kissed her forehead, nose, and lips before thanking her again.

Once the baby was cleaned up, the nurse walked him over again. That time, she handed him to Dante. Now, Dante was unable to hold his tears back.

"What's up, little one? Daddy's been waiting for you." Dante smiled and wiped his eyes. "I love you so much, Iman. The world is yours."

Dante was surprised when Sade suggested naming the baby after her sister. In a weird way, she'd brought them together. If it weren't for her scheme, he'd still be in a loveless marriage with no idea of his wife's cheating or the fact that he was raising another man's kids. Now, he had a son, he was with the love of his life, and in a year, he'd legally become Sade's husband.

EPILOGUE
Tonya

TONYA,
 This is letter number two of two. You should receive this at least three months after my death. Now that I've freed you, you owe me. I could have left you rotting in prison for a crime you didn't commit, but I showed you grace instead. You should know I did that for a reason, and it for damn sure wasn't out of the kindness of my heart.
 I need you to finish what I started. Sade Griffin has to pay for what she did. I believe there's a body or some incriminating evidence in the small body of water behind her house. I saw her boyfriend, the man she killed women for, toss three black garbage bags into the water. I want you to search that water for those bags and see what's inside.
 If it is what I think it is, call the police immediately. If it isn't . . . at least you've still got your freedom. I'm gonna put the address on the back of this letter. Please, don't fuck this up for me. Don't touch anything inside the bag. Evidence has already been ruled inadmissible once before with this girl. I can't let that happen again.

Still hating you from beyond the grave . . .
Jones

"Whew."

Tonya plopped down on the grass and wiped her forehead. Searching the lake took longer than she thought it would, but she found the three bags Jones mentioned. Because she wasn't sure how much time she had before someone noticed her, she put on her gloves and ripped a bag apart as quickly as possible.

The smell and sight of decaying flesh immediately made her sick to her stomach. She crawled over to the lake and emptied the contents of her stomach before scooting several feet away from the bags. Standing, she began to pace.

She knew who Sade Griffin was. She also knew why her ex-husband wanted her to pay. Though Tonya appreciated Jones finally telling the truth so she could be free, she didn't owe him a damn thing. Her curiosity was why she'd done as he asked, but that was as far as it would go.

Tonya retied the bag and tossed all three back into the lake. She looked around and made sure no one was watching before she tossed Jones's letter in there too. As she walked toward her car, she hummed, and a smile slowly spread across her lips. Tonya had never thought much about the afterlife, but she hoped Jones was looking up at her from hell, watching her leave. She never thought she'd be okay with letting someone get away with murder, but under these circumstances, Tonya was convinced Sade deserved a reprieve.

The End

WWW.BLACKODYSSEY.NET

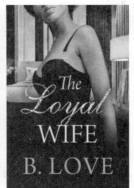
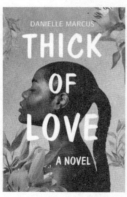